CW00840893

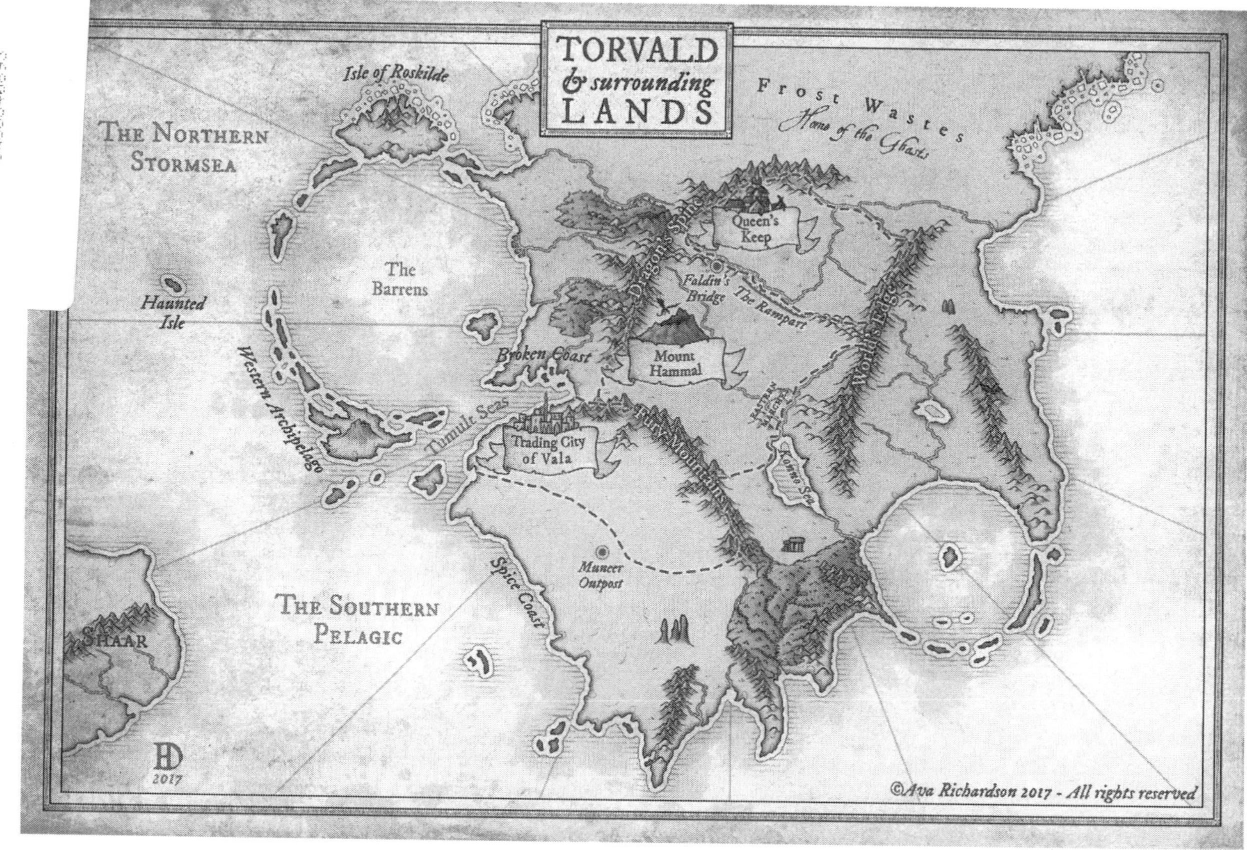
TORVALD
& surrounding
LANDS
Frost Wastes
Home of the Ghasts
Isle of Roskilde
The Northern Stormsea
The Barrens
Haunted Isle
Western Archipelago
Broken Coast
Tumult Seas
Queen's Keep
Dragon's Spine
Faldin's Bridge
The Rampart
Mount Hammal
World's Edge
Trading City of Vala
Fury Mountains
Konno Sea
Muneer Outpost
Spice Coast
The Southern Pelagic
Shaar
HD
2017
©Ava Richardson 2017 - All rights reserved

DEADWEED DRAGONS

Dragon Called

Dragon Magic

Dragon Song

This is a work of fiction. Names, characters, places and incidents either are the product of imagination or are used fictitiously. Any resemblance to actual persons, living or dead, events or locales, is entirely coincidental.

RELAY PUBLISHING EDITION, JUNE 2019

Ava Richardson is a pen name created by Relay Publishing for co-authored Fantasy projects. Relay Publishing works with incredible teams of writers and editors to collaboratively create the very best stories for our readers.

Cover Design by Joemel Requeza

www.relaypub.com

DEADWEED DRAGONS BOOK THREE

BLURB

Their only hope for their future is to unravel her past.

The Southern Kingdom is overrun with Deadweed and what remains lies scorched by dragon's fire. Plagued by the choking menace and targeted by attacks from deadly Water Wraiths, Dayie has no choice—master her magic or succumb to it. But when she and the Dragon Riders seek help from neighboring Torvald, they find a Kingdom under siege and come to a heart-wrenching realization.

They will not win the fight.

The only option to restore the wasteland that was once their home is for Dayie to travel to a mysterious site that may hold the key to her birth and the tremendous power that drives the Water Wraiths. But what she discovers is more terrifying than the enemies she already faces.

Armed with a link to her past and the song of the sea in her heart, Dayie must confront the truth of her birth in order to wield the full strength of her magic against powerful and untamable foes.

Before all hope is lost.

MAILING LIST

Thank you for purchasing 'Dragon Song'
(Deadweed Dragons Book Three)

If you would like to hear more about what I am up to, or continue to follow the stories set in this world with these characters—then please take a look at:
AvaRichardsonBooks.com

You can also find me on me on
www.facebook.com/AvaRichardsonBooks

Or sign up to my mailing list:
AvaRichardsonBooks.com/mailing-list

CHAPTER 1
DAYIE, & SOUTHERN HOSPITALITY

"K*eep an eye on them..."* I muttered under my breath, knowing that Zarr would read my thoughts as clearly as the giant Crimson Red dragon could hear my voice.

The ocean breeze was stronger than I had anticipated this morning as we flew out of the mouth of the great Taval River estuary, and Zarr's sharp dragon-senses had already informed me that the wind was bringing with it the promise of rain. Not that I could see a drop of rain or a single cloud on the horizon, of course – but then again, a dragon could always see and smell much farther than I ever could.

No, my attention was focused on the scene below – a fat-bellied ship with three masts was powering towards the mouth of the estuary, its sails displaying the purple and red colors of Torvald.

"There are dragons nearby..." Zarr's draconian hiss washed

through my mind, bringing with it the iron tang of soot. It didn't help my already tense mood.

"Where? Whose – southern dragons?" I looked around, unable to see anything.

"Not southern dragons. No den that I recognize..." Zarr's tone was heavy with a bullish posturing.

Seeing a ship flying Torvald colors shouldn't be alarming of itself, of course – Lord Ehsan, the oldest of the three Southern Lords who had taken over from the disappeared Prince J'ahillid, had told me that the South still traded with the Northern Empire, of course. But recent times had strained our relationship. The Southern Lords had been tacitly supporting the theft of Torvald dragon eggs (of which I knew only too well!) to set up our own Dragon Training Hall, and just earlier this year the Wild Company – our renegade band of wild Binshee warriors – had attempted to close the pass through the High Mountains that connected the two realms.

Trust Akeem to get all high and mighty at a time like that... I thought irritably, hoping that he wasn't going to try anything like that here and now, with the Torvaldites. But I was probably being too judgmental. I was stressed, and tired, and annoyed.

Akeem, the Captain of the Binshee Wild Company and the son of Prince J'ahallid, had thrown his loyal fighters into the defense of Dagfan, breaking a generation of suspicion and hostility between the Binshee and the Southern Lords – but that didn't mean that he was eager to see Torvald colors anywhere near *his* South.

But we need them… I thought again in desperation.

Ever since the Battle of Dagfan just a few moons ago, the South had been fighting a losing battle against the monstrous Deadweed and the Water Wraiths. Even though we had won that three-day battle in the end, the cost to the largest trading city in the South had been terrible. The docks and warehouses were destroyed, losing most of our precious stores for the winter – stores that not only fed the city of Dagfan and the Training Hall, but also a large number of smaller townships and settlements farther south as well.

It seemed, every time we achieved a victory, we only stalled the inevitable… I thought in consternation, keeping my eye on the Torvald boat as it kept a steady path into the bay, pitching a little as the crosswinds struck its sails.

Most of the banks of the grand Taval River – the lifeblood of the South – had been colonized by the Deadweed and then hacked and burned by our dragons or our foot soldiers. It was a mess, with many of the smaller port towns having to be abandoned. Fire was the only certain answer to both the Deadweed and the uncanny Water Wraith army – living soldiers made of water – but fire was no friend to houses and stores and cattle yards, either. The banks of the Taval were the prime farmland of the South, too, meaning that we were facing the prospect of monsoon season with very little food to spare.

Which was why it was so imperative that this mission went well, I thought as I looked above and behind the Torvald ship. A mission of peace, perhaps, as Lord Ehsan had sent word that the South would be willing to pay a king's ransom for a shipment of grains from the safer and wetter lands of the North.

"Screyarch!" The sky was split by the high-pitched shriek of dragon call – and it didn't come from the Crimson Red beneath me, or the small flight of Wild Company Vicious Oranges who had been holding back, skirting the river banks to look for any potential pockets of Deadweed.

"There! Moon-set and south, two female Blues!" Zarr's body trembled with agitation as he saw the shapes before I did.

The two Sinuous Blue dragons speared low over the waters of the ocean, their tails undulating behind them with audible cracks of air, and their wings beating a furious pace that set furrows in the water just meters below their long bellies.

They were from the Torvald Dragon Academy, all right – I could see the pennants that fluttered from the saddles of the two Riders that each dragon held, just as I could see the sun catch the glitter of burnished steel and spear points.

They sounded angry. They looked angry. And they were coming straight for us.

"Mine! Mine!" Zarr shouted, his words understandable to me as a gale of pride and anger—in my mind – but to my ears they appeared as his deep, challenging call. Zarr was bigger than the two Sinuous Blues who were flaring their wings towards us – he had a stockier, barrel-like chest and a much

wider wings span – but the Torvald dragons were much longer, with their whipping, barbed tails easily longer than their thin bodies by half as much again. I didn't know whether my friend the Crimson Red was proclaiming ownership of me, or of the river, or perhaps of the whole South itself – but whichever it was, the Sinuous Blues responded by shaking their heads and rattling the scales on their long necks like the sand winds in full storm.

"They shouldn't have brought dragons!" I heard a shout and turned my head to see that Akeem had joined me as we faced off against the Torvald Blues. He was dressed in his Wild Company garb: black robes and soft trousers, and with his red silk scarf that usually covered his mouth and nose, but now pulled down so that he could shout at me.

Huh, I thought. *I* was supposed to be the representative of the Dagfan dragons here, wasn't I? Even though Lord Ehsan had convinced his brothers that they had to accept the offer of aid from the Binshee Wild Company, they still wanted one of their own (*or someone they presumed was one of their own, anyway*) leading the patrol.

"It's Torvald," I called out, the exasperation clear in my voice. "Of course, they brought their dragons!"

The two Sinuous Blues snapped out their wings to their side, raising their heads so that they both shot upwards in front of us, exposing the lighter, creamy scales of their underbellies.

"Skkrrrr...." Zarr growled in annoyance. It was a classic dominance move, I was coming to find out. The more confi-

dent dragons would show off their exposed underbellies and necks, as if saying '*you think you're tough? Well – come and get me!*'

"The arrogance!" Akeem shouted, urging his own Vicious Orange Aida to perform the same movement. She was the smallest of the assembled breeds of dragons here, more falcon-like in her proportions, but the Vicious Oranges had a well-earned reputation of fierce intractability. She shot upwards in a smooth arc, high above us—

Oh no. This was what I was afraid of. I had seen this display amongst the Training Hall dragons that I was still attempting to train. The Training Hall dragons of Dagfan had been kept underground, locked in dragon cells before only being brought up a few at a time to fly with their assigned Riders and students – but that had just made them suspicious and grumpy, and so I had been adamant that Nas let them come and go freely.

Which was presenting as many problems as it was solving. The thought flashed through my mind, but I had enough worries on my plate right now with what was in front of me. The dominance flight meant that each dragon would try to rise higher and higher in front of the other, daring their opponent to attack their unprotected bellies, until one of the dragons couldn't bear the insult anymore and would dive down and forward. The goal, I think, was to hold out the longest and ascend the highest so that when your opponent flew at you, then you could attack from the higher position.

Which would not do our call for aid from Torvald any good at all – if we ended up starting a war with them instead!

"Akeem!" I shouted sternly at him, but he and Aida were already a hundred meters or so above me and rising, as one of the Sinuous Blues matched their height as well…

I still had 'my' Sinuous Blue in front of me, darting back and forth as we flew in circles over the Torvald galleon below, making little upward dips to dare Zarr into a dominance flight.

"Don't be idiots!" I shouted at the two Torvald Academy Dragon Riders, but behind their impassive horned dragon helmets, I couldn't make out if they were as worried as I was at this or whether they were egging their Blue on.

Is this how Torvald dragons always meet others? I thought as Zarr growled and soot whipped from the edges of his teeth. He was taking a breath, forcing the air to swell his chest as he tried to rise in dominance—

"No!" I clamped down on his anger with all of my will, whilst my hands gripped the harness ropes that went to the halter around his shoulders, trying my best to stop him from any of this stupidity.

"They think they're better than us!" Zarr seethed with hurt ego, and it was like a furnace in my mind. As close as our bond was – so close that some days I wondered where he ended and I began – Zarr was still a dragon: mighty and powerful – a species that had flown the skies of the earth since before humans had ever learned to build houses. My attempts to stop him was like using a feather to hold back the rain.

With a growl, Zarr rose his head and chest, daring the Sinuous Blue to strike—

But why are the Torvald Dragons acting like this? I thought. Was it because I had flown too close to the Torvald boat? Where they just as territorial about '*theirs*' as Zarr was about the South?

There was an answering, mocking hiss from the Sinuous Blue as it flew to our northern side, and I knew that I wouldn't be able to stop what was about to happen. Far above me, now just dark specks in the high, white airs were Akeem and the other Torvald Blue, each spiraling around each other and continuing to climb upward as they drew closer and closer—

Oh, sands, damn it! I swore, knowing that I only had one recourse, as I closed my eyes, took a deep breath and tried to reach for the current of magic that was always there, at the bottom of my heart—

Using my magic was not something that I wanted to do at the best of times— not after the Battle for Torvald or what the old Sorcerer of the Whispering Rocks had confided in me. It was a witch's magic, that much I now knew – but it also came with a terrible exhaustion and pain, which both the sorcerer and Mengala the Old – herself once a Witch of the Western Isles – had said was often one of the drawbacks of having these gifts.

I didn't want to use my magic because I couldn't control it properly – or what it did to me afterwards – but far more than that, I didn't want to use my mother's song on the dragons I loved. It seemed like cheating somehow, to force my bonded companion Zarr to feel things that he might not want to. But even that thought left with it the bitter taste of knowing that I had used the song within me a lot when I had first stolen Zarr as an egg from the Torvald Academy. *But I didn't realize what I was doing then,* I told myself. *Still no excuse though…*

"Mamma-la, Mamma-la…" I sang, not even having to reach for the notes as they came so easily to me now. It was the song that felt as though I had been born knowing it – a simple nursery rhyme that I had thought I made up as if it had always been there, pregnant like a seed in my mind.

But it was no nursery rhyme – or no *mere* nursery rhyme, anyway.

Mengala the Old had told me that it was one of the foundational teaching songs of Sebol; the Haunted Isle, the home of the Western Witches. My mother – a woman I had never known and whom I couldn't even remember – had taught me this song or had enchanted it into me when her ship had sunk, leaving me to be washed up on the southern coasts and taken in by my foster parents, Obasi and Wera. They had been simple fisher-folk, but had known that the power I carried was special and good – a rare insight compared to the rest of the Southlands hatred of any witchcraft and magic whatsoever!

"Mamma-la, mamma-la…" I let my voice gain in strength and could feel the rising tides of cerulean calm flowing out through me, through my words, through my hands, and into the angered dragons all around me.

Mengala had taught me the answering melodies to that song of Sebol, and ever since then it felt as though the song itself had become stronger, as if just the soothing, repeating, simple melodies themselves were the keys to greater and greater power…?

Whatever the mechanism of it was, my spirits lifted, heartened by the simple mantra –despite the dangerous beasts all about me…

"Zarr?" I whispered as I opened my eyes to see that my song had indeed had a noticeable effect – his mind was usually filled with heat and storm, but his raging inferno was now just a smoldering burn of coals. I felt the ebb of his own comfort and peace as his mind washed through mine, and knew my song had worked. Opposite us, the Sinuous Blue was no longer whipping its tail and hissing at us, but had instead turned back in descending circles around its ward, the Torvald galleon.

The song, too, seemed to have affected the dragons above us, as there was a rush of wings and the other Sinuous Blue swooped in a wide, lazy arc to join its companion, and Akeem turned back from his pursuit, looking perplexed.

Ah. Sorry, Akeem, I thought. One of the new powers that my song seemed to have was that it not only affected the creatures, plants, and animals of this world, everything from dragons to goats and even to the Deadweed itself, but the newer melodies seemed to be able to affect humans, too.

It still didn't calm the Water Wraiths, though, I sighed as Akeem flew past us, still looking warily down at the Torvald Dragons, but only with a standoffish glare, not the outright prideful fury that his face had displayed a few moments ago.

If only I could make the Water Wraiths feel like that! I thought a little sadly. Maybe we wouldn't be in this mess. Instead, it seemed as though the Water Wraiths had been *drawn* to my magical song – but not out of feelings of sympathy and affection at all. Out of obsession and anger.

"But it helps you to lead them away..." Zarr informed me, his mind a little sleepier than it had been before. I felt another pang of guilt at having to use my powers on him. I didn't want him to be soporific and dozy!

"Not dozy. Perfectly awake." Zarr pushed at me with his mind. *"I should have known the Blues wouldn't want to fight me anyway. They're too small."*

"You must be right," I said lightly, as in the next instant the cost for such magic hit me around the head like a dragon's tail.

"Ach..." I hissed as my eyes throbbed with a headache.

"Dayie-sister?" Zarr said urgently and worriedly. Through our bond he could share my pain as easily as my thoughts.

"It's fine," I said sternly, knowing that I would be. Mengala the Old, the ex-Western Witch of Sebol, had returned to Dagfan after the previous battle along with the Sorcerer of the Whispering Rocks – although both were now frail after their use of magic. Anyway, I knew that she still had some of that magewort which I could take when we eventually escorted this ship back to Dagfan, and the headache of just using the song was nowhere near as bad as it had been earlier in the season, when I forced myself to perform far greater acts of magic with it than this!

"Let's go offer them some southern hospitality, shall we?" I said, signaling to Akeem to hold back as I relaxed my grip on the harness reins and leaned forward, letting Zarr take his own course as he swirled down after the Sinuous Blues towards the Torvald boat.

CHAPTER 2
AKEEM, & THE TORVALDITES

She'd done it again, hadn't she? I thought with not a small amount of annoyance, as I watched Dayie swooping in large, graceful circles around the Torvald boat before landing in a spraying plume of water ahead of them, heading in the same direction.

She used her song on me, I thought, recalling a few strains of that haunting melody as I had been attempting to gain height over the Sinuous Blue. Still, it was hard to feel *totally* put out by her, as I knew that Dayie only used her magic when she thought that she had to – and that she didn't generally *want* to use her magic at all.

But maybe that was her magic trying to make me forgive her... I thought as I returned to the other Wild Company Riders, who similarly seemed fairly content with just watching proceedings in front of us. They must have been affected too, I thought.

"Yes, she used her magic on us..." Aida informed me, with a

touch of warmth, but it was a good-natured sort of irritation. *"But we still have our own minds, at least."*

Yes, I knew that. Dayie's magic didn't appear to *make* people do things, as far as I understood it – but just encouraged other, forgotten currents of emotion to surface. I didn't understand it, I realized as I shook my head. Even though I liked and respected Dayie—

There was a humor-filled cough in my mind from Aida that made me blush for some reason.

"What?" I said out loud.

"Nothing...." Aida whipped her tail mischievously.

Anyway. As I was thinking – I respected Dayie, and I had seen far too many scorched and burnt patches in the desert oases where other wandering witches had been hunted and persecuted to know that I never wanted her to be afraid of what she was…

But that didn't necessarily mean that I wanted her to use her magic! I had to admit. I knew that it hurt her. That it cost her.

"It is her cost to bear. She makes her own choices, Akeem. You can't save her from herself, no matter how much you might want to," Aida informed me, always so annoyingly wise. I hated it.

"Well, I can try," I said stubbornly, before turning my attention to the Wild Company. "Eyes sharp! We don't want the Deadweed or the Water Wraiths sneaking up on us! Scan the river banks!" I snapped at them, and my comrades did as they were told, sliding down through the currents of air as fleet as crows as they moved ahead of the boat.

I hope she's safe, I couldn't stop myself from thinking as I maintained my position high above them, watching the great Crimson dragon Zarr – almost as long as the galleon if you counted his tail—paddling beside the Torvaldites with his wings tucked high over his back like a swan. The small figure standing on his back with the streaming flag of white hair was Dayie, and she appeared to be talking to the forward deck of the boat, where a delegation of people in their purple and red cloaks had congregated at the railings.

"Do you want to hear?" Aida informed me, still with that mischievous note in her voice. *"Just because you care so much…"* she added with another flick of her sharp-barbed tail.

"I do care," I said quickly. Of course I did. Down there was a young woman barely into her twenties defenseless in front of a galleon of trained Torvald soldiers, probably with longbows and crossbows and two Sinuous Blue dragons! Who knows what the wrong word could mean!

"Dayie's no weakling, Akeem." This time I could sense the trill of annoyance in Aida's voice, and wondered if Dayie's mesmeric song was wearing off on her. *"And she has Zarr with her…"*

That was true, I nodded. Zarr was a Crimson Red, a 'young bull' in dragon terms, meaning that he was full of fire and attitude – and many of the Binshee were starting to call him a 'King' dragon – which is an old term for the largest of the ancient bull dragons, who could apparently be strong enough to control multiple dens instead of the more usual matriarchal 'dragon mother' set up. I ignored such talk, as the king dragons were thankfully a thing of the past.

"Yes, I would like to hear, thank you very much…" I said a little stiffly as Aida sighed and opened her senses to me.

A dragon's senses are nothing like a human's. Not only are they stronger and more acute, able to sense meat and fire many leagues before it is ever visible to the human eye – but they are also subtle, able to detect the tiniest changes in the winds as autumn tilts gently into winter; or tell when a land is sick and prone to disease…

Not only that, but a dragon can *see* places, sounds, and events that humans can only think about in the vaguest and most dreamlike of terms. Every dragon builds a picture in its mind, a 'dragon map' of smells and sounds that it will freely share with the other trusted dragons of its den or nest, creating a living, vibrant picture of the world which is far greater than the individual experiences of each dragon alone.

Which is all a very roundabout way of saying that yes, Aida could hear perfectly what was being said just a few hundred meters below, and as she rolled her mind over mind – suddenly I could, too…

CHAPTER 3

DAYIE, AMBASSADOR, MESSENGER, THIEF

"Welcome to the South!" My voice rang out over the waters as the Torvald boat slowed and stilled, reefing two of its sails in order to do so. "I am Dayie, Dragon Rider of Dagfan, and emissary for the Southern Lords…"

I had thought about how to introduce myself to this boat – as I wasn't really an ambassador, and my feelings about the Dagfan Training Hall were mixed at best. As much as I respected the Training Hall's Chief Talal for his tenacity and dedication – his methods and principles were awful, and it felt like I had spent my entire time there trying to overturn them!

And then, there was the fact that I had more respect for the Binshee Wild Company than I did for the Southern Lords – at least the mountain tribal folk of the Binshee bonded with their dragons – but it was more than that, of course. The Binshee Chiefs, as contrary and as difficult as they could be, seemed to be involved in every aspect of their people's lives, able to be approached at all times, holding large meetings where justice was decided. The Southern Lords barely ever left their villas!

However, in the end, after considering a more truthful answer of '*hi, I'm Dayie, a witch who also stole one of your dragon eggs, sorry about that...*' wouldn't go down as well, I settled just for the official line that I was here on behalf of the Southern Lords.

To be honest, I didn't think even the Southern Lords knew what to make of me either, I sighed as I waited for the response from the Torvald boat. They knew that I had magic – everyone in Dagfan now knew– but they also could see that I flew the largest dragon in the South.

(There was a proud grumbling purr from Zarr beneath me – all dragons were a bit like that; their bigger size meant they needed bigger compliments).

"Hail, Dragon Rider of the South!" a voice answered, and I looked up to see that there was a youngish man standing on the top deck prow, with short-cropped ruddy-blond hair. Even though his complexion wasn't as fair as mine, it was still a little bit of a shock to see that he and most of the people around him were fair-skinned, like me. I knew that Torvald was a cosmopolitan place (I had crept through its streets, on my way to its sacred mountain, after all), but the overwhelming majority of the faces there were still lighter-skinned, and people of all backgrounds there wore the sturdy, heavy-spun fabrics and even furs of the North.

The man opposite me wore a rich purple cloak, swept back from his shoulders to display the sculpted leather breastplate that looked like overlapping scales. At his side was a sword (sheathed) and standing just a little bit behind him was a trio of far more martial looking Torvald soldiers, with their characteristic horned helmets. From the way they stood, not to mention the pikes that they held in their hands, I figured these men and women *weren't* as impressed with having a young bull Crimson Red dragon wallowing about near their boat.

"Wallow? I never wallow!" Zarr scooped up a bit of water and spat it out in a spray. He was enjoying this, and he was enjoying the way the Sinuous Blues were slowly circling above, still not as aggressive as they had been, but looking down in apparent nervousness at his impressive bulk.

"I am Duke Robert of Flamma-Torvald, son of Princess Robba Flamma-Torvald, who was daughter to Queen Saffron and King Bower Flamma-Torvald," he said in a loud, authoritative voice.

A duke... I wondered, trying to remember anything that Fan Hazim, the Dragon Trader and thief who had kept me as an indentured servant, had said about the Torvald royal family. Not a lot, to be honest. I thought the ruler of Torvald was a Queen Nuria?

"Humans. So confusing. It is easier with dragons: Den Mother, King Bull," Zarr informed me sagely.

Hush, wyrm, I'm thinking... I chided him affectionately, and I saw the duke cock his head to one side suddenly.

"You can talk to your dragon?" he moved suddenly to the railing and leaned over with his gauntleted hands on the railings. It apparently caused a stir from his guards behind him, as they rushed to join him, before he let up a restraining hand.

Could this Duke Robert overhear my conversations with Zarr in the same way that Mengala the Old could? I thought in alarm. If he could hear dragon tongue, then that might change how we conduct the negotiations…

"Are you a friend to dragons, sir?" I called out to him, to which I saw him pull a face, look into the water and back up to me.

"Well, I don't want to be their enemy…" he said, and I found myself smirking at him.

"I don't like him." Zarr splashed his tail against the river water suddenly, and I could feel a surge of annoyance from him.

What is it? Can you sense something wrong about him? I asked Zarr, keeping my eyes on the duke as I thought this at the dragon. Duke Robert's bemused expression didn't change, but he turned his head again a little towards us as if he were trying to listen in to what we were saying.

Either he is very good at hiding his thoughts, or he can't really hear us… I thought at Zarr.

"He's probably lying. You shouldn't trust him." Zarr pulled away from the Torvald galleon a little, making me clench my jaw in frustration.

We really have to get this negotiation done right, I reminded Zarr, sensing his annoyance at the human obsession with words. I was suddenly jealous of the dragon's way of life –

they didn't have to posture and hide what they thought, ever. Mostly because they were the biggest things around, but also because dragon society was so much more straightforward. If a dragon didn't like another, then it would perform a dominance flight, and if it thought it couldn't win or couldn't make friends with another dragon, then it would just fly off.

But we need that Torvald grain, I thought with a fixed smile on my face.

The duke straightened up with a broad grin on his face. "I thank you, Dragon Rider, for your escort into Dagfan. It is an honor to finally see the great Crimson dragon of the South that I have been hearing much about!"

"He's heard about me?" Zarr's ears pricked up. *"Maybe he's not so bad after all…"*

"We have many dragons in the South," I struck a word of caution. I didn't want this duke to think that all he had to do was to butter me up and then it would all be plain sailing from there on out for him. The three Southern Lords had almost come to blows amongst each other as they had tried to agree what price they could offer Torvald for their grains and then continuing shipments of goods. We had lost so much thanks to the Deadweed that we didn't have much to give – and I had to make sure that this duke couldn't think he would just be able to ask for every coin that we had left!

"And our Dragon Riders are growing by the season," I said, which was technically true though I didn't want to let on that half of those new Training Hall Riders were little better than recruits, and the other half of the available dragons were all the smaller Vicious Oranges of the Binshee.

"But I thank you for your kind words about my Crimson Red," I tried to sound gracious. "He *is* a very powerful dragon, isn't he?" I asked, before Zarr could take offense at me not speaking up for him.

"The largest Crimson Red I've seen," the duke tapped a respectful finger to his temples, as if saluting.

"You see – I told you the human had manners!" Zarr said.

Lord Ehsan had done as much as he could to try and make Dagfan look impressive, but given the trauma of the Battle of Dagfan, that had seen our entire dockyards and warehouse district burnt and mostly demolished, all he had managed to achieve was a sort of decrepit presentability.

Silk pennants, orange and yellow and deep blues fluttered from the rounded fort structure of the Councilor's Hall, and many of the old moorings had simply been hacked away and the quays cleared of debris rather than attempting to clean them up. One fat wooden pier still jutted out into the water, however, and it gleamed golden-yellow with all the freshness of new-sawn wood.

One dock for a city, I thought, feeling a sudden intense embarrassment for the place that I was currently calling home. What would Torvald think?

Behind the dock there were still great piles of blackened rocks and bricks that the people of the city were superstitious about going near. They were the remnants of the buildings that the Deadweed had infested, and that the Water Wraiths had flooded through – but the Southern Lords had ordered their reuse, and even now I could see work teams of tired, slightly bedraggled looking city folk moving back and forth with their wheelbarrows. The air was fresh and sharp with all of the sprigs and garlands of lavender and wild thyme that people had left on these refuse piles – presumably as a way to try and ward off what evil corruption they thought still lingered.

"Dayie!" came a hail from the dockside. It was Nas, or *Lieutenant-Rider* Nas, as I should call him now. I still didn't particularly know what possessed the Southern Lords to elevate Nas above me in the Training Hall hierarchy, but I knew that during my flight to the South, and my away-missions with the Binshee Wild Company, Nas Hazim – the youth who I had grown up with and whom I had hated at first – had become a good friend of Chief Talal's. I would never have thought that the overgrown, slightly burly Gypsy boy would have been so good at strategy and administration – but it turned out he was!

"Nas, they're following right behind me," I said as Zarr walked up the stone ramp that had been used to launch the cities' boats and was one of the few pieces of dock architecture that *hadn't* been cracked and damaged at all in the battle. "And they've brought two Sinuous Blues with them…" I pointed out, as the Torvald galleon emerged into view around the distant bend in the river, once again powering under full sails.

"I heard." Nas looked dourly at the boat. "Which might explain what's going on in the Training Hall…"

I was already stripping off my gauntlets when I froze. "*What* is going on in the Training Hall?" I asked quickly. We couldn't afford to have a dragon fight, not right now, not in front of the Duke of Torvald!

"It's Irafea, she's distraught over something…" Nas shook his head.

Oh, great, I thought, quickly pulling my gauntlets back on and settling back into the saddle. Irafea was one of the oldest of the Training Hall dragons, younger than Chief Talal's Stocky Green named Gren, but still one of the first dragons to find her home here. Which meant that she had undergone all of the old and pig-headed attempts to train that Chief Talal had first tried out, before I came along. She had been the steed of one of The Seven, the previous order of 'official' Training Hall Dragon Riders who were so named because there had only ever been seven successful pairings of Riders and dragons originating in the Training Hall itself. I, myself, had replaced one of their number.

The Seven were no more now, as half of their number had been killed by the Deadweed, and in their stead, we now had thirteen dragons and rider combinations. We were a lot better off than The Seven had been, as I had insisted that the dragons and their riders bond naturally – as most of *The Seven* had drugged, beaten, or bribed their dragons to ride with them.

Irafea was one of those older dragons of The Seven who had lost her rider in the early invasions of the Deadweed, but she had never been bonded to him, or to anyone else either. She was cantankerous, and she was grumpy, and she still had a habit of ignoring the other humans and dragons alike. I was rather beginning to fear that the Training Hall would just have to keep her as a free-roaming resident, tied to her meal times at the hall and her rivalries with the others.

But what worried me the most about this situation was that Irafea was also a Sinuous Blue, just like the two approaching Torvald dragons.

"I'll go talk to her," I said, already urging Zarr to begin his hop and leap into the air-

"Wait! That's not all!" Nas was making quick hand gestures at me to slow down, already casting quick glances over his shoulder at the approaching Torvald galleon.

What now? I thought.

"It's also your friends – the wizards and warlocks or whatev-er…" Nas frowned. He was unlike the other Gypsies of Shaar that I had come to know and love. He took after his mother Fan (the woman who had enslaved me) in some of his more prejudicial, southern-leaning views against magic – even though the other travelling caravans of Shaar that I had since met had shown themselves to be nothing but generous and open-minded.

"The sorcerer and the herbalist, you mean?" I asked, knowing he meant the Sorcerer of the Whispering Rocks whom I had sought out for help with my magic, and Mengala the Old – the woman who had seemed to have sought *me* out.

Nas shrugged, at least having the good graces to look a little embarrassed at having used such terminology when he knew full well their names and their titles. "Yeah, them. They're not doing too well. We have them in the Training Hall Healer's Rooms."

Wow, wonderful... I didn't wait to hear his explanation of what was wrong with the 'wizards and warlocks' and instead kicked down with my feet and threw my mind forward. *Fly, my heart,* I thought.

And in response, the Crimson Red beneath me jumped into the air with a snarl.

CHAPTER 4
DAYIE, A DAUGHTERS' REUNION

I could hear Irafea's desperate hooting even as we swirled around the circular amphitheater that was the Dagfan Training Hall. It sat (wisely) outside the main city, along the coastal road that tracked beside the River Taval and eventually led up to the bridge to the High Mountains pass. It was an old tournament theatre from a time when the rulers of Dagfan used to have combats and races and demonstrations of strength. Almost ten years ago, the Southern Lords had thought it to be a perfect place to house dragons for underneath its packed sand floors, it had large natural caverns which had already been fitted with iron bars, to house the various animals and prisoners who had once been forced to fight in here.

Now, though, it was in a very different state of repair than those old days – if any of the old servants and Dragon Handlers were to be believed. Its stone walls were deeply rutted and scarred where the dragons had used them as scratching posts, and one entire quarter of the rounded building was still blackened and smoke-damaged from when *even we* had an outbreak of the Deadweed.

But at least Nas and Talal had listened to me about the landing platforms, I thought in annoyance as Zarr settled on one of the two wooden 'jetties' that had been built on top of the Training Hall's battlements. They were nothing like the elaborate stone platforms I had seen at the Citadel of Torvald, but they were a start – a way to encourage the dragons here to think of this place as home, where they could perch and watch the world and smell the breeze – as well as being practically useful as convenient places to launch from.

Prior to this, the circular battlements had only been the domain of heavy crossbows and arbalests, all pointing back down *inside* the Training Hall, as Chief Talal had been – and still was, a little bit – terrified of the dragons within running rampant.

Which might just happen! I thought in alarm as I hopped from Zarr's side to run to the nearest set of steps.

"Where is she?" I shouted at the nearest of the Dragon Handlers – predominantly large and burly men who had worked with goads to feed and move the dragons about, but who now doubled as guards.

"We got her in her cave!" The large Handler nodded to the open archway that led down to the Dragon Caves below, as it was obvious who I was speaking about.

Irafea's cries were muffled, but they were insistent, and most of the other dragons appeared to agitated –our other Sinuous Blue lashed her tail over and over on the sand where she had been sunning herself, and at least two Stocky Greens had taken to sharing the other dragon platform, hissing and clacking at the ground below.

The other dragons must be out on patrol, I thought as I ran across the amphitheater to the open archway, stripping off my riding harness as I did so – it was lighter than the sturdy metal thing that the Torvald Riders wore, but it was still taut, with heavy straps and buckles of leather that secured across my chest and around my hips to help me sit in place on my dragon saddle. I didn't want to be encumbered when I faced an angry Sinuous Blue dragon – and I didn't want *her* to think that I had come to make her fly if she didn't want to, either.

What about Mengala and the sorcerer? I worried as my feet took me down the stone ramp to the caves below. Nas had said that *they* were in the healing rooms here in the Training Hall – shouldn't I go to them first? It had to be their magic, I thought, knowing that both of them were suffering the effects of using too much, with the powerful enchantment they had wrought to send us flying faster to the Battle of Dagfan taking a terrible toll on their health.

Was all magic like that? I knew that my song always left me with a headache and feeling tired. But Mengala had said that magic could sometimes have a price, and for the unlucky ones, that price would be pain.

It didn't sound like something I wanted to indulge – but in the next heartbeat, I was aware that the song was the only connection that I had to my mother and whoever she was. How could I give that up?

Stop worrying, Dayie. I told myself firmly, knowing that I was just trying to find things to distract me from the task at hand. There was the loud, echoing sound of a scrape from deeper in the caverns. Like claws, rasping on metal.

I ran into the large central hallway, with tunnels with cast-iron gates, driven deep into the rock bed and sturdy enough to withstand a dragon attack. These gates had been routinely kept locked, once upon a time, which meant that you had to pass through several such gates in order to get to the actual caverns. I had forced Nas to try a system of keeping some of them open – allowing at least some of the dragons free rein to come and go at different times, and then opening up different caverns for the remaining dragons. I had thought it had been working, until I saw, in the flames of flickering torchlight the form of a rather large, burly Dragon Handler with his goad standing guard at each and every gate.

"All the gates are locked? What about the dragons that want to come out?" I said in a little sterner tone than I had been intending with the Handler. His was a face that I recognized but didn't know too well. At my approach, the Handler shuffled himself into a sort of standing-at-attention, mostly because I was an official Rider of the Training Hall now and should be able to ask for access to any dragon, at any time.

"Lieutenant-Rider Nas ordered it." The Handler nodded towards where the scraping and hissing sounds could be heard, as it was pretty self-evident why Nas had done it. No one wanted a rampaging dragon on the loose.

But it was so like the old tactics of dragon-handling! I thought in exasperation as I stepped up to the gate, hoping the look on my face would make it clear I wanted to be let through to see the angered Irafea. It was one of the things that I had been trying to show Nas, to show them all. We had to be more like how the Binshee treated their dragon companions. Yeah, sometimes their dragons lost their temper or had dominance fights, but when a dragon is agitated, the Binshee sought to try and answer its needs – which might be just to be left alone, or given more attention – but whatever it was, the answer wasn't locking it up!

The Handler unlocked the gate with his set of heavy iron keys and as it creaked back, the sound of hissing suddenly stopped.

"You'll need this." The Handler looped one of the over-large iron keys from the hoop to give to me. "She's behind the next gate, and we didn't put anyone on it, in case she flamed them."

"Flamed them?" I muttered, snatching the key and moving through at speed. *People can be so stupid!* I thought as my feet jogged down the hallway towards the distant patch of light. Dragons don't just decide, 'oh, I think I'll torch someone today!'

"Sometimes we do…" Zarr's voice was mirthful but shot through with his worry over me going down here alone.

Okay, yeah, maybe sometimes you do. But it's always for a reason, right? I thought at Zarr. Either that human had wronged them, or had attacked them, or had insulted them in some way…

"Or looked especially tasty…" Zarr prodded me.

"Now really isn't the time for jokes," I muttered under my breath as I saw that the tunnel ahead, in addition to being lit by the wavering light of the wall torch, now also had the dull red sheen that can only come from dragon cinders.

"Who says I'm joking?"

Which was true, I guess. Some of the wilder dragons of the desert ate people. But they had never had a chance to get to know people. And both Zarr and Aida themselves had informed me that there just wasn't enough meat on a human to be worth the chasing of one. A dragon had to be starving or half mad in order to attack and eat a human.

I hoped that Irafea wasn't either of these things.

"Ssssss!" A sudden rising hiss and a ruddy glow brightened up ahead suddenly. Despite everything I knew, I still flinched a little at the thought of a sudden gout of dragon flame bursting around the corner, but of course – it didn't come. I could trust my instincts. Irafea was angry and upset, but she wasn't crazy.

"*Careful!"* Zarr suddenly growled through me, and I heard an angered growl in response from Irafea. *She could sense Zarr inside my mind?* I shouldn't be surprised, I suppose.

"It's okay, Irafea, it's only me. Dayie…" I said gently as I walked slowly around the corner of the tunnel to see the black iron gate that was in place across the Sinuous Blue's cave, and behind it, the Sinuous Blue herself, standing with coils of her tail rippling and lashing around the room. At her feet she'd cindered her bedding of straw and hay, making a blackened heap of coals that sparked occasionally with red.

"What's wrong, hey?" I murmured again, wondering if I had to resort to using my song once more. My eyes were still hurting from using it before – it wasn't just the smoke of the cinders! And, after just recently feeling bad about using it on Zarr, I was loathe to do it all over again.

"You want food? You want to be out of here?" I moved forward, walking slowly but purposefully, as I knew that a dragon respected strength. But I held out my hands as I did so, showing her the key that I was going to use on her lock.

Irafea lashed her tail across the bars suddenly, making me flinch and sending me jumping back. I couldn't hear her in my mind as I could Zarr – which I had learnt from my time with the Binshee was because I wasn't bonded to her.

I couldn't understand her, but Zarr inside of my mind could. *"She wants out. Now."*

To be honest, I thought that I could see that already.

"Okay…" I thought for a moment, forcing myself to *not* do as the angry Sinuous Blue was demanding of me, but instead trying to let her know that this had to be an agreement. A compromise. I couldn't just let her go when she was this angry – what if it was one of the other Training Hall dragons that had upset her, and she tried to attack them? What if it was one of the Dragon Handler guards who had unwittingly insulted her, and she wanted to teach them a lesson?

"Dragons don't compromise..." Zarr informed me. *"That won't work. You have to offer her something."*

"Well, you want to get out Irafea?" I said as firmly as I could (my voice still wavering a little in my throat). "Then we have to work this out. Together."

She snapped her jaws, and this time threw a talon at the walls to scratch the rock. She was *really* annoyed. Maybe I had been wrong about my training methods. Maybe Nas had been right about locking her up down here until she cooled down.

No! My heart wrenched at the thought. How could that be the better course of action? To keep a wild thing locked up and out of the light, all because we humans didn't like what it wanted!?

I believe that there is a way for dragons and humans to live together, I reiterated my mantra, the very same one that I had used to petition Chief Talal into letting me try my new training practices. *Which means we have to talk to each other. Bond where we can and still talk anyway where we can't.*

"I'm going to let you out, Irafea." I came to a decision, raising the black iron key in one hand. "Because I don't think you deserve to be down here, not a strong and powerful beauty like you..." (A little flattery never hurt after all, when talking to a dragon)

Her tail whipped again, but one bright yellow eye fixed on me as she hissed. It wasn't a roar, and it wasn't scratching, so I took this to be a good sign. She was listening to me at least, which had to be half the battle, right?

"All I want from you, Irafea, is for you to tell me what's wrong…" I said evenly.

Now two lambent yellow eyes had turned to regard me, and I heard a deep, guttural rumbling from her chest as small rivers of smoke pooled from her snout.

Zarr? I thought worriedly.

"I never knew..." Zarr's tone had grown serious and not as alarmed or as defensive as he had been just a moment before. Whatever Irafea had said had shocked even him.

"Zarr – what is it?" I whispered, still holding the key.

"Irafea is a mother," Zarr said, in a sort of awe. I knew that the dragons only had two forms of hierarchy – the almost legendary 'King' bull dragons, and the den or nest mothers, sometimes called queens in the library of scrolls that Chief Talal had been collecting – every scrap of dragon lore that he could buy or bribe from any trader he could find.

These den or nest mothers would sometimes look after whole clutches of eggs that weren't even their own, acting as the heart, soul, and commander of the entire nest.

"She's a mother?" I thought in alarm. Why had no one told me this? Where were her eggs? I tried to recall everything that Talal had told me about how the Training Hall had got the Sinuous Blue.

All of the dragons in here only came to the Training Hall in one of two ways: either as an egg, or as a 'rescue' case. The older dragons like Irafea and Gren were all rescues – they had come to us thanks to Chief Talal's (at the time) pioneering work to intercept and try to capture injured or wandering dragons that strayed into the South's territory. Almost always these attempts ended in disaster – either for the dragons or the Dragon Handlers who had gone to pacify them! But somehow, the Chief Talal had managed to placate a few dragons with buckets of fresh coal, luring them towards the Training Hall where the guards threw nets and ropes over them.

All of the older dragons here had the attitudes that reflected that beginning; they were either entirely too wary, or too complacent to ever really trust humans again, or they became dependent on the buckets of charcoal to keep them happy – as it was a tasty treat for a dragon, apparently.

But what had the chief tell me of Irafea? He had walked through the caves with me just a moon ago, after the Battle of Dagfan, as I was proposing my new training plans to him. He had endeavored to discourage me (of course) by telling me all of the horror stories associated with each of the very beasts he was supposed to be working with.

"Ah, and here we have Irafea…" the older man had said as he had walked me down this very corridor to show me the curled-up form of the Sinuous Blue, her ears pricking as she tracked our movements. "She was a difficult one to catch, and no mistake! She ate two ponies and managed to break Hefel's arm!" He was talking about one of the older Dragon Handler's. "We found her near starved in the desert with a broken wing, hooting and crying at everything that moved."

Yes, that was it, I remembered now. Talal had said there'd been a particularly strong sandstorm in the near deserts, which had traditionally meant that he would take a team of Dragon Handlers out the next day, knowing that it might be their best shot to pick up dragons that had been tumbled or become lost in the storm.

"But maybe you were hooting and crying because you had lost your eggs?" I murmured to her, earning another deep and rumbling growl from the Sinuous Blue.

"She says she did." Zarr translated for me. *"She didn't come from the Torvald Enclosure, but the far northern mountains,"* he explained to me, which fit in with what strategy and history lessons I had been given here at the Training Hall about our supposed rivals, the empire of Torvald. Most all of the dragons in the northern empire came, in one way or another, from their Sacred Mountain called Mount Hammal, which was home to a gigantic crater that the dragons lived in, as well as the near citadel of Torvald, as well.

But I remembered from the tales that after the old Dark King Maddox's reign, which itself had lasted for generations and had only been overthrown by King Bower and Queen Saffron, it turned out the dragons that had been persecuted and driven from their ancestral home by the Dark King had mostly taken up refuge in the far out of the way places: the Western Archipelago, the distant northern mountains. After Lord and Lady Bower and Saffron had taken over, a lot of the old dragons came back to Mount Hammal – but there were also a good few nests out there in the wilds that did not return. It was from *these* nests that the Dragon Traders like my own used to go to in order to steal eggs, to smuggle them back to Dagfan to start our own breeding program.

"She lost her nest when poachers attacked and stole her eggs..." the Crimson Red inside of me translated the grumblings from the Sinuous Blue in front of me.

Poachers, or some of Talal's Dragon Traders? I thought at Zarr in alarm. It might even have been Fan Hazim, before I had met her. And then what – the poachers sold the eggs to Torvald? Or maybe the Dragon Academy apprehended the poachers, but poor Irafea…

"Irafea tried to hunt them down, but they had gone, and when she tried to follow them, she got caught in a southern sandstorm, and ended up in the desert..." Zarr informed me.

"Oh, you poor lady…" I said, already moving to the door, before pausing. "Hang on a minute, those are Sinuous Blues outside, aren't they…" Inside my head, Zarr went silent for a moment. He had pulled his mind away to pay attention to something – but what? I found out a moment later when his reptilian consciousness swam back to mine, now with a fierce sort of joy riding through it.

"Those Blues outside? The northern Blues – they're Irafea's daughters!" he said, and in that instant I knew that, being an orphan and never knowing my own mother myself, there was nothing that I wouldn't do to reunite a mother with her child. I moved to the iron gate and was only too eager to crank the key in the heavy lock and pull at the gate as Irafea helped me, nudging it with her snout on the other side.

"But how?" I asked Zarr and Irafea both as the Sinuous Blue gratefully undulated up the passageway, following the only route out of here. I hoped that the Dragon Handler guard had kept the main gate open after I had passed. I supposed that Torvald Dragon Riders or soldiers must have caught the poachers (Dragon Traders) themselves, and, not knowing which nest in all of their realm that they could belong to, and with no mother seeking them out because Irafea was leagues away, stranded and with a broken wing, then they must have taken the eggs to Mount Hammal, to eventually be raised as dragon-steeds if they wanted to be.

Which they had, and now, ten or fifteen years later, they had returned to the South where their mother had vanished to.

I heard a distant, muffled cry of surprise from the Dragon Handler as the large Sinuous Blue charged through the distant open gate, but I didn't hear any shouts or screams. I raced after her on foot, so that I could watch her inevitable reunion with her daughters.

Would they even accept her anymore? I thought with a shiver of panic. I didn't know how it was with dragons – they seemed to feel things so deeply that I couldn't imagine any mother or daughter rejecting each other, and surely there had to be some tiniest dragon-memory of each other in their scales or in their scent that would remind each other? That was how Irafea had known that those distant Sinuous Blues from Torvald were hers. *Just like I had my song, a gift from my mother that still connected me to her…* I realized.

"Irafea's up in the air…she's calling to her young…" Zarr

informed me as I sprinted the last few caverns up into the bright light, before rubbing my eyes and turning to see what was happening, so far above the city.

A bloomin' great disaster, it looked like... I thought. Not that I was alarmed at what the dragons were doing up there – I *knew* why they were doing it, after all. But I was alarmed at the effect that it was clearly having on the guards of the Training Hall and further across Dagfan.

There were multiple ringing alarms—one coming from the great bronze gong of the Dragon Hall itself – used as a warning and a call for the dragons that we trained. This was matched (but not drowned out) by the distant, high-pitched squawks of the cities horns as the three dragons above the city circled and flared at each other.

Irafea wasn't the largest, surprisingly – even though she was their mother. To my dismay, I could see just how thin and emaciated she looked compared to her fuller-bodied daughters. Even her royal-blue scales appeared to lack the luster and sheen of the rich, cerulean hue of her children. I knew that a dragon's scales should grow darker as they grew older, but not less rich – and Irafea had a definite 'milky' and pale quality when seen next to the others.

How could we do this to her, to them! I thought in horror, and for the first time I could see the Training Hall how Akeem (and now Duke Robert of Torvald too) must see us. Not as trying to forge a connection with the dragons, but as mistreating them.

It made me angry, but my anger was tempered by what I could

see happening above. The younger Blues were curling and coiling through the air, darting forwards and away from the circling Irafea as if they were wary but interested at the same time. They gave out high-pitched, smaller mews like animals much younger than they were, and Irafea was voicing a loud and mournful song.

Would they accept her? I worried again. They had been apart for so long. More than ten years or so.

"Ten years is nothing to a dragon," Zarr informed me strongly, and I hoped that he was right.

"But Irafea has changed so much..." I said aloud. She was one of the most cantankerous of the Training Hall dragons, and with good reason, I now understood. Would she be *able* to relate as a normal dragon should?

"Pfft!" A snort of flame and soot from the Crimson Red on the landing platform above me, and I immediately felt a little guilty. Who was I to presume what a dragon could or could do?

"Skreeee...." A whistling, encouraging sound from Irafea and suddenly both of the younger Blues launched themselves up towards her, their long, humped bodies matching hers in flight as they flew together, a curling, rolling stream of dragons.

"Yes!" I could feel the affection and fierce, savage love pouring through me - it must have come from Zarr, but to me it felt like the dragons themselves were broadcasting their joy to the whole sky.

"Skrarr!" I heard a joyous hoot from one of the Stocky Greens on the walls, and then the other Training Hall dragons joined in, in their own way – even Zarr lifting his voice to roar in song.

"Rider Dayie!? Rider – what's happening!?" It was one of the Training Hall Dragon Handler guards, running across the arena sands to me and looking up nervously. Like most of the Dragon Handlers, he had been granted the position for his size and girth – a large southern man with the dragon goad held in his hands. "What do we do – is it an attack!?"

"By the sands!" I swore, gritting my teeth in frustration. *I'm going to have to get the Dragon Handlers to join in on my training lectures,* I thought distractedly. For workers who were tasked to see to the daily needs of these great beasts, to have so little insight into their behavior was a recipe for disaster! But even my exasperation at the Training Hall couldn't match the joy that I was feeling at what I saw above me.

"It's okay. They're Irafea's daughters. What we're seeing is a reunion – and all the other dragons can sense it, and are happy for them!" I pointed out. "See how much cured fish we still have in the stores. Tonight I want all the dragons to have a feast!" I ordered, and, despite the Handler's wary looks above at what was happening, he left at a jog towards the storerooms.

I was happy with what I was seeing, as the three Sinuous Blues shot out across the city and out towards the southern hot deserts. Maybe I should have been more worried about where they were going and when they were coming, but in that moment, I could only feel gladness. *Have your reunion,* I mentally thought and congratulated Irafea, knowing that I would still have to somehow explain all of this to Chief Talal.

"No time like the present, I guess…" I jogged up the steps to the landing platform and Zarr, before we both took off to the tower of the Southern Lords, where the trade negotiations were being held.

CHAPTER 5
AKEEM, THE PRINCE AND THE DUKE

I *didn't like him,* I thought as I watched this 'Duke' Robert stand on the battlements of the Tower of the Southern Lords. He was a tallish, broad-shouldered sort of man with a thin-cropped beard, and I took him to be perhaps five or ten years older than me. He's brother to the Queen-Empress Nuria of Torvald, the son of Duchess Robba, I think?

Whatever. I was sure that his easygoing smile and his stature was the result of lots of soft living in a palace, surrounded by people who would always tell him just how great he was, and never having to fight for anything in his life.

"I don't see what he has done to hurt you yet, Akeem-brother," Aida whispered her reptilian words in the back of my mind as I watched Lord Ehsan and the others fawn over him. It was a disgrace.

He's too nice. I thought back at her.

So far, 'nice' was about the only thing that I could accuse him of, as all he had done was compliment the three Southern Lords on their hospitality for receiving him – and had even offered to help when his own Torvald Dragons had decided to take to our skies!

"Dayie explained all of that. This is a joyous thing," Aida reminded me, and I grudgingly had to agree.

Dayie herself stood on the battlements just a few meters away from our enemy, and all assembled here: Lords Ehsan, Kasim and Qadir; as well as Chief Talal; that boy-Rider Nas; the old witch Mengala and the sorcerer were all watching the distant flying displays of Irafea and her daughters. Dayie had landed on the battlements of the tower with her Crimson Red just as alarm had broken out amongst the assembled northerners and southerners at what we were witnessing and had explained to us that their older Blue was the mother of the younger two.

Even I felt a little cheer at seeing the family reunited, but I was also aware of what came next. *Will this Duke Robert demand that Irafea returns to the North with them?* I bet he would.

"Well, I cannot say how glad that makes me." The duke raised a glass of our finest southern wine to the distant dragons, before turning back to the rest of us. "I take it as a good omen, that the South and the North can work together, as one!"

"Not as one…" I muttered. *Just like Torvald to presume that we all want to join together and be just like them!* Their posturing, quite frankly, irritated me. It was all very well being generous and magnanimous when you were the inheritors of the largest empire in the world – and one that was born from the usurpation and blood shed of the Dark King! By rights, Torvald and its duke should be apologizing to the rest of us for all the riches it now had! My muttered words, however, were loud enough to catch the Duke's eye. He hesitated and looked about to ask me what I meant, before the larger Lord Ehsan jumped in.

"Of course, it is a good omen, your honor…" He took a draught of his own wine and everyone else did the same. I didn't have any wine in my hand – I wanted nothing fuzzing my senses during this negotiation.

"Omens aside," I raised my voice a little. "We still need to decide what to do about the Deadweed. And the Water Wraiths."

"And the Sea Witch," croaked a voice at our side, coming from the only two seated figures in the assembly.

It was Mengala the Old, who now seemed to well deserve her name! Something strange had happened to her since I had last left her at the battle for Shebeel. Dayie told me that the same curse had fallen onto the sorcerer's frail-looking shoulders as well, but as I had never met him before, it was impossible for me to tell. Mengala's black and pepper-grey hair was now as white as satin-cloth, streaked with silver. Her eyes had seemed to sink in her already very wrinkled face, and she could barely move her claw-like hands without them wobbling. Heavy blankets had been heaped over the small litter that she was swaddled in, with handles extending from the corners for the servants to lift and carry, just like the one that held the similarly aged sorcerer. Both of them were so frail that it only took two servants apiece to lift their bodies and litter both.

"It is their magic..." Aida informed me. *"It is like that sometimes, with humans."* Her tone was sad. *"One of the deepest injustices of the world is that not all humans can hear dragons, and the second is that of those who work magic, sometimes their bodies are not capable of holding a dragon's power..."*

Did that mean that all magic came from dragons? I thought, before attempting to push the errant concern aside. I had other things to worry about, anyway. Like the Sea Witch. Like Duke Robert.

But what about Dayie?? I couldn't stop myself from thinking. If what Aida said was true – then did that mean that Dayie was going to age right before my eyes every time that she used that song of hers? I cast a look at my friend, studying her face and looking for telltale signs. She had the fairest skin of anyone I'd ever known, but her brow was furrowed. *That could just be stress,* I thought. Or the hard life riding a dragon in the Tall Winds all day...

But no, my heart told me something else. She was *too* pale. Even for a northerner. I'd seen the tops of the High Mountains, encrusted with white frost and snow – and she looked like that. I cursed myself for not recognizing it sooner. Dayie must be wasting away right in front of all of us!

"I thank you for your concern, but this is a mission of trade, ma'am..." Lord Ehsan broke into my worried thoughts, trying to manage the apparent outburst.

"No, please, my Lord…" the Duke Robert said. "Although you are right, and I have been sent here to provide goods and grains to the people of Dagfan, I am also a duke of the royal line of Torvald. I am empowered to speak as Torvald speaks, and yes, the Deadweed is a problem for *all* of us…"

Ugh. I could have groaned. *Spoken just like a Torvaldite, look at him pretending to be generous when really, he is just trying to tell us what to do!*

"And perhaps this is the time to share with you something that we have been working on." The duke looked around the assembled party, waiting for the hesitant nods. "Liquid Fire!" he said oh-so-grandly.

"You mean, like lamp oil?" I pointed out. How backward did he think we were!? "We already use our flame pots – lamp oil incendiaries to clear the Deadweed…"

The duke made a slightly embarrassed gesture that only infuriated me even more. "Ah, no… If you will forgive me, that is not what I mean at all. Liquid Fire is similar to lamp oil in the sense that it is a liquid, of course, but it cannot be used to light lanterns and bonfires. It is *far* too volatile for that. It is the invention of the Dragon Academy itself, and it has to be kept in especially-made containers. When it is released and fired, it is much more destructive, and longer lasting than mere lamp oil."

"How lucky for you," I said, watching as Duke Robert's eyes flickered a little. *Yeah that is how much I dislike you…* I thought.

"Yes, it is lucky, I suppose." Duke Robert said a little more reservedly.

"Lucky that you have the legacy of the Dark King to draw on against the Deadweed, I guess…" I said. Everyone knew that the tyrant King Enric, who had ruled the North and half the South with an iron claw, had used all sorts of strange, noisome, belching, and fiery technologies.

"*Akeem!*" Dayie gasped in horror.

"Duke Flamma-Torvald, I am sure the *Binshee* lord meant no offense." Lord Ehsan was quick to try and put words in my mouth, while at the same time distancing himself from me and my people.

It was hard to tell if the duke had taken offense, as he kept his gaze steady on me, but his mouth was in a straight line, neither smiling nor frowning as he said, "I can see how one might think that, but I am glad to say that my father, King Bower-as-was, went to great lengths to destroy every scrap of the Dark King's legacy – all of his workshops and laboratories and hellish machines." The Torvald noble took a deep breath. "Luckily, this Liquid Fire is an invention entirely of our own devising."

I nodded, not believing a word of it. *Torvald has a new weapon. Or a new 'old' weapon, and the last time we saw things like that being used, it meant the ruin of the South…*

"I am not empowered to give away the mechanism of making Liquid Fire, alas." The Duke Robert broke his glance from me to turn and talk to the Southern Lords. "Mostly because I am afraid that I have never had a head for alchemy. But I *can* offer the support of Torvald's resources against the Deadweed and the Water Wraiths. I am sure that if you were to return with me to see my sister Queen-Empress Nuria, then she would be happy to share our good fortune with our neighbors in the South."

A trap? I wondered.

"That… That would be most kind, my lord…" Lord Ehsan nodded. "Now, let us discuss the exact trading relations between our two nations—"

No sooner had he said this, when I felt all the hairs rise on the back of my neck. It was Aida, warning me. *"Akeem – something is wrong!"*

I startled, and was already walking past the throng as Dayie shook herself also from her thoughts, and the boy-Rider Nas turn in the same direction.

"Prince Akeem? Rider Dayie?" Lord Ehsan was asking in alarm, just as the Dragon Gong of the Training Hall went off.

CLANG! CLANG! CLANG!

I didn't need Aida's urgent warnings in my mind to see what was happening out there. There was a dark, boiling tide surging up the Taval River towards us, and, when I looked closer I swear that I could see that the wave had humanoid forms and heads, as of a hundred warriors bearing weapons…

"It is the Water Wraiths!" Dayie cried, but I was already turning on my heel and calling Aida to me.

CHAPTER 6
DAYIE, THE WITCH OF THE SOUTH

I *can't believe Akeem was being like that!* It was impossible to curtail my frustrations as I raced to where Zarr was already tensing his legs and raising his wings on the battlements, waiting for me to climb up. Luckily, he still had his saddle on, and it only took me a moment to clip myself in as I heard the Chief Talal roar orders behind me. "Protect the harbor! We need that Torvald grain!"

I'll do my best, I thought. *But I think we might be doing whatever we can just to stop everyone from dying!*

Most of the dragons were out on patrol, I had earlier gathered – that meant that we only had a skeleton force of Training Hall Riders, whatever of Akeem's Wild Company he had stationed outside the city, and the city's infantry, of course – but I knew that if it got to fighting in the streets, then it would be a bloodbath. Dragons aren't good at tactical fighting in narrow city streets – or rather, they were *too* good. Their dragon fire could take out entire houses, and Dagfan was already struggling to rebuild from the last incursion of Deadweed, Water Wraiths, and dragons all at once.

We had to head them off in the water, I thought, and Zarr had already read my mind, taking great lungfuls of air and billowing his neck and chest as he forced the sacks that ran along his neck to start producing the ichor that could turn into dragon fire.

We could really use some of the duke's Liquid Fire right now, as well! I thought, allowing my annoyance with the Prince and Captain of the Wild Company to mask my fears of what I was about to face. The tide of the Wraiths was coming thick and fast, but from my height, I could see that it was at least coordinated just like the other times I had seen them fight; a line like a storm surge, but at least it only seemed to have broken white water behind it. *No Deadweed following after,* for which I was grateful. Usually the Water Wraiths were the precursor for a floating mat of Deadweed – but not this time – probably because Akeem and the other patrols had been scouring the Taval banks for days now.

"We can force the wave apart," I thought, imagining the wave diverting into two halves. That way they wouldn't directly hit the Torvald galleon, but on either side of it.

But they will hit the harbor all the same, I growled into the winds. Sometimes there was no choices but bad ones – just like how Mengala and the sorcerer's strange powerful enchantments had helped me to save Dagfan before, but had also cost them so much.

"Now, Dayie-sister?" Zarr was eager, angling his flight lower and lower towards the racing horde.

"Wait…wait…" I held onto the saddle as I leaned forward, judging when the explosion of his fire would do the most damage—

The Water Wraiths were becoming larger, the wave growing higher until their melding and coagulating bodies were now taller than the average human—easily seven or eight feet tall—their legs and feet disappearing into the surge of white water. Each one moved through the next in a constant flow.

"Now!" I called out, and Zarr roared.

From the Red dragon's maw came an explosion of flame and black smoke, thrown downwards in a lance of fire that hit the direct center of the line. Instantly, the air was filled with steam as the dragon flame clung for a few precious moments to the water, burning the magic from the wet. But the greater disruption to the Wraith army was the force of the dragon-flames strike, blasting the wave apart and sending the two halves into complicated, chaotic eddies for just a moment.

I leaned back and pulled on the reins that slung around Zarr's shoulders – not that I needed to let him know, because my thoughts and my body were in perfect unison as the Crimson Red started angling his flight upwards again, about to turn for another strafing fire-blow against the reassembling Wraith-tide.

"Wiiiiitch!"

A sound unlike the hiss, splash, roar, and torment of the waves or the beat of the wings hit me, and it was like being hit by a physical force. A wave of nausea welled up in my belly and my skin grew icy cold.

What? What is happening!? I thought.

"Dayie-sister! What attacks us!?" Zarr was confused, losing the coordination of his wings as he felt an echo of my sickness.

The froth of the water was mingling into a noise, a sound that I could horribly imagine coming from all of the water mouths of the Wraiths below. A word. *"Wiiiitch!"*

When the word came again, it was louder, more distinct. *"WITCH!"*

"Why are they saying that—?" I managed to gasp as another billowing sickness rolled up through my limbs. It wasn't pain I was feeling, it wasn't an ache – but as if I had suddenly been afflicted with every worst nausea that I had ever had in my life, all at once! My body went cold, and my limbs were shaking, and my head was feeling dizzy – and a shadow of all of those effects were being passed onto the dragon that was a part of me, too.

"No!" Zarr raged as he turned his head not back towards the city, but further up the Taval River, clearly intending to fly beyond what magical ailment the Water Wraiths had thrown at me. *"I will not have you hurt this way."*

But I didn't even know what 'this way' was as I clutched to Zarr's neck. "We have to go back. Dagfan, the Torvald grains..." I pleaded with him, but there was nothing as obstinate as a dragon, as he ignored me.

"Caaaan't Esssscaaaape, witch!" The words followed me – and as I looked over my shoulder, I saw that at least half of the Water Wraith wave had washed back up into the river and was following me!

Maybe I can lead them away, just like last time, I thought as my head spun. The waves of nausea were growing stronger, and Zarr was flying lower and lower as he started to feel the full effects of the sickness too. Was that what this new attack was? A way to drive down dragons and their Riders?

I looked over my shoulder (my vision doubling as I tried to focus) to see, in horror, that the wave of the Water Wraiths wasn't even surging towards Dagfan at all. Strangely, it had turned in mid flow, and now surged *back,* towards us.

"They're after us, Dayie!" Zarr's thought was struck-through with alarm.

Then we needed to fly, and we need to fly fast – but Zarr wasn't responding as powerfully or as quickly as he had every time before. It was the nausea, spreading between us...

"Skrarrr!" Zarr let out a whistling roar, and in my head, I heard him cry out *"Aida! Dragon-sister!"* He was calling for help. It must be bad. Really bad—

"Skreeee!" There was a burst of angered dragon calls, and two, three, four orange shapes flashed below us like hunting falcons, heading towards my pursuing Wraith army. Vicious Oranges. It had to be Akeem and his Wild Company, I thought gratefully as their angered screams of fury and the scent of more dragon fire came to me on the winds.

"Dayie-sister. I have to land. If I don't, we will fall out of the sky..." Zarr informed me, barely flapping his wings as he turned to swoop towards the southern banks.

"It's okay, Zarr, you did so well. So brave..." I murmured as he nearly tumbled towards the distant road-way. With a jolt, his claws hit the old stone and packed earth, and without my belt attached by a harness to the saddle, I would have been thrown then and there to my death. We came to a sliding, gasping halt a good few hundred meters down the road, both exhausted and feeling sick.

"Keep running, Zarr, I'll hold them off..." I thought blearily as I undid the belt and slid from his shoulder to land on the ground with a heavy thump.

"Aurgh..." that hurt. But I would use my song. It was all I had. I looked up, half expecting to see the Water Wraiths breaking over the distant coast and come seeping towards me –

But instead, there was the landing form of Aida and Akeem, performing a perfect, wide-winged landing. *Where were the Water Wraiths?* I thought, as I slid to my knees once again.

"Dayie? Dayie!" Akeem's boots thumped to the sands as he ran over to me. His strong arms lifted me from the ground as he shouted to others, landing all around us. "Heydar? See to her dragon. I'm getting her to safety!"

Why isn't he always this kind to me? I remember thinking, as the world slipped into blackness.

"It was a *Mandrake Nemesia,*" Mengala's voice labored in the dark room.

"Huh?" I said, not for the first time that evening. I was in one of the rooms of the Training Hall (despite the fact that the Southern Lords had offered me to rest in their Healing Rooms in the tower of Dagfan) but Mengala and the sorcerer, for all of their apparent age and weakness, had been surprisingly adamant about the fact that I needed to be near dragons.

Mengala and the sorcerer had completely taken over one of the three healing chambers in the hall, and had converted it from a light-filled, open room with lots of cot beds and barrels of fresh water to a cramped and dark chamber that was filled with strange smokes and even stranger oddments. I could see several pieces of blue Earthstar – the rare glowing mineral that occurred naturally underground, as well as lots of sprigs of dried flowers and herbs, and a whole apothecary's shop of fat and thin candles of various hues and smells.

"It's a curse, called the *Nemesis* curse because it targets your sworn enemy, and *Mandrake* because it sympathetically recreates the effects of Mandrake root," Mengala said. She looked little better than I felt, to be honest, but she was moving around the room with the aid of two sticks, so hunched over that I doubted that she would have even have stood as tall as my shoulder were I standing up and not lying down on the cot bed.

"Out there somewhere this afternoon, the Sea Witch was chanting over a piece of Mandrake root, and sending the terrible effects to you, through the *Mandrake Nemisia* curse," she explained as she lurched to the edge of the cot bed, pausing as she took a deep breath, before blowing out one of the more sickly candles that sat on a small side table there, her shaking hands instead replacing it with a different, faintly green one. Within moments of her wavering taper catching it alight, the calming, soothing scent of pine filled the room, and she wafted it gently towards me.

"Lemon and ginger," croaked the sorcerer on the other side of the bed, similarly using a staff in one hand, while the other shook as it set a ceramic mug of something hot into my hands.

"Thank you," I whispered, making an effort despite my still swaying head to sit up and take some of the drink. It made me feel embarrassed and ashamed to be looked after by these two, who clearly needed more help than me!

Ah. The tea was warm and spiced, sweet with honey and sharp with citrus and ginger tang. It was hot like pepper in my mouth, but it was also *good.* Within moments, my head started to feel a little clearer too.

"Luckily, you didn't have much time under the curse," Mengala breathed. "And lucky for you, the effects of a curse-at-distance are even fewer than if the Sea Witch was standing in front of you. But unfortunately, there's no magical cure. Just good old-fashioned remedies to soothe your wits and your stomach and clear the mind."

"Well, it's working. Thank you," I said. But one thing was still bothering me. "How did she know I was there? Why did she target me? How does she know I even exist!?"

"Ah—" the sorcerer coughed. "The currents of magic." It was his pet theory, of course, and I shouldn't be surprised that was how he would explain this mystery to me. He had told me that there were different currents of magical force in the world like waves, or seasons, or winds, and that they changed every now and then as different types of magic came to the fore in the history of the world. I was supposed to represent one of these 'new' currents of magic – as was the Sea Witch.

"The Sea Witch is tapped into it, and if she is sensitive enough, then she will be able to sense the flows of it. The disruptions to it."

"I thought you said that *she* was the disrupting one?" I pointed out.

The sorcerer's eyes glittered in a memory of the (slightly) younger man that he used to be. "She is. But not to her. I believe this new force of magic is about *Growth* and *growing things*, and she has perverted that to make the Deadweed, and the Water Wraiths. You, with your mother's song, make it true again," he reasoned, his voice cracking and returning as he did so. "But the Sea Witch probably believes that *she* represents the new current, and that her magic is the truer."

"Great. So, I have a nemesis now, do I?" I said, the tea, the candle, and whatever other herbs they had given me going a great deal to make me feel better again.

"She thinks *you* are hers," Mengala pointed out. "She was trained at Sebol, remember. She knows many, many enchantments that you do not, and that I can no longer cast any more..." The old wise woman looked sad – for I knew that she, too, was trained at the Western Witches' isle of Sebol – but her magic had since become a painful burden and not a joy for her.

"She must have used divination, or sensed you as the sorcerer states, and now she knows that you are the one who has been managing to turn aside her Water Wraiths and calm her Deadweed..." Mengala's face was dark. "There are tales of magical wars between witches – and mages too, for that matter"—she gave a quick look at the sorcerer— "and they have always been terrible times. Whenever those gifted with dragon magic turn it against each other..." Her voice went quiet, but I knew enough of the tales of the world to fill in the blanks.

"Danu Geidt the mage and Ohotto Zanna the witch," I said. That was the war that had torn apart the Western Archipelago, ruined the island kingdom of Roskilde and raised the Army of the Dead. "Even Queen Saffron and the Dark King," which was another war that had seen almost the entire north and south consumed with fire and bloodshed – and from whose hurts we were still recovering in many ways.

"Just wonderful." I muttered. *How am I going to be powerful enough to defeat an actual trained witch!?*

"If only we understood more about your magic, this *new*

magic…" the sorcerer sighed. "If I had my laboratory, I could perform a study – of what powers your magic, what hinders it. Perhaps I could make you even more powerful than this Sea Witch!"

"Pfft." Mengala's opinions about a mage's style of magic was obvious. "It flows from the mother. That is what we witches know. An unbroken line, of mother to daughter just like it is the Dragon's Den Mother who gives her power to her children."

"But my mother died in the storm." My voice broke in the telling. That was what my foster parents, Obasi and Wera had told me. That was what I had grown up knowing, all my life. "And my foster parents…" *They had died too, in a Deadweed attack.*

"There might be something – anything that we can find out about her would help. It would strengthen your magic…" Mengala nodded. "Where did you say you grew up?"

At that, I shrugged. It was a tiny spit of a fishing village on the northern side of the Taval River. Now long-since choked with Deadweed. "A place called Velak. It's gone now. Abandoned for the past ten years or so – that was how Fan and her Dragon Traders got me, the people were evacuating the village, and they were going to leave me there…" I said, remembering that hateful time as one of intense confusion. My foster parents had just died, and the whole village had blamed me. It was my magic that had brought the Deadweed to their doors.

Maybe it had, I thought with horror.

“Then we talk to this Fan woman. Maybe she learned something about your mother,” Mengala said.

“Or tales of your early powers, that would help too…” the sorcerer opined, but I was adamant.

“We can’t,” I said. “Fan Hazim…? She is evil. You don’t know what she tried to do to these very dragons below us.” I remember the fact that she had been lacing the dragon treat ‘Sweetbalm’ – a natural sedative for dragons – with flowers of the Deadweed, to make *her* bundles of toxic herbs that much more effective, and thus ensuring that the Training Hall kept buying from her.

Of course, there were also the years of shoves, pinches, slaps and even kicks that she had subjected me too as well. None of it made me ever want to see her face again.

But there was Rahim, Fan’s second husband (the first had died in some smuggling incident, or so Fan had told me). He was still a Dragon Trader, of course – and he wasn’t entirely unkind. He had liked to tell stories and had never raised his hand to me. But he *did* always side with Fan, at all times…. Could I trust him to tell me the truth of what had happened when Fan had brought me from the villagers?

I could probably trust him if I had Nas with me, I thought. Rahim had doted over Fan’s son and was probably far more worried about him than Fan was!

“I think I know someone who might be able to help,” I said.

CHAPTER 7
DAYIE AND HER DRAGON

"You're doing what?" Akeem looked at me as though I was mad.

Maybe I was. To be honest – everything about going to try and track down the Dragon Traders seemed crazy. Fan was a woman who had beaten me and made my entire growing life miserable. What did I think I was doing?

"I need to find out about my mother – my real mother…" I told him, and my voice sounded small in my ears. I guess it was partly the fear of seeing Fan again, but it was also our surroundings. We stood on the battlements of the Dragon Academy just as we had done before, when I had left to try and find the Sorcerer of the Whispering Rocks.

Back then – barely a couple of moons ago, in reality – we had fought and both of us had said things that I wish that we hadn't. Akeem had been determined that we had to stay and defend Dagfan. He wanted to place his trust in his dragon and his sword arm and not involve anyone else (like Torvald) or go running off after 'mystical wizards.' I think it was more than that now, as I looked at him.

"He wants to do the right thing, but doesn't know what it is," Zarr informed me.

"That's a surprisingly wise observation from the young bull," I thought at him. He made a snorting sound of laughter in my mind.

"His dragon Aida told me."

"Ah, I see…" I was surprised Zarr and Aida talked without me knowing. But of course they did, right?

"I have to go, and I'll be taking Zarr, obviously, and Nas and his Sea Dragon with me," I said, steeling myself for the inevitable argument that was to follow.

"Okay," Akeem surprised me by saying quietly.

"I'm sorry?" I asked, feeling suddenly unsure. This was supposed to be the bit where he tried to talk me out of it. Maybe I *wanted* him to talk me out of it, just so I could argue myself into feeling certain about my plan.

"Okay. I want to come with you." Akeem nodded.

I was lost. "But I thought you said that we need all of our dragons here, defending Dagfan…?" I pointed out and wondered why I was giving him the ammunition he would eventually need to argue with me.

"We can't defend Dagfan," Akeem said with a heavy sigh, and

I could see how much it cost him to say that. "Well, not forever, anyway," he said. "The only reason that we've been managing to win is because we have the dragons," he said, looking out towards the still blackened and ruined cityscape of Dagfan. "And we have *you,"* he turned back to look at me.

"Me? No. It's the Wild Company if anything…" I said, feeling a blush rise to my cheeks.

"No, Dayie – it's not. It's you. Don't get me wrong, my Wild Company are the best Dragon Riders in the sky, but in every battle we have had so far, something new has been thrown at us. If it isn't the Deadweed coordinating its attacks, seeking out our weakest points, then it is the Water Wraiths rising higher and stronger than before. And *whatever that was* that happened to you."

"The Mandrake Nemisia curse," I informed him, and it was his turn to look at me blankly.

"Anyway – it's always been you, Dayie, and your song and your connection to Zarr that has been vital in driving back these attacks. And now that the Sea Witch is using this Mandrake Noomie-what…"

"*Nemisia.* It means nemesis." I smiled a little.

"Yeah, then it is all the more important to make sure that we protect you," Akeem ended gruffly, raising his head to look back out at the city. The warm southern daylight caught his face, and for a moment I imagined how he would look when he really was the ruler of the South. *Strong,* yet kind.

"Well." He cleared his throat. "So, anyway. Lord Ehsan has

accepted the Duke Robert's offer and will be sending emissaries to Torvald to secure a shipment of this Liquid Fire he is so taken with… I suppose that if it *is* as good as the duke thinks, and if it manages to get here before the Sea Witch attacks again, then Dagfan will be better protected for a little while. At least until we can help you grow stronger in your powers."

I could see how much it still hurt his pride to admit that. "It'd be an honor for you to fly with me." I smiled at him, and meant it with all my heart.

"Do you think that's going to be enough?" Nas said to me as he loaded another satchel full of dried fruits, cured meats, and a small quantity of flour for pan-breads. We stood on the sandy floor of the Training Hall and Nas looked nervous – which was something I hadn't seen in him since he had become 'Lieutenant Rider' Nas.

It was seeing his mother again, I was sure. Fan had favored him above me and even her second husband – but that did not mean that he was immune to her slaps or sharp barbed words if she had thought that he was being slow or lazy.

"Nas." I reached out to touch him gently on the shoulder. "We're just going for information. That's all. You're a Dragon Rider now, you should be proud of yourself…"

"Hm." Nas looked at me for a moment, before pulling a face. "Get off me, stink-breath," he teased, using one of his old, favorite, go-to insults that had been so hurtful to me growing up, but was now just funny.

“Idiot,” I grinned back at him, just as there was a loud *whumpf* from behind us.

It was the Vicious Orange, Aida, landing close enough to scatter sand over us in a shower, and with Akeem sitting alert and ready on her back.

“Hey!” Nas said, spluttering as we brushed the sand from our clothes.

“Sorry,” Akeem called out, without seeming sorry at all. *What was up with him, lately?* He was dressed in his normal black robes, but had augmented it with his leather jerkin and leather arm greaves. He looked like the Captain of the Wild Company, ready for anything. “I thought you wanted to be leaving as soon as possible, Dayie?” he said to me, and I nodded, yes, I did.

But first I would need to speak to the two huddled forms sitting in the shade, in their covered litters. Neither Mengala nor the sorcerer was going to be coming with us this time, even though I knew that there was room for them on the broad back of Zarr, as I had carried them before on the long flight up from the South.

But no, the flight might even kill them… I thought as I crouched in between their two litters.

“Is there anything else you can tell me? What I should be looking for?” I said, my eyes moving from one ancient face to another.

"The key to your power is your mother..." Mengala repeated her earlier assertion. "Magic isn't like lamp oil. It isn't stuff you have a lot or a little of. It's more like a well inside of you. But to travel down that well you need to dig deeper into your own heart, your own history. By unlocking that, you will unlock the magic you need to defeat the Sea Witch..." Her voice was barely louder than a whisper.

"Well, that's not what they used to teach at the Dragon Monasteries..." the sorcerer muttered disagreeably.

"Which is probably why you look like a prune!" Mengala cackled, earning a glare – but not an entirely angry one – from the Sorcerer of the Whispering Rocks.

"Ha. I'm sure you'll be fine, if you're still able to annoy each other," I said, rising from my crouch. Our conversation hadn't really given me any clue what to ask Rahim about – maybe just getting to know a little more about my mother would unlock the depths of magic that everyone believed I had in me? I didn't know.

"Just look after the dragons while I'm away!" I said to them both.

"Of course!" The sorcerer sounded a little put out that I had even mentioned it.

"Wouldn't dream of anything else." Mengala raised a shaking hand and bid me farewell as I turned and jogged over to where Zarr was already shaking his wings and stretching out his front legs.

"You ready, wyrm?" I patted his leg scales.

"Always."

If I had any worries about how we might find the Dragon Traders, then I shouldn't have. As soon as we had risen up in bright skies over Dagfan, Zarr picked up the scent of the people who had kept me as a virtual slave for over ten years.

"It's easy. I will know their scent anywhere." Zarr said, and I guessed it made sense that he would. The Hazims were the very first people Zarr had met.

"Apart from you. The shape of you is my first memory," Zarr said, making me immediately feel both grateful and ashamed of what I had done to him. Stealing his egg from the Dragon Enclosure of Torvald. Behind us I could still hear the distant, joyous cries of Irafea and her two daughters as they gambled over the city and the river, went hunting together, and Irafea taught her children how to take sand baths – which I knew to be a wonderful way for a dragon to clean their scales. It had turned out that the two Torvald Riders of the Sinuous Blues weren't put out at all by the reunion, and were in fact over-joyed that their dragons had met their natural mother.

It did make me worry about Zarr, though.

"Why are you worried? I have you. It is how it should be," Zarr told me, as he set his course for northwards, powering us with his strong and powerful wing beats to rise up towards the Tall Winds.

"Wouldn't you like to go back to the Dragon Enclosure?" I

said, thinking of what Irafea might do now. Why would she ever leave her daughters' sides again?

"Why? My home is here, in the South with you," Zarr said, and a strong surge of his loyalty washed over me.

"Oh Zarr, I don't deserve that." I felt bad. "I stole you."

"Stole? Steal? These are human things. You took my egg, yes, but why did your hands choose my egg and not the one next to it? I think you were already bonded with me," Zarr assured me.

"Thank you..." I said, wondering at the deep feelings that a dragon had. They were capable of such overwhelming furies, but also fierce affections that I could only be humbled by. And, it turned out – a dragon could be generous-hearted as well.

"Generous? Ha!" a snort of soot from his mouth. *"Don't expect me to be sharing any fish with the others any time soon..."*

No, I didn't think that his generosity would ever go that far! I laughed as I raised my face to the winds, letting the freezing airs wash over me and take my hair. It was invigorating. I had forgotten just how good it was to fly on a dragon without thinking about fighting, or defending, flying away or towards an enemy.

"Dayie!" Akeem had pulled up alongside of me, and below and behind him I could see his second, Heydar also rising, with Nas making the fourth and final dragon of our little flight.

Oh no, had I spoken too soon? "What's wrong?" I called out, to see Akeem shake his head, pulling the scarf down that he usually wore over his face to make a sweeping movement east of our bearings.

"I've been flying these mountains all my life. If we try to cross the High Mountains here, then we'll be heading straight into the storms. There's a cleft in the range to the east of us."

"Okay," I nodded, before asking Zarr if he was all right diverting from the trail.

"The trail is in my head, silly. And even though I can handle any storm this world can throw at me – I don't think the other dragons can…" He lapped at the air with his forked tongue in what was clearly a moment of dragon humor. Behind us, I heard an aggrieved squawk from Aida, who must have overheard us with her own dragon mind, because she suddenly surged forward to the lead position, surprising Akeem.

"Aida! What are you doing?" he cried out in alarm.

"Ha. Then let's show them who the fastest dragon in the South is, shall we?" I said as I leaned forward, giving Zarr my full attention as he let out an exultant roar, and threw himself forward.

As it turned out, Zarr definitely *wasn't* the fastest dragon in the South.

"They cheated." He was annoyed as we came down again out

of the sky, the tall grey peaks of the High Mountains all around us. Akeem had been right – this was a lot more secluded, and the walls of the mountain completely cut off the difficult crosswinds.

"They must have done…" I attempted to mollify the giant Crimson Red. He had a lot of power and could surge forward with his much larger wingspan – but a dragon of his bulk just wasn't as perfectly designed to these mountains as the smaller Vicious Oranges were. Aida had easily outpaced us by using the walls, canyons and cliffs in a way that I had never seen dragons do before – swinging close-by to them in order to benefit from their wind shelter or their updrafts of warmer air to skip ahead of us. Being smaller, she could also turn and move much quicker than we could through this rocky geography.

But none were as fast as Nas and his Sea Dragon Nandor, however, who was the smallest of all of the dragons but whose wings and tail were in an almost perfect hawk-like proportion. I'd always heard said that the Sea Dragons were the fastest of dragons – and now I knew the truth of it!

"Congratulations!" I called out to Nas when I saw him alight on a ridge of rock at the end of the pass. The sun was already setting and although I knew the dragons could keep on flying for a lot longer than they had been doing so far, I also wanted to give them a rest before we found the Dragon Traders.

Or maybe I just wanted another few hours without having to think about Fan, I thought, as I watched Akeem and Heydar on their Vicious Oranges join Nas on the ridge of rock.

"Pffft. Those Oranges and Greens have bony little bodies..." Zarr refused to admit that he was too big to land on the ridge, and instead kept his head up as we soared past our colleagues, laughing—

And suddenly, we were flying over Torvald.

Just beyond the pass, the High Mountains ended abruptly, falling away into broken rocky foothills and the silvering fingers of many mountain streams, winding down to join another, much larger river on the northern side of the mountains just as we had the River Taval on the southern side. We were hit by a sudden rush of wind, however, as the temperature dropped noticeably.

"Rain," Zarr informed me morosely. He must remember the northern downpours we had trudged through on our long journey to the South when he was but a hatchling. Had that really been so recent?

The landscape ahead of us had lost the sun earlier than the South, as all of Torvald appeared bounded by distant mountain ranges – the Dragon's Spine to the north and west, the World's Edge to the distant east. But I could see the distant twinkling lights of settlements and villages, even a line of strong and steady lights that I knew to be the Torvald watchtowers.

"Dayie!" Nas shouted, and suddenly Nandor's claws scraped the walls as she launched to overtake us.

"What is it?" I asked, but it wasn't Nas who answered; it was Zarr.

"I was too distracted! Nandor knows the scent we follow, and

she has picked up something from it!" Zarr's tone was alert and alarmed, and a second later I knew why as he opened his senses to me and allowed me to feel and see and smell at great distance, as a dragon did – well, as much as my human mind could handle anyway.

"Ach!" It was dizzyingly complex and rich. Everything from the petrichor smell of coming rain and wet rocks to the damp humous of the forests ahead; a running deer under the trees; an owl on the wing; cookfires of Torvald guards in their towers…

"…RUN! Run as quick as you can…" all of the chaotic overflow of dragon information condensed into a sharp and narrow band, and I could almost *see* it ahead of us as a track, leading due northwest. It was the smell of old incense (a blend of sandalwood and jasmine that I knew so well that even I would be able to track it!), the bitter overlay of fear-sweat, and the sound of hurrying feet.

And the voice of Rahim Hazim, somewhere to the north of us, fleeing for his very life.

I didn't need to say anything to Nas or the others, as he had already leaned forward over Nandor's neck and was fiercely staring at the spot in the dark night where the dragon's senses had picked up who we were looking for. I did the same, following my adoptive brother into the Kingdom of Torvald.

CHAPTER 8
AKEEM, A DRAGON'S PUNISHMENT

There is no way we are going to get there in time, I thought, as Aida shared the dragon-sense of the trail that Nas and Dayie were following. It was hard to tell precisely how far ahead of us the Dragon Traders were – but it seemed like a long way. A loooong way.

"We'll get there," Aida said, putting on another burst of speed that almost matched up to Nandor's.

If they are determined to cover most of Torvald in a night, then we can't be reckless! I thought in alarm, and it seemed Aida had already shared my intentions as she was engaged in a hooted and whistled conversation with Nandor.

The Sea Green, besotted with Nas, was understandably put out by allowing the slower Vicious Orange Aida in front, but Aida was stern with her in that way only a true dragon matriarch can have. We might be flying over foreign soil, and they might do things differently here, but our Wild Company still knew a thing or two about flying!

Aida took the lead position and, even though she still maintained her punishing speed – it certainly wasn't as fast as I knew that she could go when she really wanted to. *Why hadn't the Training Hall Dragons studied this?* I thought, knowing that Dayie at least would be paying very close attention. That was the problem with Chief Talal of the Training Hall. He thought that training a dragon was all about learning and teaching how to fight with one – when in actual fact…

"Training a dragon! Ha!" Aida broke into my mind. Oops. *"It was I who trained you, if I remember rightly!"*

"Yes, you did," I apologized. But the point still stood – that learning how to be a dragon friend wasn't just about fighting together, it was about all the myriad ways that you can fly, use your speed, weight, direction of the air, as well as hunting, etiquette – all sorts of things!

Aida took the lead and Heydar slid in naturally on my right-hand side, a little back and a little below me. It took a while, but Nandor got the idea and copied Heydar on my left-hand side, a little back and a little behind. Flying like this allowed the group to never become too separate, and it meant that we could maintain a punishing pace over a long distance, as the dragons behind have an easier time flying in the updraft from the dragon in front's flight. It was a bit difficult to pull off with four – it worked best with an odd number, but Zarr slotted in to the right and behind of Heydar, and suddenly our flight steadied.

"How long can you keep going for, my sister?" I asked Aida.

"Until the moon rises," she informed me, which was when I would peel back to the rear of the group – Aida benefiting from the joint updraft of all of the dragons in front of her after her hard slog, and Heydar on his dragon would take my place. This was a way that no dragon would ever get too tired, and we'd always have at least most of our number rested and ready to hunt or fight should they need to.

And so, in this formation we flew onwards above the wilds of Torvald.

We were too late to stop the first wave of attacks, but by the time that the sun had risen late over the Dragon's Spine mountains and was turning the world below us into a land of golden greens – it also lit the tumbled canyon where Dayie's Dragon Traders still fought for their lives.

"There!" Aida angled her flight towards the small knot of hurrying people, and it was easy to see why they were hurrying. The river below them in the canyon had become infested with the Deadweed, and as I watched, the long vines and runners reached up to grasp at the rocky walls and race towards them…

I saw a small, terrified band of ponies, with only two people on the lead and another two ponies cantering behind along a narrow path that hugged the canyon wall. Farther behind them I could see the hump of a colorful caravan that I recognized as Gypsy workmanship, apparently abandoned in their escape.

"Rahim!" I heard Nas call out, breaking our formation to throw himself and Nandor forward.

Dammit, I bit my lip from shouting the boy-Rider back into formation. I had no authority to command him – but he really needed to know more about working as a team, especially up in the air! As it was, him cutting across our flight path threw Aida into a quick flurry of wings and forced us to change our own course.

He'd lead with his fire, meaning that we couldn't, I thought, hastily changed the attack plans that I had been devising, and sure enough, Nas did, performing a fast – and not altogether terrible – dip into the canyon for Nandor to roar out her flame on the mess of Deadweed below.

Flames and black smoke billowed out into the sky, and he was already rising out of the other side—

But he should have waited! I thought in exasperation, as all his attack had done was to give the Deadweed at the canyon floor a temporary check, not the vines that were racing up the canyon walls, and onto the path—

"Get ahead of it," I called tersely to Heydar, who nodded once and broke from his position behind me, as Dayie and Zarr deftly took his place.

"Walls!" I shouted back to Dayie, wishing that she had spent more time with my Wild Company so that she would know the whistles and hand signals that I could use with Heydar. No time to teach her now, however, as I threw my weight to one side, and Aida responded by angling her wings tight to her body, forming a quick arrow of reptilian anger. We shot at an angle towards the vine-covered walls—

"Now!" I urged Aida, and beneath me she roared her own fiery fury, releasing a concentrated plume that scored along the green wall and burst apart woody vines and greenery.

"Ach!" In that instant, my eyes started stinging. The Dead-weed must have released its pollen into the air before we had attacked. *Dammit!* My eyes were watering and feeling hot.

"Dragon-brother!" Aida was worried, but she at least had managed to close her second, transparent eyelids to avoid just such an attack.

"I'll be all right," I hoped, already fumbling at my belt for my water skin. As Aida carried me high out of the canyon, giving me time to work, I emptied the water skin over my face until it was all gone – there was no way that I wanted to go blind.

I should warn Dayie! I thought, knowing that I had told her to follow me in—

"SKREYARCH!" A powerful roar as Zarr attacked the Dead-weed, but not with flame, I saw. The mighty bulk of the Crimson Red shot into the canyon and in a quick move, flipped out his legs to scrape along the walls at both the still green and the scorched vines. Given his size, his claws actually did more damage than Aida's dragon fire had done, as he rose with great clawfuls of the twisting, shaking vegetation,

leaving barren sections of wall behind, before he dropped the vines to the canyon floor below.

There was another violent hiss, as Heydar on his Vicious Orange attacked the Deadweed from above and ahead, angling through the space between the fleeing Dragon Traders and the vines that were even now slapping themselves over the abandoned caravan. I saw an explosion of flame as the caravan ignited with dragon fire and was knocked from the edge of the canyon wall, forming a burning missile that hit the already smoking Deadweed below…

"Yes!" I thought, proud of my second – but how about Dayie? Had she been affected by the toxins as I had?

Zarr was already flaring his wings over the canyon walls, turning back to land ahead of the fleeing Gypsies… If Dayie had been hurt, then it didn't seem as though it was badly. My relief was interrupted by a loud whoop as Nas screamed past me in another long attacking run to pour flame on the Deadweed at the bottom of the canyon.

No! I thought, but it was too late. His attack was so obvious that apparently even a sightless plant could predict it—

A stand of the Deadweed's flower stalks reared up from the mess at the bottom of the canyon, with their large yellow 'pods' already opening—

"SKRARGH!" Suddenly, the scene erupted into fire and flame as Zarr landed on the canyon top above and released a plume of flame ahead of Nas, forcing the Sea Green to squawk and throw himself to one side to avoid getting roasted. Dayie must have seen the same danger that I did, and had called Zarr to attack the flower stalks before Nas could fly straight into them.

"This is a mess," I growled as I circled back around, trying to find where the knot of Deadweed was the worst.

"Nas! Nas – my son!" a voice shouted, and it was one of the two mounted figures, having jumped off of his pony and running to the edge of the canyon walls, waving his arms to the small Sea Green dragon that was even now struggling to fly. Despite Zarr's aid, they had been hit by the pollen.

"Nandor is in pain, but is taking herself and her rider to safety," Aida informed me. She sounded annoyed, but not worried – and that was enough for me. I trusted Aida's opinion better than I did my own.

Okay, then. What of Heydar? My second had been able to clear the canyon walls and top of the Deadweed, as Zarr and my own attacks had kept the main body occupied. We were winning.

The Sea Green had risen over the battle and was now swooping to land on one of the higher outcrops of rock, far away from the action. Zarr was perched on the canyon top, spewing forth great gouts of fire down to the Deadweed below, turning it into a thick mat of scorched plant matter, as the Crimson Red's much larger store of flame was like a storm all by itself.

With the battle almost over, that left the reason why we had come here, after all… I looked to where the two spare ponies had raced ahead in terror, still following the one lone rider, apparently not stopping as they raced towards the distant edge of the rocky hillsides.

Fan Hazim. She wasn't even going to wait and see if her husband and son were still alive! I was appalled at the woman's apparent total lack of empathy, but not surprised. She had, after all, remarried almost as soon as she had become separated from Rahim and Nas. Idly, I wondered what had happened to that new husband – or whether she had dropped him just as soon as she was reunited with Rahim? *It would be so much easier just to let her go,* I thought as we circled, surveying the battle. She was the one who had been dosing the dragons in the Training Hall. She deserved to be friendless, and homeless.

"And punished?" I could feel Aida's anger rising.

Yes.

I turned the Vicious Orange towards the fleeing figure, and we shot forward like a hunting hawk.

I'll say this for the woman, she was a good rider. She galloped into the stands of leafy trees, weaving between the trunks and vaulting the tangles of ancient roots. Even the two other ponies following behind her started to lose their way, their fast gallop turning into a more uncertain canter. *She doesn't even care for the animals she is supposed to look after!* I thought grimly as we shot past her.

"Begone!" she cried out, changing her direction once more as she sought to outwit us.

You can't outwit a dragon, Fan Hazim! I found myself grinning with a sort of cruel joy.

She disappeared from view often as the trees obscured my line of sight – but I didn't need to see her. Aida had her scent now, and there was nothing in this world that would stop Aida from hunting her down.

But even so, the woods she was heading into were getting denser. It would be hard to land in there to deliver justice. *Poisoner of dragons.* I felt my lip curl in disgust.

"Sssss!" Aida suddenly dropped one wing and angled the other, forcing us into a swift arcing turn towards the trees.

There was a resounding thunder of splintering wood as Aida reached out with her claws – we were travelling at such a speed that the younger tree that she struck exploded and toppled across Fan's path.

"*Aiii!"* I heard a scream and the terrified whinny of a horse as it wheeled away from the sudden tree— almost throwing Fan in the process—but the fallen tree and a scared horse wasn't enough to stop a woman like the despicable Dragon Trader. She doubled-back, heading eastwards now.

KERRASH! Aida's curling claws – each one as big as my hand – were strong enough to send another young birch tree crashing down ahead of the desperate Rider.

"You can't escape!" I called out, not knowing if she could hear me past Aida's victorious screeches.

"Shall I roast her?" Aida purred in the back of my mind.

"Not yet..." I pulled on her thoughts with my mind. "Look, she's changed course."

It seemed that Fan Hazim had finally realized that she could not outrun a grown dragon. She wasn't *entirely* stupid, then. She had found a clearing and had dismounted, jerking and clutching at the reins of the pony even though it was near frantic with worry.

"Maybe I should eat her steed, and she can watch..." Aida hissed. I wasn't entirely sure if she meant what she said or was just enjoying the thrill of the chase – but either way I told her no.

"Let's not make the poor animal suffer," I pointed out, knowing that Fan's pony was probably just as much a mistreated slave as Dayie had been. Instead, I urged Aida to land, which she did by pulling her wings wide to break her descent to the clearing before her claws skidded through the grass and moss to a halt.

"Stay back!" Fan said, moving the pony between us.

Coward, I thought.

"Fan Hazim!" I called out from Aida's back as the Vicious Orange slowly turned, lowering her neck and head in a hunting pose to face the Dragon Trader and dragon poisoner.

“The sands alone know how many lives you have hurt or destroyed.”

Aida took a step forward. I thought of Dayie, forever wary and stubborn, and never believing in her own abilities thanks to the slurs and attacks this woman had visited upon her.

“And you have been found guilty of poisoning dragons. Of sowing discord amongst the Southern Lords…” I said – although the last charge was not one that I cared that much about (the Southern Lords were, after all, only custodians to my father’s realm and far too big for their boots as it was), but I *was* very annoyed when I had heard that Fan had installed herself as some kind of councilor to them, and had apparently done her best to try and blame all of the current problems on the ‘dragon witch’ that was Dayie.

“Stay back!” she called again, panic tinging her voice.

Good. It was about time that she felt some real fear. That she saw the consequences of her actions.

“Give yourself up, Fan Hazim. Don’t make me come over there – or allow this dragon to do what *it* wants with you…” I said sternly, and Aida matched my tone by hissing a low growl in the back of her long throat and whipping her tail on the clearing dirt behind us.

“Mercy!” she suddenly called out, releasing the pony’s reins (which leapt forward from a rear and bolted into the forest as though there was a very angry dragon looming over it), and the old woman fell to her knees, holding her hands out towards me.

"Mercy?" I returned. "You're asking me for *mercy* – after everything that you have done?" Aida took another step forward.

"Please, good lord – spare me! Don't let your dragon eat me!" Fan wailed, shaking as she lowered her head. Fan Hazim was an older woman, and her braided hair that would have once been dark like all of the Gypsies of ancient Shaar, was now a grey mat of tangles. Her hands looked wrinkled, and she wore large, loose-fitting breeches and a robe top that was bedecked with beads. She looked suddenly very small and frail and old compared to me and Aida.

"Eat her? I wouldn't go anywhere near her!" Aida snorted in revulsion, the sound making Fan Hazim only wail a little louder.

"My companion won't eat you – *yet,*" I announced as I swung my legs from the saddle and jumped to the forest floor. Fan Hazim gave a little murmur of alarm as I drew my father's sword and raised towards her.

"Why should I spare you?" I snarled at her, taking another step closer.

"Please, my lord... Because I might be able to help..." The old woman shook and looked down at the dirt.

"Help?" I said, stopping my advance when the blade was just a foot or so from the woman's chest. "How under the skies could you help *me?"*

"Well, I know a way into the Torvald Dragon Enclosure..." she said, looking up at me through the matted locks of her hair. There was that twinkle of calculation again, of trying to gauge whether she could turn this situation to her profit, just like she always did. “I am sure that a Prince of the South will need to know the layout of his enemies…”

“Quiet!” I spat back. As tempting as it would be to know that information, I knew what she was trying to do. To make herself indispensable to me. To gain from the chaos and discord that she sowed wherever she was.

“I have many contacts throughout this northern empire…” Fan Hazim whispered, keeping her voice and her eyes low, as if humbled. “If ever the South comes to…*difficulties* with the North, then they will prove useful…”

It was a tempting offer, as I was already alarmed at Duke Robert’s talk of his ‘Liquid Fire’ which was surely a remnant of the old Dark King’s technology. Once we had invited Torvald troops to the South to help fight the Deadweed – would they ever leave again?

But that was my mistake. I had taken my eyes from her as I had wondered about the future, about the South and the North, and that was when she made her move.

Fan Hazim had waited until I was in front of my dragon, forming a natural barrier to Aida’s wrath. And furious she would be, as soon as she saw what I saw in Fan Hazim’s hand—

“Stay back!” Fan hissed, her hands having moved in a dizzying sleight of hand to now be holding something gingerly, half wrapped in cloth. From the edge of the white cloth I could see a deep, almost orangey-yellow hue, and the feathery fronds of flower stamens.

Deadweed.

"Sssss!" Aida reacted, crinkling her nose as she snarled at the woman who would dare to threaten me. I responded instinctively, drawing back from her as she flipped open the cloth covering to reveal a large mess of Deadweed flower heads, gesturing at me with it as she stood up, her face victorious.

Every time she moved, a small puff of the yellow pollen rose a little in the air between us. Even now, I could feel the back of my throat and nose start to scratch.

"How could you!" I said in alarm. She would seriously use that stuff – that terrible mutant weed – to try and attack us? Our entire way of life was threatened by it!

"I'll use it, by the bones and sands I will!" she said, taking a step back as more drifts of pollen rose between us.

But that was the thing with Deadweed pollen—it was toxic to both humans and dragons, and there was no apparent remedy.

"Ack!" Fan Hazim sneezed as some of the pollen must have drifted her way, too, and in that moment I lunged. The dried flower heads were the most dangerous thing, and so I flicked my father's sword to bash her on the side of the wrist that held the pollen, as I continued to jump forward—

Back, Aida! I thought as I body-slammed the old woman, hitting the floor and hearing her gasp in pain as the packet of

Deadweed tumbled to the ground behind us, the flower heads breaking apart and sending up a larger cloud of the pollen.

“Ssssscrark!” Aida sang in alarm as she jumped backwards into the air. I moved quickly, grabbing the older woman with my one free hand and stumbling in the other direction, willing my feet to push off the ground as I kept my head low to avoid the cloud of pollen.

“*Hyurk!”* I heard a grunt of startled pain from Fan as I half hauled her, half carried her out of the way to the relative safety of the trees, before I threw her to the floor, panting.

“You’re hopeless, Fan!” I muttered angrily. Maybe there was nothing that *could* be done with a woman like her. Maybe she would always try to betray and backstab anyone around her, no matter the consequences, all because she thought it made her powerful…

I raised my sword to point it straight at her black heart—

“Akeem, don’t!” A voice called through the woods. It was Dayie, running down one of the narrow paths towards me, her own scimitar in hand.

CHAPTER 9
DAYIE, NOT WHO I WAS

I shouted in alarm as I ran forwards, seeing Akeem, the Prince of the South and Captain of the Wild Company, about to run his father's sword through the body of Fan Hazim.

"Why stop him? She tried to poison me!" Zarr roared behind us, where we had alighted on the edge of the woods. It had been an easy thing to track them, as even *I* could hear Aida's angered calls and see the commotion in the clearing of the woods ahead.

Zarr had a point, I had to admit. But I needed Fan Hazim – and besides which, suddenly seeing the woman again, my tormentor for so many years, cowering before the tall and powerfully-built Akeem made me realize how pathetic she was.

Fan wasn't the figure of my nightmares anymore, I thought, as

I made calming gestures to Akeem and shook my head that this wasn't what I wanted.

"The South will want justice. For the dragons," Akeem said gruffly, but took a step back all the same. He didn't lower his father's sword from where he could lunge forward and end the Dragon Trader once and for all though, I noticed.

"I know it will. They will," I agreed with Akeem, keeping my own blade on Fan as I stopped my wild run and tried to catch my breath. "But not yet."

How could I explain to Akeem what I was feeling? It wasn't just that I needed what this old, terrible woman knew. It was also that something had changed. I no longer hated her in that ferocious, burning way I had always done before. A part of it was getting to know Nas, free from her baleful influence and seeing him grow into a young man who had an inkling – only an inkling, but still – of honor and respect.

We could be better people, despite her. That was what I was feeling. No more did I wake up with fear in my mouth or sweat on my brow as I wondered what torment or private shame she would visit on me. My arms and legs weren't purple and blue with bruises anymore – well, not from her cruel antics, anyway. I didn't even care what Fan Hazim thought of me, because what I was had nothing to do with her.

"Not true," Zarr rumbled in the back of my mind. *"You forget that I can see you, Dayie-sister. I can see your heart and mind because you and I are one thing. I can still see the shape of the pain that she put you through, in your mind."*

"Yes, but…" I murmured to Zarr as Akeem watched Fan with hawk-like intensity.

But who I was now had grown *beyond* that pain. Yes, Zarr was of course right that there would forever be a part of my heart that held her shadow, and the gloom of those long years of always being told that I was a freak, and never good enough, *that I was lazy, and cursed,* I remembered, but that pain had led me to push myself above all things. To be better than I thought I could be. To jump into my life as a Dragon Rider with both feet, knowing where I had come from.

In that moment, I realized my intense hatred of Fan Hazim had evaporated, leaving behind a more general sort of dislike that left a foul taste in my mouth. The woman of whom I had been so afraid was pitiful. She was conniving and deceitful, and a terrible mother, wife, friend, trader… But she was also weak. I had faced the attacks of mutant Deadweed and I had faced armies of Water Wraiths and even been targeted by the powerfully evil Sea Witch. There was nothing about the aging Fan Hazim that I couldn't handle now.

And I have you, I thought at Zarr, sensing how he was struggling to keep up with my emotions. *How can she ever hurt me again?*

"You do have me, my sister…" Zarr said, and a wave of fierce pride washed over me, only solidifying my certainty of what I was doing and what I needed to do.

"Dayie… Is it really you?" Fan was looking up at me with tears in her eyes. Fake tears, I thought. I had seen her pull a trick like this many times to get past a border guard or to distract a gate inspection. “You look so much taller now, girl…” she murmured at me.

“Shut up and listen, Fan,” I snapped at her, and felt a moment’s guilty pleasure when her face twisted into fury, before it dissolved into alarm as I saw understanding dawn on her face –I was more powerful than she was. *That’s right, Fan. I hold the keys to your survival now, not the other way around,* I thought.

“This, as you know, is the rightful heir to the Southern Kingdom, and besides that, the captain of a band of bloodthirsty dragon warriors…” I exaggerated a bit, but it didn’t hurt to drive the point home. “He is in his rights to demand your head for what you have tried to do to the dragons, and to me.” I let my words sink in.

“So, I think that you had better do everything that you can to try and be honest with me. No more lies. No more trying to get the upper hand, because if for one moment I think that you’re being deceitful, I will let the Prince do whatever he wants with you.” I said, and Akeem flicked the point of his sword, as if to make the point that what *he* wanted to do wouldn’t be very nice indeed.

Fan opened and closed her mouth several times, and then turned to look at me, her face becoming serious and her mouth taking on a flat line. At last we understood each other. She wasn’t going to pretend anymore with me.

“I need to know everything you know, or have heard, about my mother,” I said evenly.

"That woman Wera? I never knew them," Fan said. "Both your parents had died before I found you…"

"That, we both know, is a lie. You didn't *find* me, Fan. You *bought* me," I said curtly, my words making Akeem step forward with his sword.

"You were told the price of your dishonesty, Fan Hazim…" the Prince of the South said in a deadly voice.

Calm, Dayie, I told myself, putting my arm out to halt Akeem as Fan's eyes widened. She lied so often she did not seem to even know she did it. "And not Wera – my *real* mother."

"Your real mother…?" Fan looked genuinely surprised. "I never knew her…"

"You've always had your ears to the winds, Fan. You must have heard things. What did the villagers tell you when you bought me? What did you hear about how I came to be on the coast?"

"You were a foundling," Fan said uncertainly. "Surely you know that—your foster parents found you on the beach one morning after a particularly violent storm. They took you in…"

"What did you *hear,* Fan…" I growled. *Had I made the wrong choice?* I was suddenly very scared. Maybe this *was* all just a ridiculous idea? What if Mengala and the sorcerer had been wrong – and that I would never unlock my magic as finding anything about my mother was a dead end!

Fan frowned for a moment, then let out a sharp breath. "Fine.

I'll tell you. I met the people of Velak on the road south from the coast, fleeing the Deadweed."

That had overrun Velak and had killed my foster parents, I nodded. I had dim memories of that time – nothing much, just jostling, shouting, angry faces.

"Refugees are always good for business. Either they will have things to trade, or they want to buy back what they have lost," Fan said. "So I stopped to talk, and there you were, trailing along behind them surrounded by a scattering of goats, being ignored by everyone."

"Uh-huh." I remembered the goats, at least. Nights curled up with the warm animal smell of goat fleece.

"They called you the witch-girl, and said that you were cursed. That you could make a dog bite who you wanted, and that you could call the wild birds down from the sky."

Could I? I thought. *I don't remember doing that – had I been more powerful as a child than I was now?*

"When I came to look at you, you even called a pack of the town's dogs to stand around you, growling at everyone…" Fan said with apparent disgust.

At least the younger me wasn't stupid, I thought.

"The villagers wanted rid of you, blaming you for the Dead-weed attack – seeing as you had a way with living things anyway. Your foster parents' garden was always the one of bloom the longest and brightest, after all…" Fan shuddered at the unearthliness of what she was telling me. "They begged me to take you, and I offered you the choice to get away from there."

"You offered?" I burst out. That genuinely *did* surprise me.

"Oh yes." Fan's eyes glittered with cold malice. She might be powerless to strike fear into me anymore, but she still relished in any pain and confusion she gave me. "I gave you the choice to come with me. I wasn't going to take you on, with your perversions, if you weren't going to work for me."

"They're not perversions!" Akeem said in a tight voice, barely restrained from a shout. When I glanced back, his shoulders were shaking with his mastered fury.

Fan only smiled. "You *chose* to come with me, to take on that life, Dayie. That is probably what you forget, but it's true. You were only too eager to get away from the villagers who hated you!"

Well, that *did* sting. It seemed as though the younger me *was* more stupid than I had thought.

"My mother," I said again, shoving my shame down. "You bought me because you thought that I had powers," *'perversions'* I heard the word echo in my head, "and I am sure that a canny businesswoman like you must have made inquiries where they came from…"

"What do you want me to say?" Fan burst out in exasperation. "Of course, I asked questions. I poked around the coast for a bit, sending Rahim off to find news in the markets of witches and magic. All I ever found out was that on the night that you were found, a strange and terrible storm unlike anything that people had seen before boiled up out of the west, with clouds laced purple."

Which made sense, I think. The west was where the Western Archipelago was, and where, farthest west of all – there was the Haunted Isle of Sebol.

"Is that all?" I raised my eyebrows. "Because believe me, you haven't told me much…"

Apart from that I was stronger before, as a child, I had to concede, shelving that information away to think on later. How could I recover that magical strength? Especially seeing as I had to defeat an actual trained witch? Oh, how I wished that Mengala was here to tell me more about Sebol and what the Western Witches had been capable of!

"Fine!" Fan Hazim sneered, reaching into the pouches of her robe top—

"Easy there." Akeem moved forward a little, the blade coming within a short stab from Fan's hand.

"It's fine. No tricks…" Fan angrily pulled at something in the pouch, which appeared to be a small leather bag, drawn together with cord at the top. "This was the last thing that your mother – your real mother, that is – gave you, or so the refugees of Velak told me."

I watched as Fan carefully drew open the leather pouch and emptied its contents into her hand.

It was a neckless, with a large shell in the centre, in place on dark waxed cord.

The shell. Something hit me between my eyes and in my heart. It was the shell, a fat-bellied tear-drop like shape that I knew had one side that was rucked and pocked, and would feel dry and granular at the same time. But the other side, the inner side of the shell was a dance of iridescent colors in gentle cloud-patterns. The colors would flash and change in the light depending how you held the shell. *How did I know all of this?* I thought.

"Egg memories," Zarr informed me. *"They are like dreams of a time you can't remember. Memories of your time when you were only a hatchling."*

"Human's don't hatch out of eggs, wyrm," I muttered under my breath.

"They don't?"

But the Crimson Red was right all the same – I *did* remember that shell, or a part of my heart did. I remembered the color, and the feeling of wonder and comfort as I had held it.

Mamma-la, Mamma-la... the strands of the old nursery song rose in my memory, only it wasn't sung by me, but by someone else.

Mother? I reached out with my mind, but I couldn't catch any more than a glimpse of light-colored hair.

"I've had alchemists and scholars look at it over the years, but they say apart from the rather rare shell there, it's next to worthless." Fan shook her head. "But I kept a hold of it all the same, and the story alone of a magical child rescued from the waves has brought me many dragons from up and down the

North." She managed to chuckle a little dryly. "But I suppose that you might as well have it. It's never given *me* special powers, and it's never been worth enough to try and sell it. What good is it, then?" She threw the necklace towards me and I caught it easily with my free hand.

Ah. It was like returning home, in a way – or catching a fleeting glance of a place that you used to call home, anyway.

"The Velak refugees said that you had that around your neck when Obasi and Wera found you, and that you wore it every day without fail, until you came into my care."

Care! That was a joke, but I was too enamored of the shell necklace to pull Fan up on it. I slipped it into my pocket, taking a deep breath and feeling slightly light headed. *That necklace had been put over my neck by my actual blood-mother.* I was amazed by the thought. It was as real and as tangible a connection as I was going to get to her. I wondered if I could feel something changing in me – was that tingling in my stomach just nervousness, or was it my magical power unlocking, as Mengala had promised? Was the necklace the reason I'd been more powerful as a child? Was *it* the secret to my mother's magic?

"Right." I coughed, trying to bring my attention to the present.

"You got what you need from this woman?" Akeem's tone was still harsh.

"Yes…" I nodded. *But I had wanted to go with her.* The shame gnawed at me. Was I somehow complicit in my own captivity?

"Never think that. It is never your fault if someone else does

wrong to you," Zarr informed me quickly.

I thanked him, taking a deep breath. "Prince Akeem? I want this woman's life spared," I said thickly, wondering if this was a wise decision at all.

"Go on..." Akeem said heavily.

"We could exile her from the South, but the life of a Dragon Trader is one of constant travel anyway, and the Gypsies of Distant Shaar have long since been roaming from their homeland," I pointed out. "I do not want to be responsible for anyone being executed for their actions against me," I said. "Instead, I think it would be far more fitting if Fan Hazim was kept somewhere. A place where she could work and not roam freely again." Or at least, not for a very, *very* long time.

"Imprisonment?" Akeem said.

"Captivity," I pointed out. There was a certain fitting circularity to the fact that Fan Hazim's crimes against me had started with a sort of cruel captivity, and now she might be forced to experience the same fate.

"I'll send her back to Dagfan with Heydar." Akeem nodded that he agreed, before looking at me sharply. "You'd make a wise ruler, Dayie," he said, before tying Fan Hazim's hands behind her back.

But I wasn't dreaming about being a wise and sensible ruler at all. All that was on my mind was the newfound-old shell in my pocket.

CHAPTER 10
DAYIE, ALWAYS A PRICE TO PAY

"Dayie, is there no other way?" Rahim's usually loud and avuncular voice was small over the sounds of their camp by the Torvald woods that we had set up just a little bit earlier. The southern dragons appeared to be unsure of this new climate, moving out from the shade of the trees to try and bask on the rocks beside the fast-flowing river. I wondered how they would cope in the colder airs and frequent rains of the northern empire.

Zarr, on the other hand, appeared to be in his element, rooting around the near stands of the trees, tearing great gouts out of the earth as he hunted for voles or rabbits or whatever it was he found so interesting.

But as much as I wanted to watch Zarr play in his 'natural' environment, I had to drag my attention away instead and concentrate on Rahim's question. I nodded seriously. "Yes,

Rahim, I'm afraid there isn't – I'm sure that you understand why…"

The reason was clear to both of us, I saw in the older man's face, and the point was only proved when Fan Hazim, Rahim's wife, struggled and spat in Heydar's arms as he dragged her towards his dragon.

"Don't just stand there, you fool! Say something! Are you any sort of man at all!?" She cursed him, and I had to look away as Rahim blushed a deep scarlet. I didn't think that Rahim had ever been a proud man – how could he, when he had been ordered about all his life by Fan? When he had put up with her beating me, and putting him down all the time? But he had shame, I saw.

"Ugh! I should have guessed. You're just a coward, like all the rest of your kind!" Fan snapped at him, suddenly relaxing in Heydar's arms as the fight drained from her. "Men," she scolded, doing her best to try and look dignified, despite the way that her wrists were tied, and her arms were clamped to her sides… For the briefest of moments, something flashed underneath Fan's harsh, argumentative, bullying and cruel exterior. *Fear? Weakness?* I wondered how many men must have done her wrong, for her to hate so.

"You won't come to any harm," Akeem said sternly. "Not if you let us take you to the Binshee as I have suggested, and not to Dagfan."

"Pfagh!" Fan raised her chin defiantly.

That had been a bone of contention between me and the Prince of the South. I had said that she had to go to Dagfan, because it was the Dagfan dragons which she had hurt. They would need to see that justice had been served, at last.

But Akeem made a good point – that Dagfan, surprisingly, had much harsher punishments than the wild people of the Binshee tribes did. Dagfan still kept criminals in cages – or worse. The Binshee had an austere but seemingly fair attitude to criminality amongst their own; once you were found guilty, you could either decide to have a trial by combat, or you could work as a servant, or you could be exiled. When I had stopped Akeem running his sword through Fan, he'd thought that he had just performed a 'trial by combat' and that he had a right to take her life should he want to. I had forced him to consider turning Fan into a servant (*a slave like I had been…?* a part of me thought).

It was fair, I had to agree. I was still furious with Fan for what she had done to me – and more so what she had attempted to do to the dragons – but that didn't mean I wanted to see her treated badly, or hurt. To be honest, I was tired of even having to worry about Fan, and if I heard that she had been executed by the Southern Lords or had some horrible punishment visited on her – chopping off a hand perhaps – then that would only make me feel worse.

So, no. There was no other way forward. This was the best I could offer.

"Mother…." said Nas, looking at her with heavy brows. His voice was full of regret and shame, and I felt bad *then* – for what I was making Rahim and Nas feel. But this day had to come, and I hardened my heart.

Fan sneered. "A curse upon all of you. Upon all menfolk. You're all too weak anyway." She spat at her own son, before focusing her final words at me. "You have it right, Dayie. You have to be stronger than everyone else. You have to worm your way into their hearts and their minds to get a foothold in this life. You must have learnt that from me!" she said, and my heart turned in disgust.

How could she think that was what I was doing! I let out a gargled cough of anger—

"Shhhh, Dayie Sister!" Zarr suddenly swept his flame-edged thoughts into my mind. *"That is what she wants. She is poison, and she wishes to spread it to you. If she cannot do so at the end of a knife, she will do so with her words!"*

The Crimson Red was wiser than all of us, I thought, taking a deep breath. "Thank you," I whispered to him, drawing myself up and saying nothing as Fan was walked to Heydar's dragon and thrown over a makeshift saddle as if she were a sack of potatoes. It wouldn't be long flight until they found a Binshee camp, I was sure – but Fan would be uncomfortable the whole way…

Akeem raised his hand in a silent salute as Heydar lifted up into the skies on the back of his dragon, and I was glad to turn back to who was left and consider what we did next.

"Did you get what you needed?" Akeem murmured to me as he stepped forward to my side, his eyes large and worried.

No need to be worried about me! I thought, but I *was* a little perturbed all the same. My hand moved to the shell necklace that I now wore and felt the smooth ridges of the shell as I considered.

"I don't know," I said honestly. "Both Mengala and the sorcerer seemed to think that finding out more about my mother would unlock my own magic and would somehow make it stop hurting all the time." I shrugged. "But I don't feel any different."

"Torvald," Rahim surprised me by saying suddenly. He had moved to Nas's side and seemed to be offering what condolences he could to Fan's child.

I looked at him in confusion.

"We were on our way there, actually…" Rahim said with a nervous, relieved smile. "Fan wanted to get more dragon eggs, knowing that this war would make them very valuable indeed."

"I should have guessed." I shrugged.

"…but there's something that you should know about Torvald," Rahim stated. "Its academy has some of the largest collection of magical treatises and grimoires and studies and papers ever seen on the mainland. After the old King Bower took to the throne, he decreed that the Torvald throne would buy back any manuscript lost thanks to the Dark King, and many were the times that Fan had us sell a batch of whatever we could find to Torvald." He nodded. "If you want to know about magic, then you really have to get into the Torvald Academy."

"But would they let me?" I frowned, looking around our little cohort. Half of us were deemed vagabond wanderers, Akeem was the would-be sovereign prince of a different nation, and no one knew who I was at all!

"When has Torvald ever let us do anything, Dayie?" Nas shrugged, and my memories of sneaking into the citadel and up onto the Dragon Mountain came flooding back. "We could take the back route," Nas went on, and I thought of the path we'd taken when Zarr was just an egg, around the northern side of Mount Hammal, that wound its way up through the gorges and forests and past the old lakes, right up to the peak and the academy itself…

"I don't know…" I thought, despite the gleam in Akeem's eyes beside me. I should have known that he would want to sneak into the citadel of his rival nation.

"We're meant to be allies now," I said patiently to both Akeem and the Hazims. "I can't jeopardize that relationship for the South…"

"What relationship?" Akeem muttered darkly, but he could not have forgotten the tentative trade deal that we had struck with the Duke of the North.

"Uhr…the food? The secret of their new dragon fire?" I reminded him.

"A secret which is probably stored at the academy as well…"

Akeem said in a calculating voice. "And you and Nas have both managed to avoid the dragon's senses before…"

"No," I said out loud, seeing his plan. I would not sneak into the academy to steal anything from Torvald ever again. Those days were behind me.

"Skreayaaaarch!" Zarr suddenly threw his head back and trumpeted loudly, his alarm sweeping through me…

"Zarr? What is it?"

All our arguments and choices of where to go and what to do next were suddenly stripped from us at my Crimson Red's loud warning shout, as Zarr informed me quickly, "*Bad water. Bad water and Deadweed. Attacking the Sacred Mountain!*"

"Torvald is in danger – the Deadweed is attacking it!" I burst out, already hurrying to pick up my things and climb Zarr's back.

"What – Aida?" Akeem said in alarm, and then confirmed with his own bonded Vicious Orange dragon. "We have to go. Now." He burst into action, vaulting up Aida's leg and into his saddle. "If the Deadweed has either grown so far or has gotten so bold as to strike at the heart of the Torvald Empire, then the lands are in a much worse state than any of us had feared."

Whatever I had been planning to do when we got there—not the least of which was getting at that library of books Rahim was talking about – all of that was brushed aside as I knew that there was one thing that I *had* to do – and that was to fight the Deadweed.

The ancient citadel of Torvald was wreathed in smoke and the sky was split by the shriek of dragons.

Sweet stars and sands… I thought, as I could never have imagined seeing the citadel like this. Oh, I had known – in that vague kind of way that Torvald had suffered and survived many battles in its long centuries – millennia, even – of standing, and yet I had only ever seen it with its towering cream-white walls, its towers that gleamed with hammered bronze, and its red and purple pennants that always caught the wind. It was the sort of city that never ceased to amaze every time you saw it – no matter how many times you had seen it.

But I had never expected to see its walls that used to catch the sun look dirty and black with scorch marks, and its flights of dragons that I had seen before circling in their regimented, graceful, and exact flights now a scattering, boiling mess of crow-fight.

"It's almost got to the outer settlements!" Nas shouted, a little way ahead of us on Nandor.

The flight northward towards the citadel hadn't taken us long as Zarr and the other two dragons had fought their way high into the colder airs (*not the Tall Winds, but something else – a different river of air that was unique to the North*) and then swooped downward again in a long, shooting flight that ate up the leagues in terribly fast time.

We had arrived in the late afternoon, and the sun was even now fading and burning the western sky, turning the walls of

Torvald dark, and giving the entire city a somber air. Not that the land outside the citadel and the mountain that it sat on was dark – instead, it was alive with reds, oranges, and flickering yellows.

Deadweed, I saw to my amazement. I had thought that particular dark masses below us must have been woodlands, but the darker shapes convulsed and surged forward – banks of Deadweed, as thick and as large as trees, eating up the land beneath it as it approached the outlying settlements.

Torvald was a citadel that terraced up the sides off Mount Hammal, but any successful city, I knew from my extensive travels with Fan, attracted to itself smaller neighborhoods of warehouses and shanty towns, market-sites and eventually entire small townlets, clustering along the wide pounded-rock roads that stretched out from the high walls. I could see the small eaves and chimneys of such settlements stretching out along the roadway, congregating every time that there was a crossroads, or a bridge or an inn. It was to these outlying places that the Deadweed was threatening to engulf…first.

"There's just so much of it…" I said in horror. Even though the Dragon Riders of Torvald were amazing, technical fliers – swooping in exact formation and attacking in waves – I had never seen so many different attacks by the Deadweed happening all at once. *How had it managed it?* How had it managed to travel this far inland and not be noticed, or stopped?

"Bad water…" Zarr screeched in my head, turning his snout towards one of the many streams that snaked down the high

mountain, through or around the citadel in deep culverts, to join a larger network of canals and rivers. It seemed that one of Torvald's greatest strengths (apart from the dragons, that is) its technology, had also become its greatest weakness.

I scanned the waterways that crisscrossed the landscape outside of the citadel, and, at the exact same time that my eyes found them, my body shook with nausea as I saw the surge of the Water Wraiths, stepping out of the canals and crossing the roadways, fields and meadows, spreading the Deadweed behind them as they did so.

"Dayie!?" Zarr thought in alarm, flaring wide his great wings so that we broke from our reckless flight into the battle. He could sense my distress.

"It's okay – I'll be okay…" I said, even though my vision was already doubling. "It's something to do with the Water Wraiths, it's like I can sense them in my mind…" I explained out loud, although I was sure Zarr knew that already.

"I can sense them like a bruise... It is the same for you – but much worse..." Zarr informed me, already turning back, away from the other Dragon Riders.

"No – we can't go! We can't leave people defenseless down there!" I pointed out, my anger and frustration marrying with my vertigo and nausea. This was a little like the *Nemisia* curse that the Sea Witch had sent against me, and a little like the sickness that my magic had always provoked within me, but all horribly rolled into one. Was this some new trick of the Sea Witch? Or was it just that, as I grew stronger in my powers – so my failings and drawbacks grew stronger too?

"I cannot let you be harmed!" Zarr wrapped his warm heart around me, and his fierce loyalty, and love flooded through me, along with his desire to tear the world apart from its roots should he have to. Dragons do not feel as humans do – they feel far, far deeper.

And then something happened.

In my mind, and in my body, some of that dragon warmth spread from Zarr, through the connection and into me. It felt like a raging fire – but it wasn't painful. Instead, it felt joyous and uplifting, purifying even, filling me with a fierce energy that made me want to stretch my wings and screech at the sky—

"You have no wings, little sister..." Zarr was saying, but his voice sounded muted and far away next to this volcano of savage strength racing through my limbs.

"I have given you too much..." I heard the Crimson Red say, and the bubble of my elation burst.

Zarr was giving me his strength, I realized, remembering how he had done the same before – but unknowingly, during our frantic, magical, and quite frankly eerie flight from the deep southern deserts to Dagfan. At that time, it had been a magical working of Mengala and the Sorcerer of the Whispering Rocks that had 'drawn' on Zarr's innate magical power as a dragon – but it was obvious to me now that Zarr was able to send his strength to me directly, whenever he wanted. My body was enervated and whole.

But, as inspiring and as touching as it was, I couldn't let Zarr give me any more. "No," I said sternly, my own voice resonant with authority... I pushed at Zarr's connection with my mind – *no, not my mind, my heart,* I knew. I might hear Zarr's thoughts in my mind, but our bond was through our heart – I reached towards Zarr with my heart, and halted the reckless gift.

"We're going back," I said, full of certainty, and in that instant Zarr turned on a wingtip and threw us back towards the line of Water Wraiths. I was in tune with the Crimson Red in a way that I hadn't before. My thoughts were full of a dragon's fire, and his senses overlay my own. *Is this what it is to be fully bonded?* I thought – or was this my magic enhancing the bond that I had with him? It seemed that even my eyes were keener, making out every individual Water Wraith as they marched and swept forward, and even the leaves on the trees fluttering in the baleful wind ahead of the unholy army—

"*STOP!*" I called out, reaching with my mind and my heart and my magic, and something uncurled within me. It was the magic that had been hidden within me all this time, which I had only ever had the smallest access to before, through my mother's song.

"*Stop,*" I repeated, and my voice was lilting and musical in my ears. I was singing the word, just as I sang the magic before—

And something passed from my outstretched hand and out into the world.

But nothing appeared to happen, not at first, anyway. Not that I was worried, I could *feel* the current of strong fire and water magic flowing out through me, changing the invisible currents of the world beneath me, growing, gaining strength—

WOAOWOWWOAO—

The fluttering leaves in the trees that hedged the first townlet started to tear from their seats as the wind rose. And rose. And rose some more, until the branches were swaying and creaking, and the tiles from the nearest roadside Torvald warehouse were being torn from their moorings—

"This wind has teeth, little sister!" Zarr roared, angling his wings so that he could ride the strong currents of air that had swept up out of nowhere and were even now blowing hard against the tide of the Water Wraiths.

"It does," I smiled, feeling the exhilarating flush of power. I had called the wind, even though I did not know how I had done it. But when Zarr had lent me his strength – *his life,* a part of me tried to say – it had seemed so simple.

That sorcerer was right, I thought, laughing. There are currents of magic running all through the world, unseen to us. All you have to do is to tap into them and you can summon the wind's teeth, or the water's unstoppable nature, or the rock's intractability…

"Dayie…?" This time when the Crimson Red's voice rose in my mind, he sounded less sure of himself, and even his voice – usually as close as my own heartbeat, sounded muted and far away. I could feel his worry for me. His worry that I had gone too far.

"I'm fine, Zarr…" I laughed back at him, as I swept my hand

across the landscape, gathering the storm winds towards the line of Water Wraiths. Below us, the gales started to howl and whine as wooden gates were torn from their positions and smaller trees bent so much that they snapped and exploded in wood fragments—

The effect that this unnatural hurricane was having on the Water Wraiths wasn't as destructive as I would have liked, but as I watched, the front line of the Wraiths collapsed back into their watery brothers behind. The unnatural spirits were losing their humanoid forms under the onslaught, being thrown back and losing the white foam of storm seas as they were pushed back towards the canals.

"It's working, Zarr! Look – it's working!" I called out jubilantly.

"Skreyarch!" The commotion that I had created had drawn the attention of a flight of Torvald dragons who were fighting the rising winds far above us, before finding their wings and joining the violent flows of air instead of fighting them. They rushed, thrown like the leaves being torn from the trees towards the lines of Water Wraiths, releasing their dragon fire as they did so.

Phoom! Phooom! The missiles of burning red fire exploded against the built-up banks of the canals, hitting the Water Wraiths with gouts of flame and smoke, sending steam into the air to obscure the lowlands.

"Keep on going! Keep on!" I was shouting, as Zarr beneath me lifted us up, out of the way of attacking flight to circle around. We were shaking in the air, losing height and gaining it in turns as Zarr fought to maintain his position with the aggressive storm that I had summoned.

"Dayie-sister!" Zarr's voice was a bark of worried frustration, but it was something that I had to ignore. We were going to win, and my magic was instrumental to that victory.

The dragon flight tried to wheel around to attack again, but the storm winds were too strong and had already carried them far out from the canals and over the mats of Deadweed – opportunistically, the Torvald Dragon Riders fired again, and another knot of Dragon Riders took their place to attack the canals.

I rose my hand and the winds with it, meaning to dash them against the Water Wraiths with full force—

"Little sister, I said STOP!" This time, Zarr rushed into my mind on wings of flame and inferno – wrapping his fierce heart around me and choking me with a savage, reptilian love. It was a dragon's love, which meant that it was comfortable seizing its young in powerful jaws to control it-

"*Hyurk,"* I gasped, as I felt my eyes closing and my hand lowering. My body felt no longer my own as Zarr bent his powerful will over mine and forced me away from the magic—

What are you doing!? I thought in alarm, mumbling the words because even my face felt thick and sluggish.

"You must stop. This isn't you," Zarr growled.

How was he to know what was me or not? I thought indignantly. Of course, this was me. This was *all* me. I had pushed the Water Wraiths away with just the power of my mind, I had summoned the storm with just the magic inside of me… It seemed that Mengala and the sorcerer were right, as soon as I had reconnected with my mother in just a small way – finding the shell necklace that hung around my neck, then I had grown stronger, I might even be unstoppable…

"No. Nothing is unstoppable, little sister." Zarr was already wheeling away from the battle, heading higher and higher over the storm that I had created and turning in an arc towards the sacred mountain of Torvald itself.

Zarr – the battle! We have to go back! I thought at him, but he was implacable.

Clearly, I wasn't as invincible as I had thought, as I could barely control my own body, it seemed…

"No," Zarr said. *"You are not invincible. Nothing is invincible. Not you, not dragons – even the sun and moon will one day change in their course..."* he stated in his (very annoying, I thought) quizzical dragon nature.

But... I could have screamed in frustration at him.

"*Look, my sister...*" Zarr did something to my mind, opening up my awareness to something on the other side of my magic that I had not even been aware of—

Pain.

A wave of nausea rolled up through me from the balls of my

feet right up through the top of my head, bringing with it stabbing, shooting electric pains—

No – why? I could have sobbed in misery, and, as easily as the pain had appeared, it vanished as I felt Zarr seal it from my mind, blocking it behind the wall of his fiery love.

"That is the pain of your magic. It has not gone away, but only grown worse. You were so caught up in the flows of your power that you could not feel it, so I am holding it for you... but I cannot do so for long..."

What? I shook in my seat, my guilt and alarm so strong as to even shake the dragon's control of my subdued body. I had thought that I had conquered my magic. That the side-effects had gone, somehow…

Akeem! The thought tore through me as I looked around in my misery. I had completely forgotten about them in the rush of magical power. And what about Nas and Heydar, too? Were they still fighting? Had the hurricane I summoned affected them, too?

I couldn't see them. I had no idea if they had survived or fallen – why hadn't I been looking out for them? I cursed my ignorance.

I have been so stupid, I thought, all my fight leaving my body as I realized what I had done. Zarr had offered me his dragon strength – his heart and his fire – and I had used it to unlock my magic – maybe the shell necklace had helped, and it was the combination of the two: me remembering a slight hint of my mother's love and the surging fire of the dragon's soul that had allowed me to glimpse everything that I could be…

But the magic had still come with consequences, hadn't it? I had been fooling myself that I was cured of the magical illness – the necklace wasn't enough to heal whatever trauma I had with my magic, and I had unknowingly blocked out the pain—

The pain which Zarr now held for me. My heart jumped in shame. What had I done? What was I doing to him? How was this any better from what the sorcerer and Mengala had done to him, asking him to give of his life to feed their magic? The tides of savage joy had evaporated from my system, and behind us the unnatural storm, too, had started to die down. In its lull, the Torvald dragons had thrown themselves into the breach left, sending their fires against the Water Wraiths and the Deadweed. I think that they might have turned back the would-be invasion, but I was too disappointed in myself to find much joy in that victory.

Oh Zarr…. I thought at him, *I am so sorry…*

"Don't apologize. It is already been done. And I did what I wanted to do, to save you," Zarr sent the thought at me, but I could tell how tense he was as he fought to control the pain that he had somehow taken from me and held apart.

Just give the pain back to me, I can take it, it's rightfully mine…. I thought at him, only to hear a stubborn silence from the Crimson Red as he flew me over the citadel and up the steep banks of Mount Hammal itself.

There, rising above us like a fairy-tale was the dark crown of the Dragon Academy with its two impossibly tall towers, encrusted with strange copper or brass instruments like gongs or horns. The battlement walls were topped with lanterns, and I could see lighter-skinned faces running back and forth between them as we soared over the walls and the buildings inside, seeing snapshots of different practice grounds and courts, a garden – and we were heading out again, over the other side.

"Skreych!"

"Sssss!"

I could hear the warning hisses and whistles of the dragons on their landing platforms back at the academy as the massive Crimson Red and me flew over – we had not announced ourselves, we had not flown any flags to declare our intentions, and I was fearful that they would launch to attack us.

Where are you taking me? I thought, now starting to feel sleepy, even in the middle of this chaotic and violent evening. Zarr still held my mind in a fierce grip, and the warmth of his heart made it difficult to stay awake.

"You should sleep, then. Don't fight me, Dayie. I am trying to save your soul, silly human!" Zarr said as we flew over a saddle-back ridge of dark rock and small, scrubby bushes. I thought that maybe he would ease over the ridge and we would glide down to that long and still fishing lake, and the hidden waterfall cave where I had hidden with him as an egg, and where I had first heard him in my mind.

But no, Zarr kept his course straight and true, until the high rocks dropped away into the impossible large, rounded crater that was the Dragon Enclosure of Torvald.

A small, not-quite asleep part of me panicked. Wasn't it considered truly bad dragon etiquette to arrive at another's den unannounced, uninvited?

The Dragon Enclosure below us looked like the maw of an extinct volcano, and the rising air from it as warm as I remembered it being the last – and first – time I had ever been in there. *When I had stolen Zarr,* I thought in alarm. There were various platforms, rises and dips of rock, and half of it was covered with a thick vegetation that reminded me more of some of the irrigated gardens in the South than up here in the North.

And, of course, the place was filled with dragons – what I had thought was a large, creamy-white boulder below us suddenly raised its head and looked up at us with golden, flashing eyes. A *Giant White!* I thought. Hadn't it been a Giant White that had been nursemaid to Zarr's egg?

The Giant White dragons were the largest of all dragon-kind (although there were legends of Gold Dragons that were even larger), but when Zarr was a hundred years old or more, then he might just be near the size of the Giant White.

"Sssss!" Smaller dragons, much smaller dragons rose in raucous, angry flocks to warn us. *Messenger dragons,* I thought sleepily. A little like the breed that we called Orange Drakes that we had in the South – smaller than the Vicious Oranges even, and rarely bigger than a large wolfhound, if that. But these Messenger dragons were smaller even than the

Orange Drakes, and despite their hisses, I found myself looking at them fondly. They were cute.

"Hah." Zarr give a distracted sort of snort in the back of my mind.

"What's so…" I managed to mumble, before yawning.

"*You're almost asleep. Good.*" He was lowering us in ever tightening circles into the Dragon Enclosure, flying smoothly and gently even though I knew that he must still be in the tremendous pain that he had taken from me.

I don't deserve you as my friend... I thought as the dark of unconsciousness washed up to claim me.

"Too late." His reptilian voice growled against mine, tumbling me over the edge into a deep, and dreamless sleep.

CHAPTER 11
AKEEM, IN HIS ENEMIES' HOUSE

"Where is she? Where is the girl on the Crimson Red?" I hissed as soon as my boots hit the floor of packed earth. *Torvald soil,* every fiber of my being told me, making my teeth grate and my every nerve jangle.

It didn't help that I was surrounded by the high battlement walls of the one place in the world that had been the cause of so many sleepless nights for me, ever since my father had disappeared a few years ago.

The mighty Dragon Academy of Torvald. So old that it is said to be the earliest place in all of the Midmost Lands where dragons and humans had come together. It had been rebuilt and torn down and fortified and expanded and abandoned and repopulated many times, I knew from my father's history scrolls – but to me it had always represented one thing:

Torvald's power.

My father had known this, and that was why he had been insistent on starting the Wild Company. Torvald's real power wasn't in its mighty trade routes, its fleet of ships, nor its armies of foot soldiers. It wasn't even in the many leagues of lush growing lands and plains that Torvald had at its disposal – at least half of which had been stolen by the ancient Dark King anyway, and so Torvald had no right to at all! The oldest of history scrolls even tell of a third, Northern Kingdom, that once stretched up to the distant ice wastes and filled with a stern, mountainous folk – what had happened to them over the centuries, huh?

They had been consumed by Torvald, just like it always did to everything it came into contact with, I thought bitterly.

And *how* did it do all of this? The scholars all claimed it had been the Dark King Enric's evil magic that had swept over the land – but that was an easy apology for a much deeper problem: that Torvald had the primary access to the sacred Dragon Mountain, and that was the seat of its real power and always had been.

And here, in the shadow of these stones, was where the famous Dragon Riders of Torvald were trained. I forced myself to breathe calmly and control my anger. I was at least self-aware enough to know that while my anger at this academy was justified, it was heightened by the fact that they had kidnapped Dayie from me!

"My Lord Akeem," said the Torvald Rider who had greeted me in the skies after the battle and flown me here, guiding me to the home of my enemy.

I should never have told him who I am... I felt my lip curl in annoyance.

"You had to, dragon-brother. And I tell you, Dayie is safe. I can sense her sleeping..." Aida hissed in the back of my mind, but I brushed her attempts to mollify me away. Just because she was sleeping, that did not mean that there wasn't a Torvald guard waiting to put a knife to her throat.

"She is with the dragons, Akeem!" Aida hissed back at me, something which she had already told me once before, as well, but even that wasn't good enough for me. I needed to see her with my own eyes.

Yes. With the dragons of Torvald, in the Torvald-controlled enclosure, I thought back.

"We will get to the bottom of this, I promise you, my Lord," said the man warily. He was a tall, athletic man with hair that bounced into a tangle of dark curls as soon as he had removed his horned helmet. I was surprised at how old he looked, almost my father's age, with piercing blue eyes. He had announced himself as 'Captain Daris' and had stated that even though he had been surprised to see our different sort of dragons at the battle, he had known that his duke had gone to make alliances with the South.

I had let him assume that we were just emissaries from the South –a peace envoy even– in response to Torvald being gracious enough to send their very own duke to the aid of Dagfan.

"Isn't that what we ARE?" Aida snorted fire in annoyance. *"We're here to ask for help for Dayie, after all..."*

I coughed to hide my temper, *I am no peace envoy....*

"Skreeee!" A whistling shriek echoed as Nas on his Sea Green dragon Nandor swept down to join us on the wide landing arena inside the Training Hall, Nas wide-eyed and pleased at everything around him.

I could have groaned, wishing that I hadn't sent Heydar off with his bundle of trouble, Fan Hazim. Heydar might be a joker, but I had been through enough battles and long years with him at my side to know that he would be able to see through the glamour of this place and already have formulated three battle plans in case we were ambushed. The boy-Rider Nas would be useless in that regard; he seemed enamored of this place.

It's alright, but it's not the Binshee way, I thought, casting my eyes around, pretending to be as impressed as my colleague, when really, I was scoping for hidden archers or crossbow-men. There were wide archways through the internal walls that segmented different training areas, wide enough for a dragon to walk through comfortably, I saw. There were large barrels and equipment lockers stacked all around the walls, and above us were large landing platforms that clearly had been designed into the very masonry itself. It was a well-designed building, I conceded – if you like keeping people running about from room to room, building to building, instead of being out on the hills and plains.

We Binshee preferred a more natural approach... It was the

dragons after all, which were the whole point of the exercise, so it was the dragons that we allowed to teach *us* what they wanted. The Vicious Oranges of the High Mountains liked the high mountain caves and the sudden cliff-top drops, and so it was to these places that we travelled to befriend them. We learnt to fly by clambering and clinging onto the dragons from an early age, always dangling over precipitous drops that would mean our death if we lost just one handhold or our feet slipped.

No wonder the Dragon Riders of Torvald fight like they do, I considered. All flying in exact lines, exact flight paths and with carefully orchestrated moves. I even felt sorry for the poor dragons and all of that routine that they had to follow.

"Pfagh!" Aida once again let out a small flame of laughter, although I had no idea if that meant she was agreeing with my comment or not.

"If you will just wait here a moment, I will send word to Queen-Empress Nuria of your arrival," this Captain Daris stated, and I saw the first shadow of nervousness cross his features. Was he hiding something?

"…and I am sure that she would be honored to receive you at the palace, instead of here…" he said, turning to his second Rider (every Torvald dragon had two Riders, unlike ours) who was a woman with blonde hair, nearly in her middling years. She nodded to the captain in a wary sort of way, clearly concerned about what they were taking part in.

They probably want to hide the secrets of the Dragon Academy from me… I knew it. "The academy is fine for me, captains," I said curtly. "I am not used to palaces, and am but a humble warrior after all – all I want to know is where my friend is, and why she was taken into your Dragon Enclosure!" I ended on a slightly firmer note.

Captain Daris shot a worried sort of look at his fellow Rider, who gave a very faint shrug before nodding. "I'll inform the queen," she murmured to her friend, turning on her heel and proceeding to jog across the grounds to the gates.

"And ah, well, we *should* really wait for the queen's wishes…" Captain Daris said lightly, tapping his chin with his gloves as he looked over at me appraisingly. "But maybe there is something that I can do here, to assuage your fears…" I narrowed my eyes as he turned to the Stocky Green that he and his fellow Rider rode, and leaned forward so that he had one palm on the side of the creature's neck, just behind the ears. I knew that Aida liked to be scratched there as well, as it was hard for her to reach the smaller, delicate scales back there.

It's probably all for show, I thought skeptically. *Pretend to the foreigner just how closely bonded they are with their dragons…*

"Akeem!" Aida thumped both of her front feet on the ground suddenly, making Captain Daris and his Stocky Green look around in alarm.

"Don't question another's bond of friendship!" my own dragon-friend berated me, and I lowered my eyes. Ouch. Maybe she was right.

"Right, well..." Captain Daris coughed and stepped back from his Stocky Green, which was even now sitting back into its haunches and preparing to launch itself into the skies. "I have had a word with my friend, and she will go to the enclosure and enquire with the matriarch just what the situation is," he said with a slightly wary grin.

"Can't she just talk..." I muttered irritably as I waved a hand by my temple, knowing that it would be much quicker for the dragon to talk to this 'matriarch' of theirs through the dragon-thoughts they could share.

"Ah yes, of course," Captain Daris said. "But the dragons here have their own customs." The man gave a respectful nod in the direction of the enclosure. "A matriarch demands respect, just as much as any queen does."

It seemed like a silly way to do things, and I was about to tell him so, when Aida gave me the mental equivalent of a prod in the back of my mind, and I coughed as I stumbled forward a step.

"She was brought up in the enclosure." Captain Daris had apparently not seen my small embarrassment, as he was nodding up at the Stocky Green, his eyes shining with emotion as she jumped into the air and snapped her wings out in a thunderous *clap* of air. "She'll have some news for you, I promise..."

"Mhm." I managed to nod and only half-smile, feeling a little more self-conscious. After Aida's rebuke, this man's clear bond and affection he had for his own Stocky Green dragon made me reconsider things a bit.

Maybe not all the Dragon Riders are bad, I allowed. *Not the ones bonded with their dragons as I am with Aida, anyway…*

"Perhaps you would like to refresh yourself from the battle while you wait, Lord Akeem?" Captain Daris was pulling off his gauntlets and gesturing towards where a low building had been built against the outer walls. "You'll find washrooms in there, and I am sure that the cook will have food ready to be eaten."

"I'd rather wait here," I said stiffly. As much as I *might* be able to trust some of these Torvaldites, it didn't mean that there might not be others who were eager to sink a knife into the back of a Southern Prince!

There was a flicker of uncertainty in Captain Daris' eyes, before he inclined his head. "As you wish. I will be one moment." He turned away from us and walked to the far end of this training yard, where a small wooden door led to another part of the academy. I waited until he had gone, then I turned back to Nas, to find him still looking around the Training Hall with apparent awe.

"They've got everything here." He nodded to the platforms and buildings and guard towers. I knew what he meant, I could smell woodsmoke and cooking meat, and could even hear the clank of a smithy hard at work…

"How many?" I said.

"Huh?" Nas looked at me.

"How many Riders do you think this place can hold? Fifty? A hundred?" *Far more than we had at Dagfan,* I glowered.

"Well, when I used to come here with uh..." He looked down but not before I saw the memory of his mother and what had happened to her flashed over his face. "Anyway – before I went to Dagfan, we used to trade here once a year. The people we talked to said that they had...let me see now..." He scratched his head, trying to remember the figures.

Heydar would never have forgotten such an important piece of information! I inwardly groaned. *Why didn't Nas tell me this before?*

"Five flights – or 'wings' they called them, and was it ten or twelve dragons every wing?" he said.

"And two Riders per dragon, that makes...." I rocked a little as I toted up the figures. "As many as sixty trained battle-dragons, with a hundred and twenty Dragon Riders..."

"I know, incredible, right?" Nas completely missed the point. "And that is only scratching the surface of how many more dragons there are in the enclosure!" he said.

He'd been into the enclosure, hadn't he? I remembered suddenly. *He might know a way in. A way to get to Dayie?*

No sooner had I said that, when there was a sound like the mountain itself was splitting in two, a deep and sonorous rumbling noise.

BWAAAAARRM!

"'Ware treachery!" I hissed at Nas, my hand immediately moving to the pommel of my sword as I backed away towards Aida.

"No – Akeem, it's not...." Nas was shaking his head and grinning. *Did he think I was being foolish?* "It's the Dragon Horn. *The* Dragon Horn – surely you've heard of it?"

I had, but I had never heard *it,* of course. I followed Nas's pointing hand up to the tallest tower, encrusted with lots of bronze-colored dishes and devices, telescopes and horns. None of them looked large enough to be making such an earth-shaking racket, but the very top of the tower had tall, arched windows which I guessed the sound had to be coming from.

"Skreeyargh!" There was a shriek from across the walls, as the sky was filled with the sound of the returning Dragon Riders. I watched in agitation as they landed on the high parapets and landing platforms, each one able to hold five flapping, whistling, and clacking dragons at a time, until I saw that there had to be at least twenty-five or thirty up there.

Half the entire Dragon Rider army, I thought. Where was the other half? Still out there chasing down the last of the Deadweed? The Torvald Dragons, of course, instantly realized that there were two dragons here that did not belong. They craned their necks and immediately made smaller, whistling sorts of noises at Aida and Nandor.

"Sssssss...." Aida raised her head on her long neck and whistled back at them defiantly, showing off her neck and breast in a clear display of confidence – despite the fact that we were far outnumbered and many of the other dragons above us – the Stocky Greens and even a couple of Crimson Reds, were far larger than she was.

That's my girl... I grinned, standing in front of her, one hand on my scabbard, and the other on the hilt of my sword. If any of the dragons or their Riders decided to attack, they would not find me shirking from my duty—

Clang! In that tense moment, there was the jangle of chains and the thunk of heavy bars as the front gates of the Dragon Academy groaned open. I couldn't see any people on our side moving them, so I figured that the two attendant guard towers must have interior workings inside.

"My Lord Akeem, please – be at peace..." called out Captain Daris, hurrying back from the doorway, followed by six others in white tabards, pulling small trolleys laden with what looked to be food. The captain was looking stressed, and I wondered if it was because of me, or because of the Deadweed, or because of the new arrivals now cresting the outside the walls and heading for the open gates.

BWAAAARRRM! The Dragon Horn greeted the fast-moving procession on horses. They had flags and banners, and half of their number appeared to be fully-armored knights.

"Make Way for the queen! Hail, Queen and Empress Nuria!"

CHAPTER 12
DAYIE, A DRAGON-SHAPED WARMTH

"*Will she be alright? What's wrong with her?"*

People were talking about me. Again.

My body was aching, and I didn't want to wake up yet. For a long, terrible moment I wondered if this was Fan's caravan, and that I had suffered another of the terrible old woman's beatings last night. Why couldn't I just return to my deep and comfortable slumber, where all I remembered was dreaming of dragons?

Fan's been taken captive to the Binshee, I suddenly remembered, and, in that sleepy way that happens, the memories started piling in: we had tracked the Hazim family down, and I had stopped Akeem from killing her so that she could give me my mother's necklace. The necklace that seemed to help me connect with my magic. My magic that…

Had hurt Zarr. I started at the memory, gasping.

"She's waking up…" the voice murmured. It was dark. And warm. Where was I?

"It's not her I'm worried about, it's the dragon…" muttered another voice, a woman's, and one that I didn't recognize.

The dragon? I thought in alarm. They could only mean Zarr!

I groaned, forcing my heavy eyes to open and pushing myself up from my prone position. But my head was swimming as if I was feverish, my vision doubled and blurred, and I thought I was going to be sick. I panted, screwing my eyes shut against the dizziness as I tried to regain my composure. I was in a cave. No, not a cave – a nest. The floor underneath was in fact a bed, made of thick carpets of moss over straw. It smelled fresh and forest-like, and I had smelled this scent before. *A dragon nest!* I realized, as I rubbed my eyes. But my hands were shaking, and my body felt like I had been put through a mill.

"Easy, easy…" said one of the muttering voices, and it was one I recognized. as he sat down next to me. Akeem. Suddenly, his hands lightly touched my shoulders, holding me steady, but so cautiously I imagined him wondering if he was hurting me or not. He wasn't. It felt good, actually – to be held and cared for. He started to firmly rub some life into my back, and I hadn't realized how stiff I had been, until my neck and shoulder muscles started to relax…

"Zarr…" I said, as light flared and I twisted toward its source to see who was with me in this dragon nest. There was Akeem crouching behind me and seeming intent on not letting me move too much, and further away, down the humped incline of the moss, straw and sand, was a young woman with midnight-black hair, pale skin, and in a fine purple dress. A *very* fine purple dress, I realized as she made a gesture with a hand and behind her sparked a lantern, being held by a taller man with curly black hair, dressed in riding leathers.

And there, half-curled on the other side of me was Zarr.

Why didn't I sense him immediately! I thought, all concern of where I was and who these people were (and the fact that the man with the lantern had a very large sword strapped to his waist) fleeing from my mind as I turned to my brother and my closest friend, the great Crimson Red.

"Wyrm…?" I said, moving my hands to his paler under scales. He was lying on his side, his wings folded neatly and his bulk pressed against the rear wall of the cave. For a terrible, awful moment I feared the worst—

That was until a heavy sigh rattled through the Crimson Red's body. He was alive, at least, but he wasn't awake – and I couldn't hear him in my mind.

"Easy now, Dayie, one thing at a time…" Akeem was saying, but I rolled my shoulders and shrugged him off.

"Get off me, you lumbering idiot!" I snapped at him, not caring that I was talking to a prince or who these other people were who could overhear us. "My dragon is wounded!"

"Your dragon isn't wounded as such," the black-haired woman said in a clipped and precise sort of tone. It was a perfect Torvald accent— no hint of a burr, rasp, or accent like the

Gypsies of Shaar or the Binshee or anyone else for that matter might have had.

Whatever. I ignored her. *What was wrong, why couldn't I hear Zarr!?* I thought, pressing both of my hands against his belly as another nervous jangle of nausea rolled through me.

This was something new. And alarming. I had spent so long living with a dragon in the back of my mind that I had almost forgotten what it had been like before I had met Zarr (before I had stolen his egg, I meant). It had been so lonely, I recalled. I had always thought that was, quite rightly, because I had no friends before. There was Nas, of course – though back then he hadn't been my friend but my rival, and Fan and Rahim weren't my parents or my mentors either – they were taskmasters who treated me with varying degrees of cruelty.

Now, I rather thought that loneliness would have always been a part of my life without Zarr. Maybe those of us who *could* bond with a dragon, and who *were* able to share our minds with one would always gravitate to these noble beasts – and would never feel complete without them?

I don't know, all I knew now was that Zarr was hurt. I did my best to reach forward to him with my mind, passing through the thin, insubstantial walls of my skin and—

There! I could feel a dim shadow, far on the edge of my awareness. A dragon-shaped warmth, but it was distant and far away.

"You gave me strength twice before, Zarr…" I muttered, feeling as though I were pushing my mind through black treacle to get to him. “There must be a way that I can do the same for you…”

But how? I had no idea how Zarr – or any dragon – did the things that they did, from being able to talk with their minds, to apparently being able to give some of their magical, in-born strength to others. *What had happened? What was it like?* I tried to recall – it had felt like Zarr had wrapped his mind around me.

No, what had he said? I knew that was wrong. In the fragmentary moments I remembered, Zarr had said that he bonded with his heart, not his head. Maybe that was it?

He had thrown his heart at me, wrapping me in it, and that fiery, eternal warmth like the heat of a sun; like fierce, tooth-and-claw love, had washed into me…

I was not a dragon. I had no internal fire. But I had my heart…

“I remember you as an egg…” I reached out to him, not with my thoughts and my mind, but in my heart, with my memories. I remembered carrying him in my hands, the slightly pocked nature of his shell, the warmth of it, the feeling of wonder at the tiny life it carried.

Thump! I remember the noise that he had first made. The tiny thuds and cracks he’d made against the inside of the shell, which had so pleased me that I had ended up naming him *Thump* for the first moon or so of his life.

Before I found out what your real name is. It was Akeem who had told me that, who had been told by *his* dragon, Aida. She was a matriarch to her own den, her own nest somewhere, and so apparently could see deep into the hearts of other dragons – enough to share the names that were written on their souls.

And when I had said that name out loud for the first time, it had felt so right. As if all the pieces had finally slotted into place, or of trying on a new pair of boots to find that they fit perfectly….

I remembered the shared howls of exultation as we had flown together through the skies, shouting and cawing just for the joy of feeling the Tall Winds against our backs and the endless sky as our home—

"Dayie-sister!" Something passed between us, and I had no word for it other than love. I could feel the shape of the dragon in my mind once more, and it was warm and vital – but weak.

And suddenly, in terrible pain.

I cried out, as the pain jumped through Zarr and into me.

"No, what are you doing, silly newt! Back!" Zarr breathed his fiery words into my thoughts, sending my mind and my heart tumbling back into my own small and fragile body with a shock that was almost like being kicked by a pony.

"Ugh…" I groaned, opening my eyes to see that I was now lying on my back, staring at the ceiling of the cavern, with the Crimson Red breathing in a deeper, huffing and puffing way just beside me. I opened my mouth to ask what had happened, but instead all I could do was cough and groan and roll onto my side—

"Dayie! What did you do?" Akeem was at my side, dabbing at

my face with a cool and damp cloth, before getting me to drink a little cool water. He sounded annoyed, and worried.

“I couldn’t feel him before,” I said. “I tried to find out what was wrong, to give him some of my own strength…”

“Foolish,” stated the other lantern-carrying man sternly, and Akeem hissed, his body suddenly tensed at my side. The strange man and woman were muttering together, conferring on some matter or another, until the man cleared his throat and repeated in a louder voice what his companion had said just a moment before.

“Your dragon is not wounded. Your dragon has been trying to do the impossible, and it is making him ill,” his voice was stern.

“Do the impossible?” I gasped, finally able to sit up at last, even if I had to hold my head in my hands. “What are you talking about? My Zarr can do anything…”

“If only it were true,” the black-haired man said. “But dragons aren’t invincible. And they certainly cannot seek to sever the bond that they themselves had created with their Riders…”

“Sever the bond!?” The words were so terrible that I forgot my addled pain and looked up. Is that what Zarr was trying to do? Had he had enough of me?

“Not willingly, or even aware of what he is doing I think.” The man’s mouth was a flat line of disapproval. “But it amounts to the same thing. Zarr has been working to wall a part of *you* away from yourself.”

My pain, I knew. The magical agony that rolled through me every time that I used my magic – which was actually very, very similar to what I was feeling now…

"And you and he are the same," the man continued. "Once bonded, a dragon and their dragon-friend can never sever. You become one thing, in a way. A creature with two bodies. There will always be a place in you which is Zarr, and a place in Zarr which is always you…"

"Mhm." Akeem made a disapproving grunt in the back of his throat. "At least he speaks the truth…" the prince muttered to me. "We Binshee teach the same. Two become one, up there in the sky."

"But why would he ever want to sever that bond with me?" I wailed, unable to stop myself. He had just pushed me away, back into my body, after all. But if he had been trying to close himself off from me, it had failed, as I could once again feel the shape of him in my mind – even if it was distant and muted.

"I must assume that he doesn't want to, but if he is trying to hold a piece of yourself apart from you, then that is effectively what he is doing. He is causing a great imbalance in your natural bond," the man said.

I hung my head. "He is holding my pain for me. Or he was," I thought as my body shook. "He must be trying to keep all of that terrible, awful stuff away from my mind."

"Sounds probable." The man nodded heavily. "But he can't do that. It's the same as trying to sever a bond. He cannot erect walls between you, no more than you can. So, no – the Crimson Red is not *wounded* – he is ill – and it is your illness that he is suffering from and only a matriarch can set it right!" the man ended sharply.

As if I needed another excuse to feel terrible.

Zarr had carried me to the Dragon Enclosure just last night, it seemed – or so Captain Daris, the man with the big sword and the curly black hair told me. I had dim memories of seeing the greeting flights of the smaller Messenger dragons, but after that everything was pretty vague. Zarr had collapsed almost at the same time as I had, but he had somehow managed to negotiate with the Mount Hammal Enclosure dragons that his Rider – me – needed aid, and they had showed him here, to what Daris said was one of their birthing caverns, currently not in use.

"We don't understand it yet, but the dragons are able to heal themselves not only with their…" Captain Daris struggled a little for the right words, "*hearts…souls…?* But they also seem to get a great supply of healing, strength, and confidence from these caverns…"

We were walking through the different levels and terraced ridges of the Dragon Enclosure, on a path that I actually remembered from my time here. Even so, I stayed behind the captain and remembered to look puzzled and awed at the sights around me - it wasn't hard when there were so many dragons about!-- as he led us to one of the higher 'balconies' of rock that climbed the interior walls of the crater. Captain Daris was in front, along with the woman in the fine dress, and Akeem hovered behind me as if he was afraid I was about to keel over and fall down the cliffs at any moment. There was less vegetation up here, and the various dragons that had ventured up here were sunning themselves on the rockfaces.

And there were a *lot* of dragons around us – far more than I had seen before. It seemed that only a fraction of the available dragons eventually trained to become the fighting 'wings' of Torvald, and the others used Mount Hammal in a fairly natural way.

"We don't force them to bond, of course…" Captain Daris stated when I asked him about it. There was something about this fresh mountain air that was clearing my head and easing the aches in my limbs, and although I told myself it was the exercise and the *not* using my magic, I was also thinking that it might be something to do with this mountain itself. I remembered Zarr's heart skipping a beat as soon as he had spotted it on the horizon and that shared feeling of joy at the sight. *Did dragons have a religion?* I thought idly. *A set of beliefs they lived by?* And if so – just how important were places like Mount Hammal to them?

"But the students already at the academy come up here to train, and they naturally spot the dragons that take an interest in humans. In time, the bonded dragons encourage those curious dragons to choose their Riders," Daris explained. "Lord Bower and Lady Saffron had reinstated a very old custom from the time before the Dark King, when for three days of a year, those curious dragons that wanted to establish a relationship with a bond would be guided to take to the skies over Torvald and hunt for their human. They could swoop down anywhere in the citadel or the surrounding lands, choose their human and return to the academy…"

"Just like the Binshee!" I exclaimed. Although I had never seen the *actual* Choosing Ceremony of the Binshee. During my time with them, I had taken part in their morning training which had comprised of the dragons flinging themselves from their caves to snatch their Wild Company Riders from where they stood, and Heydar had told me it was a reaffirmation of that willing bond, that *choice.*

"We have to instate something like this at Dagfan—" I started, before Akeem coughed and suddenly stumbled into me.

"Hey!" I wobbled on the path, but his strong hands caught my shoulder. When I looked over, he was glaring at me. *What had I done now?* I thought. Oh yeah, made my dragon ill…

"Really? You *don't* have a Choosing at Dagfan?" said the only other person in our group – the woman in the fine dress and the long black hair. I wasn't sure who this person was – maybe one of those 'scholars' and 'dragon experts' that Torvald was apparently stuffed with? She certainly hadn't ventured any introduction yet, and appeared pleased to hold herself apart from the rest of us. *Torvaldites!* I sighed irritably.

"Well, not exactly, in fact, we—" I began, before Akeem suddenly stumbled once again, stepping on my foot this time.

"Ouch!"

"Oh, I'm so sorry. I must be tired from the battle…" Akeem

gripped my upper arm. “I. Must. Be. More. Careful,” he said in clipped tones, before resuming his pace.

Oh. I suddenly understood what the Prince of the South and the Captain of the feared Binshee Wild Company was going on about. *Shut up, Dayie – the South wants to keep its secrets,* I paraphrased, and rolled my eyes. I didn’t think that Torvald was anything but interested to hear about our dragon practices, but whatever. I wasn’t the rightful prince and Akeem was, after all…

“You were saying, Rider Dayie?” the woman said imperiously in her perfect Torvald accent.

“Oh, you’ll have to come for a visit, madam.” I avoided her question. “I’ll be more than happy to show you…”

Apparently, what I had said was at once completely horrifying to Akeem and terrifically funny to the woman and Captain Daris.

“Oh well, maybe one day I will…” The woman chuckled. “But it probably won’t be any time soon, will it, Captain Daris? What do you think?”

The captain suddenly swallowed nervously. “Oh, uh, anytime that you decide to go then it would be our honor for the Dragon Riders to accompany you, my lady…When your brother gets back from the Southern Trade Treaty, perhaps… ma’am, I am sure that we could…”

Your brother. I suddenly realized who I had been speaking to. *A brother who had gone to the South recently. To negotiate a trade treaty.*

Duke Robert Flamma-Torvald, older brother to Queen-Empress Nuria.

"Oh," I said, feeling stupid. Why hadn't I figured that out before? Catching Akeem's 'I told you so' glance, it only made me wish *he* had found a way to tell me that I was lying around, almost fainting and throwing up in front of the most powerful woman in all the midmost lands, if not the entire world.

Knowing who she was made me reappraise the youngish woman who walked ahead of me now. She was older than me, older than Akeem easily – but probably younger than Captain Daris. She walked with a quiet confidence that must be the result of growing up here, surrounded by an entire city full of loyal people and— not least to say— fire-breathing dragons. I had assumed that she was some kind of Dragon Academy scholar, as she had seemed knowledgeable, but not overly eager to offer advice about my condition, or to step too near to Zarr or me.

Her clothing was fine, of course, as I saw earlier – and on closer scrutiny, I realized just *how* fine it was. A heavy, multiple-layered and quilted dress of purple; a very expensive color to make, but of course- what problem was money to a woman who could control any trade route this side of the moon? I wondered idly if that purple had been achieved by trading rare indigo from the South. The dress had a heavy banded embroidery at the hem, and the hem itself appeared thicker so that it wouldn't catch and snag on the rocks. Her belt was of a shining chestnut-brown leather, burned with a design of chasing and intertwining dragons. *Of course the woman wore dragon insignia – she's Miss Torvald herself!*—And her elbow-length gloves matched the belt. On her back was a half-cloak, wrapped and tied to one side, but I could see that it was black on the outer, and the inner folds were a deep scarlet red. *(Colors of House Flamma,* I recognized from one of Fan's many lectures on who not to annoy, or to steal from during our trading visits).

She wore no overt jewelry though, apart from small bluish earrings like sparkling tear drops, and a very fine silver neck-lace. No crown. No circlet. No sign of her office. I wondered if she was trying to be undercover.

"I see you are surprised to discover who you are speaking to?" the Queen of the World said to me lightly.

"I, uh… I've never talked to a queen before." *Or is she an empress?* I thought. Wasn't an empress an 'excellency' or were they a 'Majesty'? Highness? Your Grace?

"Good!" Nuria gave another of her small chuckles. "I would dread to think that I had some rivals cropping up…"

Akeem coughed suddenly.

Oh yeah, wouldn't his mother have counted as a queen? I thought, before remembering that no – she didn't. It had been a tradition dating many hundreds if not thousands of years that the only king and queen was in the North, and everywhere else had 'princes' and 'princesses' – even if they weren't related to the Flamma-Torvalds.

I could see why it would annoy the hell out of Akeem. Why couldn't the South declare its own king and queen whenever they wanted? Why couldn't Roskilde and the Western Archipelago do the same?

"You are not to be blamed for your ignorance, especially if I purposefully worked to conceal my title from you," Nuria said, and I could see that she was proud of this small deception. "I rarely get to travel without a complement of knights, advisers, councilors, more knights, more courtiers..." She sighed. "But this is a situation that requires the attention of a queen." She inclined her head not to me, but to Akeem.

Oh... I thought, feeling even more stupid than I had done already – which was quite a feat, really. *She must know who Akeem is.* And who can negotiate with a prince other than the monarch? That was also probably why she hadn't put on her formal airs and graces as well, I thought, my mind racing ahead as I thought not like a diplomat – but like a trader. When I had been a Dragon Trader, we had done more than steal dragon eggs and trade for scraps of dragon lore to sell to Dagfan – we had also brought and sold items all along our routes to fund the journeys. We had pretended to be entertainers, tumblers and acrobats in order to find the tastiest bits of information in whatever village we passed through. You never knew what might be important, after all. The fact that Old Mr. So-and-So had lost all his cattle last winter could be the gossip you needed to buy some cheap yearlings a few leagues over and sell them to Old Mr. So-and-So at excellent rates.

In short, I was pretty good at reading people and situations, I like to think.

Queen Nuria wants to try and put the warrior, practical Prince of the South, at ease, I thought, and to show him that she is a woman who is even *more* practical and secure in her own home. That she is so powerful that she doesn't need knights and people bowing to her…

"Mhm." Akeem just gave a very brief, and very fake smile and a nod as he acknowledged Queen Nuria. He would have made a *terrible* trader, I thought, as every facet of his body was radiating disapproval.

Nuria continued speaking. "You see, not only am I here to talk with you about the threat facing both of our peoples, but my good Captain Daris here has also enlisted my help to speak to Queen Jexia, daughter of Queen Jaydra."

I was lost. "I thought you said there weren't any other queens about?" I burst out, earning a horrified look from the still-clearly nervous Captain Daris. *Oh right. You're not supposed to question a queen's words.*

There was the slightest pause from Nuria, and I wondered how many times in her day people really *did* ask her things. Clearly not often enough.

"Queen Jaydra was my grandmother's dragon, whom the Lady Saffron rode from the Western Archipelago against the Dark King Enric, and who helped to reinstate the Dragon Enclosure here," Nuria said gravely. "With great sadness, after my beloved grandmother passed away many, many years ago, Queen Jaydra decided to take the Western Track across the oceans, as many once-bonded dragons do when their human partners die," Nuria said this in a matter-of-fact way, but her voice wasn't as exact and clipped as it was before. She had loved her grandmother very much, and I felt instantly sorry for her – if a little jealous as I never had the opportunity to have a mother, let alone a grandmother!

“Ah, your graceful highness,” I tried to be as formal as possible, “I have heard of the Western Track. That is where the Western Witches went after their matriarch died…”

“Quite.” Nuria frowned a little. “Although we still haven’t managed to discover *what* precisely the Western Track *is,* or where it leads to. But our scholars who were last in touch with the sanctuary of Sebol tell us that it must be some sort of sea route, but one that is stranger than normal seas, and can only be travelled by dragons and those magically-inclined.”

Everyone has magic. I remember Old Mengala’s and the sorcerer’s words. *It’s just a different sort of magic for different sorts of people.* It was easy to remember, too, the magical flight that Mengala the Western Witch – who had trained at Sebol – and the Sorcerer of the Whispering Rocks who had trained here at the academy – had cast me and Zarr on, and I wondered if that was the same thing as this ‘Western Track.’

The Queen-Empress was still explaining, however, “and Queen Jaydra’s daughter at the time, Jexia, naturally succeeded to become the new Den-Mother and Queen of Mount Hammal. And that is why I am here, as it would be impolite for a queen to not be the one to negotiate with another queen.”

“But, uh, your excellent-ness,” I fought for the right title, “why are we negotiating with Queen Jexia?”

"Oh, my dear, please stop with the titles!" Nuria tinkled a high-pitched, silver-bell sort of laugh. "They can be complicated and take a lifetime to get right, but we do appreciate the effort. Just call me Queen, or Lady Nuria, please." She cleared her throat. "We are here to negotiate for the rest of the dragons to rise up against this new threat. The Deadweed. The trained and ridden dragons of Torvald will obviously fight with us, but what I saw last night – and for the two long days of battle before that – is that we need both more dragons and more knowledge of our enemy. Both of which, I hope Queen Jexia can provide." She nodded at Captain Daris, who surprised me by gesturing to me.

"And, if you don't mind, your friend the, ah, prince," Daris looked about as nervous as I was to be addressing foreign dignitaries, "has requested that we seek an answer for your malady as fast as possible. Especially now, as it seems that your dragon is endangering his own life!" He said the last part with a bit of a grimace, and I felt myself blush once more. *Yeah, I know. I'm a terrible person.*

"We hope Queen Jexia might know a sort of dragon-magic that can help you and your bond-partner," Daris said heavily, turning back to walk ahead up the ledge of rock to our destination: the cave of the Queen of the Dragon Mountain.

CHAPTER 13

DAYIE, AND THE QUEEN OF DRAGON MOUNTAIN

"Do you think we should have brought something too?" I hissed at Akeem, as I looked at the strange collections of offerings that sat outside the cave of Queen Jexia. There was a battered horn helmet (one horn missing) next to a fragment of purple and green cloth, almost tattered away to nothing. On the other side I could see that someone had left the large, burnished scales of dragons – red, white, green, still shining and catching the late sun. There were giant claws, a dragon's tooth looking so ancient that it could have been fossilized or carved from the rocks of the mountain itself…

"Oh, these aren't gifts," Queen Nuria said lightly as she approached the cave first. "They are more like…*memories.*" She gestured to the scrap of the banner. "That is a fragment from the old Torvald banner, which we have to replace every few years or so – before House Torvald married to House Flamma, that is…" Another gesture to the scales. "That is a scale from Zenema the Giant, and that over there is the helmet of King Seb Smith, the lance of Orichalkor, the melted Double Crown of Queen Hilary."

I had never heard of half of these names, but I could see the reverence that the Queen and Captain Daris placed on them. Torvald had a rich history, after all – I knew that there had been more wars and battles fought on the slopes below us and in the sky than in almost any other place in the Midmost Lands.

And surely, if anyone were to know how to stop the Deadweed and to heal Zarr, then I would find the answers here, right? I hoped nervously. My head still felt a little muzzy, and, despite the enervating effect the sacred Dragon Mountain was having on me, I knew that my body was still weak. Was that my enforced slumber that Zarr had wrapped me up in when he took my pain? Or was it just the battles I had been a part of recently – or the magic?

Anyway. All of these were questions I hoped to get answered – but right now, my attention was caught up in what was happening at the mouth of the cave.

The queen of the citadel stood in the middle of the opening, and called out into the darkness beyond. "Great Queen Jexia, it is I, your sister queen in the human lands. Please, come and talk to me, woman to woman, queen to queen…" She spoke in her exact perfect tones but her voice rose and lilted with a certain musicality. Zarr liked it when I sang to him – and I wondered if there was a connection between music, dragons, and the magic of song.

"Queen Nuria." The wave of presence rolled through me, as

strong as if it were a sudden breeze, but one of power and fire and force. *I can hear her. In my mind,* I thought, looking up in awe at Akeem who was nodding, wide-eyed. *I thought only bonded partners could share their minds?* Clearly, what I thought of as the rules of the dragon bond didn't apply to queen dragons…

The dragon's head appeared out of the darkness, and I was surprised at how small it was. The Queen of Mount Hammal was smaller than Zarr by a long way, with sea-green and turquoise-blue scales. *She's a Sea Dragon?* I thought – but knew that also wasn't quite the truth. There was a line of red and orange scales skirting her sides and belly, and beading her legs. I rather guessed that perhaps one of her parents had been one of the faster, smaller, and hawk-like Sea Green dragons of the Western Isles.

Which had to be Jaydra, the old Queen Saffron's dragon, right?

But this Jexia looked larger and with a broader face, as though perhaps her father had been a Stocky Green. She had grown two extra horns as well, that swept back past her larger, more traditional horns on her temple. There was something indescribably *powerful* about her, and I tried to work out whether it was in the slow and cautious way that she moved – as confident and as steady as a queen in her own domain, or whether it was the magic that radiated from her mind like heat from a fire.

Jexia stepped just a little way out of her cavern, bringing with her a wreath of smoke, before settling down onto her haunches and belly like a cat as she stared unblinking at the smaller human woman standing in front of her.

"My Queen, I thank you for all that you have done to allow the Riders of Torvald to bond and train with your siblings and den-mates." Queen Nuria inclined her head a little. Enough to be respectful, but not enough to lose the fact that Nuria, herself, was also a queen.

"Your presence, your strength, and your wisdom continue to guide all of us in these dark days, just as it has ever since you took to this cave..." Nuria said, and I realized that it wasn't just Zarr who liked getting compliments – it was *all* dragons, apparently, as Queen Jexia let out a deep, encouraging and throaty purr.

"I am here to ask for your aid once more, as I am sure that you know of the danger that threatens our borders – and almost up to our very doors!" Queen Nuria said gravely.

"I do," Jexia stated. No more, no less.

"We would ask you to help in the defense of Torvald – to lead the rest of the enclosure dragons into battle beside us, and to encourage them to fly alongside our Wings of Dragon Riders, to drive this magical weed from our lands!"

There was a pause as the mighty queen looked steadily at her human counterpart, before she raised her snout just a little to sniff the air gently. *"No."*

What? I thought in alarm. The Torvaldites had like, a *really* good relationship with their dragons—everyone said it. Why did the queen say no!?

"But, my queen…" Nuria also seemed a little taken aback by this response, and I saw twin spots of high color take to the woman's cheeks. "Surely the den-mother of the entire Sacred Mountain of the dragons could defeat the Deadweed! There is no limit to your powers, your reach, and your abilities, after all!"

Nuria's trying to appeal to Jexia's pride, I thought. It was a taunt, of sorts – and I worried at the wisdom of taunting any dragon, let alone this one.

"Ssssss…" The Queen Jexia let out a slow, bubbling hissing noise which made me take a step back cautiously. Had Nuria offended her? Were we about to see the Queen and Empress of Torvald get eaten?

"Ssssusss-suss…!" The hissing grew a little louder and turned into a slight coughing melody.

She was laughing. The High Queen of the Dragons was laughing at Nuria.

"Your compliments are welcome, and I appreciate your confidence in me, sister-queen," Jexia chuckled. *"But of course, my powers are not limitless. No one is unstoppable, or invincible. Not even the Queen of the Sacred Mountain."*

Her words echoed so strongly what Zarr had told me, that they stuck in my mind like a barb. I had thought myself invincible for just a brief moment – and look at the damage that it had done.

"And so also, I presume, the Deadweed cannot be unstoppable, either," Queen Nuria countered. "But in order to defeat it, I need more dragons and their dragon-fire," she said, bravely not giving up her request. "Our own Liquid Fire just isn't enough, and neither is it as hot or as fierce as anything you and your brood could produce…I need you to fly with us, noble Queen."

Jexia's chuckling stopped as she turned her head back around to view Nuria full-on again. Even though this dragon wasn't the largest that I had ever seen (clearly), there was still something deeply unnerving about the sight of a dragon glaring at a human.

"I am not fond of repeating myself, Queen Nuria – but for you, I will. I cannot do this thing that you ask of me – and what is more, I WILL not, either," she intoned.

Nuria rocked backwards on her heels in front of the larger dragon, and Captain Daris flinched, looking concerned and worried about what he should do. Steady his monarch? Step in to speak? But what can he do, I thought. This was a matter between queens, not lowly Riders… The moment of tension stretched long, as the dragon appeared to dare the human to argue once again.

Luckily for everyone perhaps, I was half-ill, exhausted, and my heart was already at breaking point anyway, with the state that my Zarr was in. All this talking while my dragon was ill! While the Deadweed rampaged freely across the Midmost Lands, it appeared. I wanted to tell all of them – the queen included – to get a hold of themselves, put aside all this posturing and concentrate on what really mattered!

I had also never been very good at respecting my elders – not

Fan, and not anyone else for that matter, either.

"Queen Jexia?" I spoke up, earning an aghast look from Captain Daris beside me, as if I had just insulted everyone on the ledge. "Why won't you fight alongside your den-mates, the ridden dragons?" I said.

There was a moment of horrified silence from everyone around me – but I was through with caring. *I want Zarr healed.* I wanted the Deadweed and the Water Wraiths gone from our shores. I wanted the Sea Witch stopped – and if that meant I had to speak some home truths to a dragon, then so be it.

But I realized I had seriously underestimated the situation, as the full force of Jexia's mind rushed into mine, knocking down all of my barriers, leaving me vulnerable and exposed in a way that you do before a mighty storm.

"Who are you, little human, to speak to me this way?" her voice thundered through my mind, so loud that I let out a cry and stumbled to my knees. I couldn't think anymore, as all that occupied the inside of me seemed to be this queen dragon.

"I…" I stammered for an answer, but the ruler of the Dragon Mountain did not wait for my slow human-shaped thoughts. Instead, I felt her knocking over my memories and rooting through my psyche as if I were a trough of water with glittering fish hidden inside.

"I see, Dayie, you call yourself…" the queen mused, teasing out the information. *"A human girl from the South. But you are not from the South after all, are you? No, not really…"*

I knew that my almost platinum-white hair and my fair complexion gave me away, but I rather thought that the queen was finding out more about me than even *I* knew. Or let myself know.

"That is right, there are walls within your heart that even you are unaware of..." the queen purred in victory, sensing my weakness. I could feel no malice or cruelty from the queen, for a giant predator like a dragon, contrary to popular belief, is rarely ever cruel – but they are still predators.

"You have your mother's gift," the queen said to me.

She could sense my mother inside of me? Through me? I felt like I was a tiny bit of flotsam on the top of a boiling sea – I flailed and tried desperately to get to the memories and the truth that the queen found so easily, but I couldn't. Whatever I had not let myself know – the storm that took my mother's life perhaps – those barriers still held strong against me, forming an impenetrable forgetfulness.

"Ha. I am not so powerful as to see into the past that you yourself have no knowledge of. But I can smell the traces of your mother scattered through your soul like fingerprints in wax. She was arrogant, your mother. Arrogant and stubborn, and thought that she could be better."

How did she know all of that? What part of me told her that?

"It is written in your character, Dayie, daughter-of-the-sea, sister-of-the-air. You think you are self-made? Well. Here is a dragon-lesson for you then, just as you sought to give me a human lesson on loyalty! No one is ever entirely self-made. We

are born with the gifts of our parents. We take on their souls at a young age, forever making who we are meant to be. It is what you do with what you have been given that creates your own heart, which you may one day pass on to your children, and so the cycle continues..."

The queen dragon was saying this like it was a bad thing – but her words – although sounding fatalistic, merely spurred me towards hope. *You have your mother's gift within you.* I latched onto the thought. This magic that threatens to kill me every time is something that I can use. That I can control!

"Your arrogance is your downfall, as is often the case with those who use magic," the queen intoned heavily. I felt judged, but I would not back down.

"But – my queen..." I gasped, still on my knees before her. I forced the words out of my mouth once again. "Why won't you fight with the Dragon Riders! The Deadweed threatens us all!"

Another muttered gasp from the humans around me, and from the look on Nuria's face, I could see that even she thought that I had gone too far, to directly question Queen Jexia's decision.

A pause, and the rifling through my mind stopped.

"You are arrogant, yes – but you are also stubborn, little girl. And that, at least, is a quality that a dragon – even a queen – can admire," Jexia stated. *"I said that I cannot and will not rouse the rest of the enclosure dragons because that is not the dragon way. We may have matriarchs, den-mothers, and*

queens – but I do not order them to do things for me! Loyalty to one's mother is given through love, not fear."

"I… I do not understand what you are trying to tell me, Queen Jexia…" I blinked and rubbed my eyes. My headache was returning with a vengeance.

"Of course, you do not. Because you did not have the opportunity to truly know your mother. Another reason why you have no respect for me," Queen Jexia explained with a hint of teeth to her voice, before continuing with her original point. *"I cannot order these enclosure dragons to fight the Deadweed if they do not want to, because dragons do not follow orders. And they have not bonded with a human, so they are free, in their hearts and minds, to choose totally as they wish."*

I nodded that I understood, more to get her out of my head than anything else. By squinting through my headache, I could also see that Nuria, Akeem, and Captain Daris had heard the words, as their appalled looks were mixed with deep concern over the news. There was no way to rouse the rest of the enclosure dragons against the Deadweed. They might fight, or they might not – the choice was entirely up to them.

"At last, you understand," Queen Jexia said, sounding impatient. *"It is tiresome to have to constantly be explaining myself to a small human mind. However, I said before that I appreciate your stubbornness, Dayie daughter-of—the-sea, and so I will say this: I will fight with the bonded dragons against the Deadweed – but the rest of the enclosure will have to make up its own mind for itself. I will not argue for the battle nor against it."*

And with that, Nuria let out a sigh of relief, and one that I could well understand – surely having such a dragon as Jexia – small and older, perhaps, but filled with power – would be a strong ally.

But was it enough? I still worried. The South had almost entirely ceded its coast to the Deadweed and the Water Wraiths. Only the interior oasis and settlements still held out, thanks to the difficulty of the Water Wraiths to cross the burning sands. And Dagfan, I hoped. Dagfan still held.

The South wouldn't stand for another season, I thought. And now the same thing was happening to the North as well – and the sands alone knew how the Western Isles were faring against this onslaught…

And Zarr was still in pain.

"Lady Queen!" I burst out, feeling the pain of my headache match the pain of my heart over my friend. "I have one more request of you…"

It had felt like the queen dragon had been preparing to leave my mind, as the awful pressure of her presence had lessened, leaving me feeling oddly disorientated, as if my own thoughts did not fit me anymore. But my apparent arrogance at asking for more – or my stubbornness, perhaps, only worked to slam her presence once more into my mind – and this time I was knocked to the floor.

"Dayie daughter-of-the-sea. I have already been very generous with my time. Do not think that my good graces can be taken for granted."

"Not for granted, Lady Queen..." I stammered. "But...my dragon, Zarr..." It was hard to manage the words under such a mighty and baleful intelligence, as well as the pounding headache that it was inspiring in me. Instead, I just opened my heart to her once more, this time, thinking about Zarr the Crimson Red, what he meant to me, and how ashamed I felt for putting him in so much pain.

"I know what has been happening, girl." Jexia stated. *"Zarr is in my den, after all. Or should I say that Zarr has returned to my den?"*

Oh no. This was one of the things that I had been dreading. What if Zarr's own parents were here, and were furious over my theft? Wouldn't they have a right to rip me limb from limb for what I had done to their family?

"Yes, they would have that right." Jexia intoned, picking up on my thoughts with hawk-like awareness. *"So it is lucky for you, that Zarr's parents passed away some time ago. Zarr was an orphan, which is why he was being nested by Oliea, the White Nursing Dragon, when you found him."*

"Oh." I never knew, I thought, before I understood then what had drawn me and Zarr so closely together.

Zarr never knew his parents, just like me. No wonder we had bonded and had been so perfect for each other – until he had taken my pain away, that was.

"Yes. Zarr loves you so much that he is trying to save your soul by almost sacrificing his, you silly girl," the queen intoned. *"But luckily for you – I stand by what I said earlier –*

that dragons do not take orders. If they did, then I would be able to order Zarr to stay away from you, and your reckless use of a magic that you cannot yet control!"

Ouch. It was like getting slapped. My heart stung.

"And yet, I can also see that it is his love for you, his loyalty to you, that forces him to do this great service for you, just as it is your stubbornness, your loyalty and love towards him that seeks to ask for MY aid, even when you know that I am already angry with you!" Jexia hissed over my body. *"It is because I respect that stubbornness, and Zarr's courage, that I will grant you this boon."*

"You must travel to the Dragon's Spine Mountains, to the place they used to call Telumeh. There, you will find an ancient dragon, far older than me, who is called Selm. Selm was wise and ancient when even I was a newt, and it was often said by the other older dragons of this very enclosure that Selm had been one of the greatest healers of dragon-kind... and that it was to him that dragons and their Riders would go to if they had a problem. I advise you to seek Selm of Telumeh out, before your dragon suffers anymore!"

And with that, the queen had left my mind and I flopped over to my side, panting as if I had just run a race. Against a dragon.

But although my body and mind *felt* as though I had lost in that race – I remembered that I did now have the information that I needed to cure Zarr.

CHAPTER 14
AKEEM, DRAGON-TALES AND PRINCES

"Telumeh." I repeated the strange, northern-sounding word. My apparent confusion was matched by the looks on the queen and the captain's faces opposite me.

We were in one of the drafty, freezing-cold stone rooms of the Dragon Academy, the queen standing by the open window, looking out over her citadel (*no wonder it was so cold!*) while Captain Daris and I congregated around a large, ancient, work-scarred table. The captain had called for maps to be brought and the scrolls necessary to find this strange dragon place, and it was over these that we pored.

Outside, I could see that the lights of the citadel far below us had started to come alive – like tiny wavering stars dotted in rows and strange constellations down there. The noises of the academy and the mountain beyond set my teeth on edge. It wasn't the high whistling winds of the deep deserts, and it wasn't the echoing ululations of the sand foxes, or the haunting calls of the Southern Ibis. No – outside I could hear the distant, muted noises of rough and sharp barks, or the sudden squeals as some small creature met a grisly end.

I didn't like it up here in the North, I thought glumly, turning back to look at the maps of a land that I had never travelled across before.

"Yeah, it's not visible on Denbarr's '*The New Torvald.*'" Daris indicated the largest, most detailed, and also the most recent map of the Northern Kingdom. It was a fine-looking map, I had to admit, the vellum was thick and yet still soft, and pressed to a very fine, smooth texture, upon which a fabulously detailed scene had been painted.

"And it's not listed here, on '*Bower's Census.*'" He thumped a very heavy book onto the table. When I opened it up, I saw that its paper was almost as thin as spider's silk, and with fine black writing on every page, listing place names and numbers alongside various small symbols such a drop of water, or a stylized tree, or a yellow dot. *Resources,* I thought – wells, timber, gold?

The South could really do with something like this, I thought, and surprised myself when I realized that just a few hours ago I would have meant that the South needed this actual book detailing the resources of our traditional rival.

No, what I meant now was that the South needed to perform its own census with just as much detail. The oases that were scattered across the desert of course were the key feature. There was no map of them that I knew to exist, and instead their exact locations lived on in the minds of the caravan leaders, desert pilgrims, or Binshee tribes. Imagine what prosperity would flow if everyone could see their locations? Could pick their own routes to deliver trade where it needed to go, rather than having to suit the needs of whatever powerful chief controlled the local caravans?

Not that there is going to be much trade in the South for a long time, I grumbled to myself. Not with how fast the Deadweed was spreading.

But it did make me think about the relative treasures of Torvald and the South. One of our strengths were our hardy people, and the goods that we could produce that no one else in the Midmost Lands could. There was the resin and the oil from the scented trees which was always in high demand, as well as the various types of herbs and shrubs that only we in the South could grow thanks to the heat, and not to mention the rarer types of gemstones that apparently hid in our mountains.

The South should be a rich nation... I thought, my mind looking back, beyond our current difficulties. Why wasn't it?

I already knew the answer, of course. Everyone did. The south 'bickered' as they called it in the North. In reality, you might as well say that several of the different tribes and territories were in a fully clandestine and bloody war with each other. They called them 'bandit attacks,' of course – but everyone knew that it was really just some tribe's warriors dressed in desert blacks.

No, the strength that the South lacks is this, I thought, looking at the scrolls and the maps. *This organization was the secret of*

Torvald power... Apart from the dragons, that is. I knew that the old King Bower, now dead for a good few years, was lauded somewhat as a scholar of sorts, and had excelled at putting in systems to record what areas needed to be rebuilt after the Dark King's tyranny, which meant knowing precisely who lived where, what road went where, and what condition that road was currently in, as well as where every dam and bridge and lighthouse was, or could be.

It was that kind of detailed picture of the country as a whole that the South needs, I thought. Although just a small realization, it was one that gave me pause. Why didn't the three Southern Lords see this? Why hadn't they tried to unify the South, rather than playing at their games of negotiating between one tribe and another, one village against a chief, and so on?

If I was in charge... I growled.

"Is there really no mention of it?" Queen Nuria sighed, breaking her contemplation of the citadel below as she turned to regard our work with cool appraisal.

I had been insistent that we find this 'Telumeh' place immediately, and had half expected the Captain Daris to propose that we would be flying there tonight. But no. Instead, Nuria had announced that she would be taking Court at the Dragon Academy this evening (and it had already been dusk then), which meant there was a whirl of activity as Torvald knights rushed through the academy to set up checkpoints and guard details here and there, and acres of food were cooked and brought up from the kitchens.

One of the many things that I was thankful for was that the Binshee *didn't* have such pomp and ceremony that it took hours to have a simple meal before you could get on with your work! I was impatient to locate this Telumeh, and to take Dayie and Zarr to this dragon Selm. We needed her magic, and we needed that giant Crimson Red in this fight!

And... Well, I was her friend, wasn't I? How could I waste my time when she and her bond-partner are in pain?

After the 'meeting' with Queen Jexia—which seemed a bit more like a tournament of wills, to be honest—Dayie had elected to stay in the Dragon Enclosure, with her Zarr. I was mildly surprised to hear that she wanted to stay in the same place as the queen dragon did, but I wasn't surprised *at all* at her sentiment of staying next to her bond partner in times of duress. The sacred sands and stars alone knew that I would be doing the exact same thing were I not here.

I hoped that a night spent in each other's company would do Dayie and Zarr a world of good, but I had no way of predicting whether it would help or hinder – what if Zarr grew even more ill? How would Dayie react to that?

The boy-Rider – Nas – was downstairs in the Dragon Academy, hopefully not giving away all of Dagfan's secrets as he asked questions and made new friends. I couldn't begrudge him his wonder, of course – I just wished that he had a lot more common sense! Torvald might be our ally – but they were still a rival nation-state. Our relationship with them relied on the fact that we could barter, bargain, even threaten or beg when we had to.

"No *Telumeh* listed anywhere that I can see…" Captain Daris frowned as he flipped the scrolls to look at different, older maps.

A slight groan from Queen Nuria. "Although my grandfather did much to rectify the damage, we lost so much thanks to the Dark King's reign… And Torvald has such a deep history, my clerks are *still* working to uncover all of it…"

"And, if you forgive me, Your Highness, unless we go back to speak to Queen Jexia for clarification…" Captain Daris murmured in a troubled voice. None of us in this room thought much of the likelihood of the queen helping us out any more than she had already done.

Everywhere has a deep history, Your Highness, I thought, my tiredness giving way to irritation.

"Dragon tales." I heard Aida's voice in the back of my mind. She sounded as tense as I did, and I wasn't surprised – being a matriarch far from her own lands and in another queen's territory must be excruciating.

"Not excruciating, dragon-brother…but these Torvald dragons are a very quiet sort! There is not the bickering that I am used to!"

Ha. Vicious Oranges were named so for a reason. But anyway. *Dragon tales?*

"We dragons have our own legends and histories and names, as you well know," Aida explained. *"But we usually call places for what they sense-like, Place-Where-The-Water-is-Always-Fresh, or Place-Where-Redulant-the-Dragon-Died.*

Telumeh is not a dragon name…but that does not mean that the tales of the dragons haven't passed into human memory, becoming folk tales and legends."

I felt a surge of fierce love for my dragon once more. Aida was surely the wisest of all dragons!

"Don't think that too loud near the Queen Jexia!" I heard Aida's soot-filled laugh, but I could tell that she was also pleased with my assessment of her abilities.

"Folk tales," I said out loud to the captain and queen. "This *Telumeh* might have become forgotten to the people of the North, but that doesn't mean that legends of Selm the Healer have."

"Explain." Nuria frowned as she looked at me. Once again, her casual commanding attitude raised my hackles, making me wonder if I would ever be like that were I to one day become the legitimate Prince of the South….

Before I could show my annoyance, however, it was Captain Daris who unwittingly stopped a diplomatic incident. "Brilliant idea!" he said, proceeding to start shuffling the scrolls and books until he had unearthed older, fragmentary tomes. "I have no idea why I didn't think about it before!"

Maybe because you do not have the benefit of an Aida, I thought proudly, as the captain kept on speaking.

"You are right, my queen, that Torvald has a deep history—"

Why does everyone keep saying that!? It annoyed me.

"…and before it was Bower's New Torvald, we had the Dark

Years, of course, but before that we had the Old Dynasty of the Flammas, and way back even before that we had the Dragon Monasteries…" Captain Daris appeared enthused by his subject. I attempted to wait patiently.

"Anyway, although it is very hard to find tell of the exact locations of those older ages, we often find clues in songs, stories, legends…" Daris started looking through the scrolls, muttering under his breath. "What did Queen Jexia say? The dragon's name was Selm, and that he was some kind of healer…"

"And that they had a cave in the mountains." I drew a finger down one of the map's depiction of the Dragon Spine Mountains. They were large, stretching the entire way from the coast up to the icy snows of the far north.

"This Selm might even be dead by now, of course…" Nuria shook her head.

"I doubt it, Queen Nuria," I said. "Your Matriarch Jexia would have been able to sense it, and besides, it takes a lot to kill a dragon, Your Highness." I turned back to the far more detailed map of '*New Torvald'* and started carefully tracing my finger down through the mountains, scanning for any sign of a Selm or a dragon, as inwardly I wondered, *just how little does this Queen Nuria know about dragons, that she doesn't even know that her own Queen Jexia would be intimately connected with the dragons in her territory?*

But then again, I had yet to see Nuria talking about her dragon, which meant maybe she wasn't even bonded with one!

Unfortunately, in a land which had dragons, there appeared no end of dragon names. *"Dragon's Leap, Dragon's Grave, Drakespear, Wyrmtower..."* I groaned in frustration, until my finger paused at one place. "Healer's Rest." It looked to be no more than a tiny place high up in the Dragon's Spine Mountains, with a tiny blue blob of a lake.

"Where is that?" Daris looked over, following my pointing finger and showing me the larger 'catchment' area that part of the mountains belonged to.

"Jodreth's Uplands, we call it that whole area," Daris stated.

"Jodreth?" Nuria frowned. "I know of it, of course – it is my job to know, after all! It's a wild, very sparsely populated area. A few hill farms who run their goats and sheep up into the mountains. Not much else. But that name though, *Jodreth*, I've heard it before..."

"He was one of the first Dragon Mages of the ancient Draconis Order, Your Highness," Daris said seriously. "Going right back to the foundation of Torvald and the Three Kingdoms."

Three Kingdoms but with only one king, I couldn't help myself. But there wasn't the time for my bitterness. I cleared my throat. "So we have a place which must have been associated with healing, and whose region is named after a Dragon Mage." I nodded. "It makes sense that if this region was named after this famous Draconis Order Mage, then surely it also follows that Jodreth travelled here a lot? That they had a reason to travel here? A powerful dragon healer, perhaps?"

"Let me see now..." Daris turned to the scrolls, unrolling and winding through roll after roll, raising dust as he did so. It took an interminable long time to find reference to Healer's Rest, but he did in the end.

"Ah, well, here in *'Bridgette's Miscellany of the Middle Kingdom'* – which is what Torvald used to be called – it says:

'There is little noticeable about the mountain wayside called Healer's Rest, in the region known as Jodreth's Uplands, other than that it is comprised of a small and very ancient looking dragon statue next to a clear but narrow mountain lake. In a cliff above the lake sits a large cavern, with no recent signs of habitation. However, local shepherds claim that their grand-parents used to come up here to leave small offerings at the shrine and would in turn get healed of their ailments. Clearly a wild country fanciful tale, only made worth noting by the fact that the gentlemen that I spoke to referred to this place as Telumeh, and not Healer's Rest at all!"

Captain Daris looked up at me. We were both grinning. We had found it.

"I'll tell Dayie," I said, feeling energized by the prospect of getting into the air and on the move again. Despite how hospitable they were trying to be, there was something about all of these stone walls and narrow passageways here in the North that didn't agree with me.

"Wait a minute, Lord Akeem," Nuria said in her commanding

tone, and the shock of hearing her use my title made me pause as much as anything. I was used to just being called Akeem, or captain – but not lord.

"It would be unwise to fly straight into the Dragon Enclosure without an actual Torvald dragon and Rider at your side," she stated.

"I'll go with him," Daris nodded, already packing up the scrolls.

But it seemed that it wasn't just caution that had made Nuria speak out. She nodded at Daris. "Leave the papers, I'll sort them out myself. Go and ready your dragon, Captain Daris, while I have a little chat with the Lord of the South here."

Huh?

Nuria turned back to the open window, waiting for Daris to quietly shut the door behind him (a momentary flash of the looming Torvald Knights on the other side of the door, standing guard wherever the queen would be from now on, I gathered).

"Prince Akeem," she said, but still did not turn to look me in the eye.

Uh… "Yes?" I said, feeling confused.

"I have been meaning to speak with you since I was informed by the academy that you had flown into our lands. I wanted to extend my thanks to you for fighting on Torvald's behalf just last night," Nuria stated formally. I was surprised at how suddenly bureaucratic and ceremonial her tone had become.

"The Deadweed and the Water Wraiths threaten us all," I said. Was that it? She had just wanted to thank me?

No, it wasn't.

"Any day now and my brother Robert will be arriving back from the coast road with the details of the Dagfan Trade Treaty. I have heard word that it went well, and that Dagfan is eager to request both food *and* our new weapon: Liquid Dragon Fire." She half turned to look at me for a response.

"I don't speak for Dagfan." I shrugged. It still made me wary to think of Dagfan – or any part of the South for that matter – becoming reliant on Torvald trade and protection. That was the very thing that my father had *not* wanted to happen!

"Yes," Nuria nodded slowly. "As far as I understand it, the South is ruled over by the three Southern Lords – all brothers, who each negotiate different loyalties and contracts between the various cities and desert chiefs?"

"Mostly," I said dismissively. The Southern Lords didn't control the wilder deserts, nor the Binshee tribes. Their position was a precarious one, as they were nominally only a 'council' waiting for my own father to one day return, but in the years since he had left, they had become ever more powerful.

But power had not made them wise or grateful at all, I considered. Each of the three Southern Lords worked to manipulate or strengthen the tribes and towns that they had in their power, and quite often the surreptitious 'bandit attacks' were actually one of the Southern Lords moving against another, or making sure that their brother did not gain *too* much in the constant war of influence.

"I'm going to be blunt, Lord Akeem, because you fought alongside my Dragon Riders against a shared enemy. Torvald likes to keep its friends," the Queen of the largest kingdom in all of the Midmost Lands said.

Were we friends, now? I wondered.

"I respect *history*, Lord Akeem."

I wish she would stop calling me that!

"Given Torvald's past, I was brought up with the value of history and tradition drummed into me from an early age."

"You said your grandfather had to rebuild the realm after the Dark King."

"Precisely." Nuria nodded gravely. "We lost so much, and in that aftermath, I saw my mother and father struggle to negotiate a way through."

"Okay…" *Why was she telling me any of this? What was the point?*

"I discovered that the people primarily want very few, but constant things: for their rulers to be loyal to them, to protect them, and to provide for them when they are in need. That is all."

I nodded. My own father had voiced pretty much the same sentiment – that a true king or a ruler was really a servant of the people, and that their position came with many great responsibilities.

"There are some rulers who know this fact, and there are many people in positions of power who do not." She looked up at me sharply, and I saw what she was getting at.

She knew about the situation with the Southern Lords. She knew the South was always on a knife's edge, and that we had been doing our best it seemed – even before the arrival of the Deadweed – to compete against their own countrymen and women.

"I value those who understand the burden of leadership, and I think that the people of *every* land will, too," she said lightly. She was dancing around the shape of something, and I thought I could discern what it was.

Was the Queen of Torvald saying that she would support me if I rose up against the Southern Lords?

The thought was too big to think, or to feel clearly. Of course it was something that I had dreamed about, in my darker moments, late at night and annoyed with the way that the South was intent on tearing its own eyes out… But that would mean Southerner fighting Southerner, and as much as the idea excited me, it also repulsed me in equal measures.

She has no right to say these things to me! My confusion was swept aside by my temper—always quick to rise—which made me clench my fists suddenly.

"I see that I have offended you, Lord Akeem," Nuria said. "And while I offer my apologies for causing you upset, I am *not* sorry for saying what I did." She ended on an infuriatingly blunt note. "Call it a queen's prerogative. Just as you have a prince's right, too. We of all people can speak honestly to each other."

"Are you offering Torvald troops to overthrow the Southern Lords?" I said, my voice a low growl in my chest. I couldn't think of anything worse for the 'will of the people' of the South!

"Sacred Stars, *no!*" Nuria blinked and managed to look genuinely shocked by what I had accused her of. "That would be called *collusion* or quite possibly an *invasion* in the scrolls that come to be written about our time…"

Here comes the 'but'… I thought.

"However—"

Ha! I knew it! The empire of Torvald was always going to be the same as it ever was!

"—were you to one day become the ruler of the South, then I believe that Torvald and the Southern Kingdom would be stronger than ever before," she said.

I squinted as I looked at her, and found that she was staring straight back at me in frank appraisal. *Queens are like dragons; they really do have no regrets*, I thought. I searched through her words to try and see if I could find any hint of treachery or manipulation.

"I thank you for your, uh, vote of confidence." I chose my words carefully. "But the people of the South already have a monarch, which is my father. Who will return." They were the same words that I had repeated to myself many, many times over the years since his disappearance.

"I am sure," Nuria nodded in respect. "I have no wish to cause distress, Lord Akeem. But these are important matters of state. Important matters for both of our kingdoms – for the world, even. They need to be talked about."

This Nuria was uncompromising. It was a quality that I liked, but her trying to encourage me to declare myself as the rightful heir, and to spark a civil war, I really didn't like.

And besides which, my father will return. I know he will!

"My father is already the ruling Prince for the South, my lady," I said, my voice sounding thick in my throat. "Now, if you will excuse me, I have a flight to this Healer's Rest ahead of me…"

"*Prince* Akeem," Nuria called out to me, her imperious tone making me halt with one hand on the door. "Your father may indeed return – which Torvald will be happy to see – and we may defeat the Deadweed – I hope – but know this: that *your family* is the royal line of the South, and the grip of the Southern Lords cannot last forever. Torvald awaits the day that we can treat with allies on our southern borders."

I didn't say anything as I opened the door and walked out. I just hoped that through all of this chaos my father *would* return, and he would know what to do, because I sure as the sands run dry, didn't.

CHAPTER 15
DAYIE, A RECEPTION

"Can Zarr fly?" Akeem had asked me that morning, his heavy, sharp brows creased with worry.

The Prince of the South had found me in the nesting cave where Zarr had first been led, and where he had spent all of his time since fitfully sleeping and trying to contain the pain that he had pulled from me. After my meeting with Queen Jexia of the Dragon Mountain, I was left feeling even more strung out and tired than I had been before. It was a sort of bone-weary tiredness that affected my mind more than it did my body.

It's the bond, I knew, deep in my heart. I still felt the nauseous pain of my magic's curse – but it was a muted and distant ache against my soul. Zarr had taken so much of it, and that act of his was creating a new sort of weariness, as if half of my soul had been scraped from the seat of my body.

But spending last night dozing against to the Crimson Red had made me feel better, at least – and I liked to think that perhaps Zarr felt better for it too, as he had not whimpered or growled in his sleep as far as I remembered.

The situation made my heart break – but there was hope. There was still hope. *Akeem found Telumeh,* as he had told me everything that had happened in his own meeting with the Queen-Empress of Torvald. I just had to hope that this ancient Selm was still alive and still lived there.

"I can fly." Zarr had surprised me by answering the prince's question. I had immediately pressed him to talk to me, to share the pain back with me, but he would not. I just had to hope that whatever this Selm could do, that at least they would be able to stop me transmitting the magical curse through my bond to my dragon-brother.

So, it was with a heavy heart that I eventually took to the skies on Zarr, with the Crimson Red barely responding to my questions, and instead holding his soul awkwardly away from mine as he climbed into the skies.

Our flight consisted of Akeem and Aida, Nas on Nandor, of course me and Zarr, but also Captain Daris and the woman called Mel who was his second Rider (or Dragon Fighter, they called her position, and Daris was a Dragon Navigator) on their Stocky Green Torvald dragon.

We flew due west for the rest of the morning, Daris and Mel leading the way towards a line of grey hills on the horizon that eventually became a hazy mountain range skirted with clouds and then, finally, sharp peaks dressed with snow.

So these are the Dragon Spine Mountains, I thought. I had only ever seen them in the far distance before, and I had always wondered what they looked like up close. They weren't as sharp or as tall as the High Mountains – called the *Fury Mountains* up here in Torvald—and so they appeared to be not also heavy with the constant storms that the High Mountains got. Instead, they just appeared…*massive.* Great shelves of rock and bodies of stone which stretched for leagues in all directions. They looked old and established in the same way that you can tell the difference between an older crooked tree with heavy stems and branches and a younger, but more vigorous one.

At midday we stopped on the edge of the hill-lands, Daris directing us towards a small meadow by the side of a winding river. All around it was the patchwork mosaic of fields and open spaces, edged in hedges or singular trees. Flocks of sheep and goats fled in panic away from us, and at that I felt a tiny flicker of amusement from the Crimson Red beneath me. It gave me great joy to see that he could still take joy in the simple pleasures of being a dragon, after all.

To my surprise, however, there was more commotion going on underneath us as we swooped in. There were people, villagers, running *towards* us instead of away.

"Daris?" I called out in alarm as he did not stop. Had he even seen these people?

But my surprise turned to a deep confusion when, as I landed, I realized that these people were *happy* to see us.

"What news from Torvald!?" they called out as Zarr finished his landing run and panted in the colder, higher airs.

"Hail, brave Dragon Riders!" one of the youngest amongst them – a child barely old enough to be out on his own, and yet still with a shepherd's crook many times his size— shouted excitedly to us.

We didn't even get this kind of greeting in Dagfan! I thought, stunned by how respected we were. Even when the shepherds and field workers realized that I, Nas, and Akeem *weren't* actually Torvald Dragon Riders (we did not wear the characteristic uniforms, nor have the horned helmets of Daris and Mel), they still did not seem scared or taken aback by us. If anything, these simple folk appeared even *more* intrigued with who we might be and how our dragons might be different than the Torvald ones.

"He's the largest Red I've ever seen!" one of the shepherds said, an old-timer with hair that grew around his face like the petals around a flowerhead.

"And this one – she's a Vicious Orange!" the man's wife gestured towards Aida.

Aida and Nandor performed their part perfectly, of course, drinking up the attention and flaring their wings or cawing to the skies to the shrieks and cheers of excitement from the villagers. Zarr, however, who was usually always so eager to show off and to hear a compliment or three, was subdued. He did not snap or growl at the pestering villagers, but he made it clear by tucking his snout in under his wing that he did not want to be bothered as soon as he had eaten his fill of river fish.

"Let him sleep for a bit," Akeem advised me, leading me away from Zarr's spot beside the river and back to the crowd where a couple of campfires had already been lit for the midday feast. "We won't be here long, but you should hear this," he explained as he took me through the throng to where the old shepherd with his funny facial hair was already regaling Daris, Mel, and Nas with tales.

"Oh, yes, I've been on Jodreth's Upland all my life! Babe, child, boy and man!" He clapped his hands. "You say that you're going up to Telumeh, are you?" A dark look crossed his features. "Is there something wrong, in that case?"

"Why would there be anything wrong, sir?" Daris said with a laugh – a very fake laugh, I thought, and it seemed that the old shepherd noticed it too, as he fell quiet for a moment.

"No one goes up to old Telumeh unless there's something wrong with them," he said in a softer voice, although the throng nearest to us had similarly fallen quiet anyway, entranced by anything to do with dragons it seemed.

"It's funny you call it old Telumeh…" Akeem prodded a little.

The gaffer shrugged. "It's what my grandfather used to call it, and his grandfather before him. No idea what it means, or who called it that first as there's no town or temple or any houses at all. Just the statue."

Daris asked him about the place, and the gaffer described a very deep and very cold but narrow, kidney-bean shaped lake at the bottom of a cliff. It was a local custom in these parts of Jodreth's Uplands to go bathing in that lake once a year, at the turn of winter into spring. Even though the water was freezing and could be dangerous, it was supposed to be a restorative – and it was true that all of those who *had* used to bathe there every year seemed to live long and healthy lives...

On the far side of the lake, opposite the cave was supposed to be a weatherworn block of stone shaped into a dragon. "Although all features have long since been abraded away by wind and ice and sleet and mountain weather!" the old man said. "There might have been a name carved at its base, but no one knows what it reads now – as it could have been the name of the dragon, or the place, or the craftsperson who built it for all anyone knows!"

It certainly sounded like the place Akeem and Daris sought, and this was only further corroborated when the old man ventured that there used to be an old tale of a dragon that lived in that cave that could grant wishes. He laughed a little self-consciously (as did several other of the villagers and shepherds), but one of them – an old woman with hair like snow, raised her voice.

"Now, now, Gaffer Frams! You know better than to be laughing like that at the good sense of people!" she scolded him. She wore simple homespun, drab clothing, and her face was deeply lined. Something in her no-nonsense attitude reminded me of Mengala the Old.

"My great grandfather went up to the cave and asked to be healed of the pain in his knees – and he was!" the woman called out.

"Stories!" one of the villagers accused the woman good-naturedly.

"Is it, Ellison?" she rounded on the younger shepherd just as vociferously. I was beginning to like the old woman already. "What if I told you that I sent my own granddaughter and her babe up to Telumeh last year, telling them to ask for a cure for the croupy cough – and didn't little Esme get better over night?"

This apparently was a fact that few could deny, and it created an appraising wave of grumbles and whispers from the crowd around us. I suddenly looked at Akeem beside me, and I could tell that we were both thinking the same thing.

If all the local villagers were now convinced that Telumeh – or Healer's Rest— really can cure all their ills, then the cave is going to be a very busy place in the very near future!

"We'd better get Zarr up there, now." Akeem nodded, gesturing for Daris and Mel's attention as I slipped back through the crowd of people, and back to the Crimson Red.

To see Deadweed, poised to wrap itself over him—

"ZARR!"

The Deadweed had crept up the riverbank and had somehow

managed to hide its own scent from the dragons. *More tricks of the Sea Witch!* I knew with certainty deep down in my gut. The Deadweed was changing, evolving, adapting – and the Sea Witch was doing her best to make it the world's most dangerous weapon.

I was already running across the meadow, my sabre singing from its scabbard as Aida, Nandor and the Torvald dragon let out trumpets of alarm at my discovery.

"Get the people back! Back!" Akeem shouted, but my eyes were only on the vines that were whipping back in the air, losing droplets of the river water that had birthed them – to suddenly race downward towards my unprotected Crimson Red.

"Skrgh?" One of Zarr's great, golden eyes opened and, in awful slow motion the reptilian pupil widened as he registered what was about to happen-

I can't let it.

Without thinking, I threw out my free hand and my own voice rang out, loud and clear in a wordless melody that I didn't even know that I knew.

"Ullale-luu-lahle-luu-lahl-!"

There was something of the same haunting lilt of my mother's 'Mamma-la' song, but beyond that I couldn't say at all where this new 'song' came from. It couldn't even be described as a song, as there didn't appear to be any verses, or choruses, or words. As I ran forward, chant-singing at the descending mutant weed ahead of me, I couldn't help but feel as though what I had discovered *wasn't* a 'song' or a 'spell' at all, but that it was just the raw manifestation of whatever magic I was calling up.

There was a sudden shimmer in the air between me and Zarr, and something kicked through my chest like when you stand too close to a dragon landing, and you feel the impact its mighty bulk has on the ground through your own body even though the dragon never touched you.

This 'kick' of energy shimmered through the air, and I heard the snap and splintering of twigs as *whatever* I had cast slammed into the outstretched vines.

They snapped as if a great weight had been swept against them, breaking on their stems to release droplets of their strange oils, and the air filled with the acrid scent of the Dead-weed's sap immediately. Where my curse-wave had hit the large fleshy leaves of the vines, the leaves shook and tore, as if the magic was a wind, and that wind had teeth…

"Skreyargh!" By now, Zarr had woken up and was already bounding awkwardly towards me as I prepared to shout and wail my curse-song at the Deadweed once more.

"Dayie – look out!" The desperate shout came from Akeem – as suddenly the world was being thrown to one side as I hit the scrubby grass and was dragged towards the river.

"Ach!" There was a sharp pain in my ankle. A tiny sliver of the Deadweed vine had managed to snake across the grass unseen towards me as I ran towards the Crimson Red and was even now trying to carry me to a watery grave!

I fought it, but it was dragging me too quickly, making my elbows and hands and back burn with pain. There was grass and dirt in my mouth and I didn't know if I would choke to death from soil before I ever managed to drown from water.

"Skrargh!" Suddenly, I stopped as Zarr slammed a foot down on the weed, careless of how its thorns must be pricking straight into his pads, his head darting in and snipping at the weed quickly.

No, Zarr – it's poisonous! I wanted to shout, but it was already too late. The pain and the tension on my foot suddenly eased, and Zarr spat out the torn and bitten pieces of Deadweed, his mouth frothing with smoke and bile.

"Spit it out!" I said to him frantically, which he did – sorta. He turned and roared his dragon flame back at the still advancing Deadweed, not checking his anger this time as the ball of molten fire almost took apart the entire near half of the meadow, and the reaching Deadweed vines that had sought to kill him.

But the battle was far from over. "Get out of here you two – there's more coming!" Akeem yelled, already vaulting onto Aida's back and pointing with his sword farther downstream. Looking around (and blinking back the tears in my eyes, though whether they were from the dragon smoke or the Deadweed sap or pain, I couldn't be sure), I saw a dark thicket racing towards us around the bends and snags of the river.

More Deadweed.

Not only had the Sea Witch found a way to make the Deadweed seemingly 'invisible' to dragon senses, I was also starting to believe that my nemesis had found a way to detect where *I* was, and this was her attempt to silence me for good. Why else would a thicket of Deadweed travel so far inland, following water courses and yet ignoring local villages?

I had to stop it. I struggled to get to my feet, then collapsed on one knee again as my ankle couldn't take any weight. Looking down, I saw that it was already visibly swelling, and the skin taking on a ruddy, waxy sort of look.

Oh, sand's teeth! I swore, but that didn't look good. In the South we have a very healthy and one might say cautious approach to poisons. There were so many creatures in our daily environment that could either bite, sting, or scratch us and deliver a deadly toxin that it was only to be expected.

I have to get that foot cool, and then I have to drain the poison before it gets into my blood... I was thinking, but I was already feeling woozy, and the approaching Deadweed was already heading closer.

"Please, Dayie, no more...!" Zarr hissed into my mind, his heart's voice sounding tight with pain and worry. His shadow fell over me and, with incredible delicacy but at the same time incredible speed, he nimbly plucked at my shirt with his jaw and lifted me up high into the air before wheeling me around to his back. As soon as we were touching again, I could feel our bond all the closer. He was in pain, and it was getting worse now that I had recently used my magic.

"Zarr, no – you have to give my pain back to me. You cannot

keep doing this!" I pleaded with him, remembering precisely what had happened in the battle outside of Torvald.

"I don't have to do anything I don't want to!" the Crimson Red said in annoyance, before leaping (awkwardly) into the air, and turning in a wide circle towards the west, flying as hard as he could.

"Zarr! What are you doing? Where are you going – Akeem! Nas!" I stammered in shock. This really *wasn't* like the proud and boisterous Crimson Red to ever back down from a fight...

"Not backing down. Making the fight fairer." His voice was a pained scowl against my mind. *"I am taking you to this Telumeh, and this Selm. You cannot fight injured, and neither can I,"* he said, and that was that.

There really is no arguing with a young bull dragon in full flight, especially if you are the one clutching at its back scales.

CHAPTER 16
DAYIE AND SELM

I could feel the poison rising in my blood. A hot, uncomfortable, aching sort of pain that was spreading from my foot where the thorns of the Deadweed had punctured my soft leather shoes. I cursed the fact that no one had thought of making a Deadweed-resistant leather suit. I cursed *myself* for not thinking of it.

"Hush. Stop beating yourself up. Think about getting better." The Crimson Red's voice in my mind was a tight needle of emotions as he concentrated with all of his might to hold back the tides of magical pain that he was drawing from me.

The magic, I thought, as the ground beneath us rose and the trees grew sparser, clustering in the valleys between the ever-rising mountains. Mengala had said that my mother's song could be used to heal… I wondered as I felt the throb of pain from my foot once again. But to do that would mean the inevitable curse that went with my magic—pain for Zarr.

"If it saves your blood, then do it!" Zarr's voice was full of fire. The pain that he held must be eating away at him, making him angry. Just hearing him was all I needed to realize that *no,* there was no way I would use the Mother's Song. Not if it would inflict more pain on my bond-partner.

"I'll be fine," I hissed through clenched teeth, and, as Zarr flew faster and higher, I could only pray that it was true.

The path that the villagers had indicated climbed for several leagues through the rocky hills. Then, as Zarr swept over the brow of a ridge, a sheer cliff face appeared unexpectedly opposite us with a thin, bean-shaped lake at its base. Telumeh – or Healer's Rest.

"Zarr – can you sense any other dragons here?" I croaked, trying to figure out if I was too warm. *Oh no—a fever?* I thought in alarm.

"There are." Zarr's words were tight and controlled, and he didn't explain further as he descended towards the lake, and the shale and shingle stretch of land that sat opposite it. I saw a hunkered down shape not far from us – a rock sculpture, weatherworn and smoothed in places, but still bearing the recognizable form of a dragon.

And there was a man standing beside it.

"Skrarrr!" Zarr trumpeted, though whether it was a challenge or a welcome, I wasn't sure, as my thoughts were starting to feel thick and slow. I'd only had a small wound from the

Deadweed thorn – which was nowhere near as bad as if you were hit by the strange plant's pollen – but still. How deadly was its resin? I wondered as another wave of nausea and pain washed up through me.

With a scattering stones and clods of earth, a loud crunch and several thud-thumps, Zarr landed awkwardly on the 'beach' in front of the statue, – but the man didn't even move.

Am I hallucinating him? I thought.

The figure wore ragged robes, the hem and shoulders frayed visibly, and parts of the black cloak greyed and spotted with dirt and dust. He had a heavy hood pulled up around his shoulders, but his head was bare – and bald – and on his chin grew a long, wiry-grey beard. Even as my vision doubled and refocused, I could still see the bright sparkle of his eyes as they seemed to stare directly at me.

I have seen a robe like that before, I thought, trying to work out where. In each of the man's hands were tall and stout staffs, which he leaned forward on.

"Who are you?" Zarr's words echoed in my mind, tinged with the snarl of challenge. The man, however, did not seem fazed at all by being growled at by a very large Crimson Red Bull, and just stood silent.

"Excuse me, sir…?" I managed to gasp, as my hands fumbled on the straps from my saddle to my belt. It took me several attempts to get them open, and to half slide, half-fall to the earth beside Zarr.

"My sister!" Zarr's head immediately turned to nudge at me gently, huffing his warm, sooty breath all over me.

There was a scrape, and the man ahead of us turned with difficulty, leaning on both of his staffs as he negotiated the rocks and rough land. Whomever he was – he was leaving us to our fate!

A black robe, very old and covered with dust. But the other one I had seen had been carefully preserved...

I tried to fight through the feverish thoughts and remember where I had seen a robe just like that!

When the man had got to the end of the lake, he turned to walk up what I now saw was a small path that climbed the side of the cliff, to the large cave opening at the top.

"Zarr?" I whispered, seeing the man pause and turn back to look at us. "I think that he wants us to follow him."

"I smell dragon-sign," Zarr said, but he wouldn't share his senses with me as he usually would when trying convey something important. *Oh no,* I would have groaned, had I the energy. *Zarr must be in so much pain if he doesn't even want to share his senses with me!*

"Where? I whispered, watching as the man leaned forward, dragging his feet with the help of the twin staffs further up the path.

"Up there." Zarr breathed some soot up to the cave.

"Well, we came here to see a dragon...." I pushed myself up to my feet and tottered after the ancient man ahead of us.

"*Hm!*" I heard Zarr's annoyed grunt, before suddenly I was being lifted off of the ground.

"Hey!" It wasn't doing my nausea any good to be picked up and dangled through the air, as Zarr very daintily held the back of my shirt and deposited me into my seat on his back. He wasn't about to let me hobble up the path, when he could fly.

There was only one place to go, which was the wide ledge at the top of the cliff, in which sat the large, and dark, cave entrance. It took Zarr only three wing beats to hop into the air (while I clutched at the saddle and his shoulder scales, too disorientated and tired to re-tie the saddle straps to my belt), and to alight on the ledge with the furious thunder of his wings. Even through my own nausea and rising fever, I could sense the agitation and nervousness radiating from Zarr's quivering limbs. He was in another dragon's territory, he knew, and that usually meant that he had to wait until he was either challenged or accepted by the occupying dragon.

And this dragon – Selm? – hadn't acknowledged him yet, though it must surely have sensed and heard our arrival!

Just as before, I slid to the ground beside Zarr's feet and knelt there panting for a moment as the waves of discomfort washed through me. My weakened state must have given the strange old man time to arrive, as the next thing I heard was the crunch of feet and wooden poles on the ground ahead of me. When I looked up, there were two – no three – of the same figure. I blinked and they coalesced into one. The man was looking at me again with that same, sharp-eyed glitter, but said nothing as he stumbled past us to the mouth of the cave, leaning on the rocks of its entrance.

"...my friend, come, my old friend...we have visitors again," he mumbled and muttered, his voice barely raised more than a whisper. This guy was ancient, his skin tight and stretched in that way some people's does as they age, the skull that hid inside his flesh visible.

The sorcerer! That's who else had looked so old, and worn an ancient black robe. But the Sorcerer of the Whispering Rocks had looked after his garments, clearly – while this man hadn't.

What had the sorcerer said? That the black robes were the historic and traditional attire of the Dragon Monks – a group of people who used to study and graduate at the Torvald Dragon Academy, before the Dark King Enric, and before Lord Bower and Lady Saffron restored it to its original function of training dragons and their Riders. From what I recalled, both of these black habits had the exact same cut and style. This man had to be a Dragon Monk, like the Sorcerer of the Whispering Rocks – but wouldn't that make him very old indeed? The sorcerer had looked aged when I had first met him, his magic prolonging his life even *before* he had aged visibly before my eyes. That meant that *this* Dragon Monk had to be positively ancient!

I had kind of accepted the fact that the sorcerer was indeed, magically old. Maybe it was the fact that everything about the sorcerer was strange and surreal – from where he had lived to what I had seen him do. He had appeared to be a figure out of another time, so it was strange to see someone else cut from the same cloth, so to speak.

There was a sudden change in the air, an updraft from the cave at our side, and I could *feel* the arrival of something pressing against my mind.

"The dragon – it comes!" Zarr reacted how any young bull dragon would react, lowering his head and baring his teeth at the entrance to the cave as the darkness was suddenly disturbed by two small flickering and glowing red lights, which grew larger and brighter and resolved themselves into the tiny gobbets of flame that the gigantic dragon was flaring from its nostrils.

And gigantic was no exaggeration.

First came the scarred head, far larger than Zarr's own, and filled with teeth longer than my torso. It was a Giant White dragon, I was surprised to see, as they seemed to be the ones who, of all the dragon breeds, absolutely loved living with others in a den. Zarr had once told me that the Whites were the largest of the dragon breeds (although individuals of any species might grow pretty large, depending on their age and health), the Giant Whites often became the natural Den-Protectors and egg-carers in a busy den.

Maybe that is what Dagfan's Training Hall of dragons needs, I thought, trying to distract myself from the terrible size of the approaching wyrm as it crawled into the light.

The White blinked slowly, its eyes were milky and opalescent.

Either it was so old that it was going blind, or it had lived for such long periods underground that its eyes had clouded. It *looked* old, too, with heavy folds of skin and scales like a human's wrinkles. Just the old dragon's head alone was nearly a quarter of Zarr's total size. This White was big, even by the standards of other Whites.

"You have come for healing?" whisper-muttered the old man on the two staffs.

Isn't it obvious? I shuddered where I still crouched beside Zarr, and nodded. "The Deadweed attacked us, and my foot got caught…" I said warily, still unsure who this man really was. "And my dragon is ill…"

"Hm." The man nodded, gesturing with one of the staffs at me. "Selm can see the state that the Crimson Red is in. *Your* healing will be simple, but your friend's will be longer…"

"You can heal him?" I asked the dragon, not the man, and my hope sparked that Selm would be able to deal with all the pain that Zarr held. *My pain,* I had to remember. "It's… It's not his pain to feel…" I added as another shiver ran through me.

"Selm is very old and knows much more than we do," the man whispered. "If Selm can heal your friend, then he will."

"How much?" I said, for as a Dragon Trader I had learned that nothing ever came for free. "What do you want in return?"

The man lurched a little on his two staffs, as if I had insulted or accused him of something.

"No payment. Magic isn't a service, it is a gift," he said quickly, stepping away as the giant White's head turned to me.

Zarr hissed warningly at the ancient dragon who stopped and blinked at the Crimson Red for a moment.

"It's okay, Zarr… I think…" I said, my vision swirling with sickeningly dizzy waves.

Zarr stopped hissing, but instead of calming, he proceeded to make an angered grumble deep in his chest as Selm the White turned his head back towards me and sniffed at the air over my crouching form very delicately.

"What do I have to do?" I asked, but Selm the dragon only *huffed* at me in that way dragons have and that I had seen Zarr do a hundred times before. It was a steady exhalation of warm, sooty air from the dragon's nostrils and partially-open mouth, usually as a sign of affection. I was immediately engulfed in that warm, familiar sent of charcoal and bitter smoke, but what was different was the impact of *feeling* that washed over me at the same time.

It was like when Zarr was able to send his strength and life force to me merely through the bond we shared. I could feel this vast dragon mind pressing down on top of me, and then the presence washed over and through me – filling me with a sense of peace and affection that was entirely different from Zarr's savage and fierce love.

But…why is Selm doing this for me? I found myself thinking as tears rolled down my face. I didn't deserve this, did I? I was Dayie. The witch. The outcast. The thief and the orphan.

"Of course you deserve this!" Zarr's grumbling stopped as he sensed, too, Selm's mind on the other side of mine.

There is no way to share minds with a dragon without learning a little bit about them. This is the reason why dragons almost never lie to each other (although, they love to play jokes on humans). I knew from watching Zarr and the other Training Hall dragons interact, that there was a level of honesty from dragon to dragon which must come from the fact that when they talked to each other with just their minds, a picture of their own soul, their motivations, and feelings were transmitted at the same time.

So it was in this way I learned a tiny fragment about Selm.

He was old. Truly old. Older than even the reign of the Dark King, and it was up here that he had sought to hide in a new territory during those dark years of persecution. Selm had seen kings and queens and monasteries and academies come and go, and it seemed that the only interest that the Giant White now had in the world was just a desire for it to be whole.

I could sense that Selm had a profound respect and a deep love for the world itself, and so had devoted his mind to finding older, more fundamental ways to heal.

"Good." Zarr noticed the same thing in Selm, and I could feel his approval.

All of this understanding hit my mind in an instant and was just as quickly blown away by a sense of absolute calm that radiated from the dragon above us.

"Oh..." Zarr's tone was one of awe. *"He sees the world not as it is, but as it was. As it could be again..."*

I didn't understand what he meant.

"We dragons build memories and senses of places and people and each other as we grow older. Den mothers pass on some of that picture to their hatchlings..." Zarr attempted to explain. I knew that every dragon had a sort of a 'picture' in their head, but one that was built out of the scents that they had encountered, the sights, as well as the subtle nuances of feelings or intuition that their great hearts could encompass. It was more than just a map of all the places that they had been or other dragons had told them about (by sending their sense-pictures to them, as Zarr had done with me), it was a story as well. Or lots of different stories, all woven through each other. It was their version of history – at once confusing and contradictory and interknotted with everything else, as more dragon pictures could be added again and again on top of the older...

"Selm is the keeper of a memory that is passed down from his mother by her mother by her mother, by..." Zarr's tone was reverential, even, and I knew the whole concept of the den mother was almost an article of faith for the dragons – another reason why the Training Hall had to change!

"And that memory is of a time when the humans and the dragons did not fear or hate each other," Zarr said. *"A time of endless skies and lands that were lush and overflowing with life. Before the world was changed."*

What changed it? I thought, and I caught a glimpse in my

mind – perhaps a picture from Selm? – of a sky choked black with ash, with gobbets of burning fire raining down. I whimpered, squirming where I sat at the horrible image of a world burning—

But just as easily as it had appeared, the image vanished, and once again the peace flowed through me. I didn't understand what Selm had done, not really, but the picture-memories in my head changed. I could see a land that was whole, vibrant with trees and rivers and life; birds in the skies, dragons crying far above them, creatures moving down between the woodlands… Through Selm, I got a glimpse of every speck of life here in this land, which I knew somehow instinctively was the whole world – and every spark of life felt *right* in a way that was hard to describe. *Like everything was exactly where it should be,* I thought. *Doing exactly what it was meant to do.* And the force of that hope seemed almost so strong that it could remake the world.

And remake me, it appeared – for my pain had gone.

"What?" I realized that I didn't feel hot and sweaty, or feverish, or nauseous or dizzy. If anything, I felt energized and confident, as I slowly unfolded my limbs and eagerly tore off my shoe to look at my wounded leg.

Which was completely healed, apart from a small curl of white scars that had been the puncture wounds of the Deadweed.

"Tell him thank you…" I murmured, amazed. *How could just a picture of hope have such an effect?*

"*Memories, like stories, are powerful things,*" Zarr informed me.

I was a little too stunned to even think what to say next, but it seemed that I didn't need to. Selm had already turned his attention to Zarr. There was a low, guttural croak from the old White, and an answering chirrup from Zarr.

"Zarr?" I asked, as the White slowly moved back into its cave, and for my bull Crimson Red to follow him. My dragon did not appear to even hear me – which was impossible, I knew – as I lived inside his mind as much as he lived inside mine. What hidden conversation were Zarr and Selm having that was so engrossing that Zarr would forget about me? A small part of me felt a flare of jealousy that I was not invited to be a part of this healing – but it was instantly subdued by the gratitude that I felt towards Selm for healing my dragon.

"Your friend will be fine," whispered the only other voice besides me left. It was the old man, now seated on a boulder with his awkward legs spread out before him and panting as if he had run a race.

"Oh, I don't doubt it…" I said, my heart still light with the feeling of peace and joy.

"But Selm told me to tell you that it may take a while…" the man croaked, shivering a little and I could see him massaging the gnarled knuckles of his hands. He was cold, and I wasn't surprised as it was dropping cold up here in the mountains.

"Let me gather some firewood," I said, eager to be able to help this odd couple in whatever small way that I could. I might even be able to catch some fish in that lake for a meal.

It didn't take me too long to gather the firewood, and the vitality that was singing through my body made the task joyous instead of arduous. Still, the sun was starting to redden low in the sky when I finally managed to build and spark a bonfire near the cave entrance, and near enough to the old man so that he could at least warm his pained legs.

Which struck me as a bit odd, now that I came to think of it. "Why hasn't Selm healed your legs?" I asked him, trying to not look directly at them for fear of hurting his feelings.

"These old things?" The man pulled a weary smile at his own body. "Because I am already whole as I am," the man said and then explained.

It was a disease. A type of wasting disease that attacked his joints and made it more painful to move, every year.

"But still, can't Selm heal that too?" The dragon had, after all, miraculously neutralized the Deadweed poison coursing through my own blood as well as healing the wounds that the thorns had left in my body. Half a dozen other such minor injuries on me were gone too, I knew instinctively. No sore back and shoulders from flying. The sprain I had done to my shoulder felt gone, and I couldn't feel any twinge of the bruises or muscle aches that came with leading a life as a Dragon Rider.

"Perhaps. If he really tried – but I am happy with what years I have had, and this illness is something that has been coming to me for a long, long time," the man whispered, his voice mixing with the pop and crackle of the burning logs. Above us the stars started to come out, one by one, bright and beautiful. "What I have learnt in my long years at Selm's side is that some pains are not wounds; they are not *injuries* that our body and mind aren't supposed to suffer. Selm's magic sets right what is out of balance, whereas this illness of mine comes from my own age, and a life that should never have grown this long…" the man said.

"How old are you?" I whispered into the fire, earning a wry grin from the monk before he answered me.

"My name is Tian, once a proud Dragon Warrior of the Academy, before I donned the habit of the Dragon Monks," he said, saying these things like they were something I would understand instinctively.

"It was always the way, back in my time," he said, "that there were two. A Dragon Warrior and a Dragon Monk, or mage," Tian said, and a look of sorrow crossed his features as I realized that he must be thinking about his partnered Rider. Who wasn't here anymore…

"But, in time, after a successful life of riding dragons and fighting for Torvald and all the rest of it – I returned to the academy to begin re-training as a Dragon Monk. I was getting too old and slow to wield a sword or throw a javelin anyway," Tian stated, once again looking faraway for a moment. "I was bonded to another dragon, a long time ago, but eventually I lost him and my fellow Rider… I was alone, so… I took the habit, and wandered - seeking a cure for my heartsickness."

"I'm sorry," I offered. If losing a fellow Rider was anything like the bond that a Rider and their bonded dragon-friend has, then I knew that his heart must still be riven in two by the loss. But to lose your bonded dragon, as well! My mind couldn't contemplate the heartbreak that he must be experiencing.

"Wait, you two are not bonded?" I said, surprised because Tian seemed able to hear what Selm said.

"We have a…*rare* sort of bond." Tian looked confused as he searched for the words. "When I first came here, I thought that Selm would be able to heal my broken heart, but he could not. I studied with him. I fished for him. Set fires just so we could enjoy the warmth, tried to learn the ways of wholeness that he knew so well. In time, after the first ten years or so, and then after another ten, I realized that I could even sense him whenever I couldn't see him…"

"You bonded" I said, surprised. "I thought you could only bond once in your lifetime?"

"Not necessarily, but it is very unlikely that any heart – human or dragon – *could* bond a second time," Tian explained. "As you know, bond-partners give their hearts completely, and so the loss of our partner changes us forever."

I nodded.

"So, yes – I think what we have is a bond. Or maybe my studies in Dragon Magic helped me to come close to his mind. I don't know. All I know is that Selm is the wisest being that I have ever met, and that I am happy to stay here and continue to learn from him for as long as he will teach me," Tian stated.

The man made it sound like he had been here for a *long* time, *and* that he had a *long* life before that, too.

"What Selm does – what the pictures inside Selm's head does – is to restore your soul to whole once more. To help you grow into who you *could* be, as far as I can make out," the man whisper-said.

"But there aren't many people left that I *could* be, now," Tian said with a wry smile. "I have already far, *far* outlived my years thanks to my studies, and this illness is something that I am glad to accept for the price of so much life."

Just like Mengala and the sorcerer, I thought. This Tian had become preternaturally 'preserved' by the magic that was within him, and, although he seemed very happy – I did wonder just what this meant for me, as another magic user. Was I going to end up like him and the sorcerer and Mengala? Did I want to?

Before I could voice my own concerns to Tian, there was a sudden jolt through me as if I had been prodded with a pin, and with it came a fast-rising sense of optimism and hope, and-

"SKREAYARGH!" There was a jubilant, victorious roar from somewhere deep in the cavern before us—a voice I would know anywhere – whether in my ears and in my mind as I knew that was Zarr, somewhere inside the mountain beside us. It washed into my thoughts with that same residue of calm and hope I had experienced from Selm's healing. A little jealously perhaps, but I closed my eyes and kept my awareness on Zarr, basking in the feelings of strength and confidence and total, pain-free life.

"He's done it," I said, relief filling me.

The pain that Zarr had been hiding from me was gone, and it hadn't jumped back into my head as I had almost expected it too.

"Dragon-sister!" Zarr's voice was eager and triumphant as his awareness slammed into mine. Gone was his previous taciturn, or angered irritation. Instead, it was like he was a young hatchling once again, full of enthusiasm and joy as he washed through my emotions and heart.

"We are whole, once again," Zarr said in my mind, and I heard with my ears the sound of the great beast thundering back up through the cave ahead of us. With a rush of soot-filled air and open, lolling jaws, the Red burst from the cave to leap lightly and deftly to the ledge beside me, before shaking out his wings in a gale that almost put out the bonfire I had meticulously crafted.

"Hey, wyrm!" I batted at his scaled leg affectionately, and in turn he silently mock-roared at me, before carefully pawing at the floor until he had stretched out along the ledge, his belly curving around me, the fire, and Tian.

"We are one again…" I agreed, not able to help myself from grinning as I leaned back against the warmth of his belly scales. Just that simple act of enjoying each other's company was almost as healing to my soul as whatever Selm the ancient White dragon had done to me, to be honest.

To my utter astonishment, the old dragon was also emerging from the cave, moving slowly and snuffing at the night air carefully, as if he really *was* blind. But instead of coming all the way out of the cave, Selm settled half in and half-out on his front haunches, before setting his large head on his front paws on the other side of the fire to us.

"What happened in there?" I whispered at Zarr, wondering if it was rude to ask, but neither the Crimson Red, nor Selm or Tian seemed to mind.

"I sat down. And Selm breathed on me, as he had you…" Zarr's voice was drowsy and peaceful. *"But then…something else happened. He showed me the picture of the world before…"* he stated, struggling to transmit to me what it was he had experienced. After my own strange healing from Selm, I understood a little.

"Dragons – all of us – we're bigger than we think…" Zarr attempted to articulate the profound thoughts he had received. *"You know we dragons make a picture of the world around us, in our minds…"*

"Of course." I nodded. "But Selm gave you – me – us – he gave us a picture of a time that was so long ago. Before either of us were alive…" I pointed out. How could that help with Zarr's pain? "It's almost like that memory picture of that time is still alive…" I pointed out. "That we're carrying a story of the past forward into the future…" I couldn't make out how this mystery fit together – but I could *feel* that the edges would meet somehow.

And it was Zarr, working with my thoughts and realizations, who brought it together.

"The pain – your pain – our pain – is just one part of a much larger picture. I realized I could let it go," Zarr said, but there was still a shadow of a worry at the back of my mind, despite the Crimson Red's ebullience. "But Zarr, my heart – what is going to happen when I have to use my magic again? When the pain comes back? I can't help but pass it through our bond to you."

Zarr's optimism was undimmed, however. *"Then I will be ready. I am able to release it out into the world now. You will not harm me, Dayie-sister,"* he said happily, even though I still had my misgivings.

"Dayie, daughter-of-water," Tian cleared his throat to say.

Who else had called me that? I thought. Someone had. Wasn't it Mengala? I scratched my head trying to remember the reference. *No. It was Queen Jexia, the Matriarch Queen of the dragons of Torvald.* She had called me 'daughter-of-the-sea' and 'sister-of-the-air.'

"Why did you call me that?" I asked.

"Selm reads it on you," Tian said simply, as if that explained everything. "The Queen of the Sacred Mountain saw those names within you and named you so – and Selm is able to read that."

This was all getting too weird for my liking. It was like Zarr and Tian and Selm were all suggesting that they could see more about me than even I could!

Tian the Dragon Monk must have seen my puzzlement, as he gave a chuckling wheeze, and said, "Take heart, Dayie. No one means to intrude on your mind, but Selm cannot help it sometimes. He tells me that he saw in you the great wound that you bear…"

What wound? I thought a little defensively, before suddenly the rest of Queen Jexia's words came back to me. That I was emotionally damaged because of being an orphan. Because I couldn't connect with my own mother, who was the woman who had given me my magic.

"I'm doing okay," I managed to say, sitting forward over my knees. I didn't want to be lulled by the warmth from Zarr behind my back.

"If you were, then you wouldn't be here," Tian said in the same gentle tone.

Ha. Maybe he's right there…

"But, after Selm has news for you. For the *both* of you," Tian said happily, prodding at the coals around the edge of the bonfire with his staff.

"He has been considering your plight. The magical wound inside of you, Dayie, that you cannot fix and that will always make your powers erratic…" Tian stated all of this as if he knew everything about me. I wondered if he *did* in some way, because Selm had shared the picture of my soul with him? It wasn't an entirely comforting thought, to be honest.

"As well as the rise of the new magic within the land, and the Deadweed and worse that it brings…" Tian stated heavily. "Selm believes that he knows who has caused this tragedy to the world."

What?

CHAPTER 17
DAYIE AND THE SEA WITCH

"A few years ago, Selm and I received a visitor in the dark of night..." Tian intoned, his croaky voice creating a sing-song melody with the crackles and pops of the fire. Above us was the dome of the night sky, and in the distance the mountains glowed eerily pale with the reflected light of the moon.

"Much like the pair of you, she arrived out of the blue, out of nowhere, and came seeking aid," Tian stated. "Although it is not so unusual for people to come here for aid, they are usually simple shepherd or mountain folk who do not seek to meet with Selm, but make offerings and hope that their questions are answered." Tian explained. "Selm can see the hearts of these folk, and knows that they would react to him with fear were they to actually see him, so he usually just heals them from a distance, hidden in his cave..."

I was once again struck by how gentle the old White was, and what a rare soul the dragon must be to care so much for the lives of the poor peasant humans around here, even to the point of remaining hidden so as not to scare them!

"But this woman was alone, and she did not have the same sort of heart as the others who usually come seeking aid," Tian said, and the White gave a small huff of sooty air from his nostrils, as if in comment of the woman.

"And who was this woman?" I asked, wondering just what all of this had to do with the…

"Oh," Zarr said, as if his news was an afterthought. *"Tian said they knew who the Sea Witch was. They told me her real name is Saheera."*

Saheera. I turned the strange name over and over in my mind. It felt odd to put a personal name on the figure of the monstrous 'Sea Witch' who I had started to think of in more legendary, nightmarish sorts of terms – a woman made out of seaweed and drowned sailor's bones – not a real woman at all.

Saheera, I repeated her name in my head. That was the name of my nemesis. One that I had never chosen, and yet who seemed determined to destroy me and my dragon. Just hearing the name made my heart beat faster and my stomach feel queasy. It was like seeing a sword drawn from its scabbard… Full of threat and foreboding even if it hadn't done anything yet. "She came *here*?" I burst out." Why didn't anyone tell me?" *Why had Selm shared this information with Zarr and not me? Did he think that I couldn't handle it?* There was a rattled breath from Selm as he lazily opened his myopic eyes a little.

Oops. Maybe I shouldn't be quite so angry with the fire-breathing dragon who was just good enough to heal me and my dragon... "Sorry," I said a little shamefacedly.

"Hm." Tian was less forgiving that Selm, it appeared, who casually closed his eyes and breathed a little deeper, as if he was dozing. I knew that he wasn't, though, as his ears were still flicking a little, turning to catch the sources of distant noises and hoots from the mountains.

"Back then, we did not know who this woman was. Or what she *would* become," Tian said heavily. "Her future was not written. She could have been anyone. She could have been a great healer one day, perhaps. Or a truly phenomenal witch, like old Chabon, the Matriarch of the Western Witches once was..."

'Instead, Saheera chose a different path," Tian said. "We did not know what her path was until now, until Selm saw into your minds, and saw all of the battles that you have been fighting with this Deadweed, and saw the return of this type of magic."

"This current of magic," I repeated what the Sorcerer of the Whispering Rocks had told me.

"Precisely." Tian nodded, looking at me appraisingly. No wonder that he should understand these terms, I thought, as both he and the sorcerer had been trained as Dragon Monks.

"This magic is not altogether unfamiliar. Selm had seen the source of this current of magic before. In the form of a woman named Saheera - she was one of the Western Witches," Tian explained. "One of the ones who stayed behind after the rest of Chabon's coven left this side of the world."

I nodded. This much we had figured out for ourselves.

"Like most of the Western Witches left behind, she took to wandering, not having a home anymore, and not wanting or willing to stay on the Haunted Isle – the traditional home of the Western Witches."

Which also made sense and was just what the Sorcerer of the Whispering Rocks had claimed, that, when he had gone to try and locate what had happened to Chabon's coven, he had found the Haunted Isle of Sebol little better than a sanctuary for the half-crazed.

"What happened to her?" I asked.

"She had heard from somewhere, perhaps one of the ancient scrolls that were once housed in the Sebol libraries, that Selm had one of the true pictures of the original world in his head. And she had come to learn of it," Tian said, rubbing his hands in front of the fire. "She was convinced that her magic was a way to bring the world back into balance. To reverse all of the evils that the Dark King had done, and to make the world truly whole once more…" The old man looked into the fire. "She imagined a time when there would be no wars between nations over such petty things as pride, or timber, or gold. The world itself – the plants, the seas, the beasts in the field and the birds in the sky – would be as important as the humans in their cities and the dragons in their skies, and there would be no need for conflict and strife. The poor people of the world would no longer have to pay taxes. No person or thing or place would be above any other. There would be no disease or illness, even…" Tian shook his head sadly.

"Doesn't everyone want that?" I murmured. "Isn't that the same picture that Selm has in his head and heals people with?"

"Saheera's dream was a noble one, but it wasn't the same as Selm's vision…" Tian stated. "Saheera wanted to force that change. To remake the world into what she thought it should be. The world in balance, how it was, is not something that can be forced, but it has to be allowed to grow, you see… When Selm told her this – Saheera grew mad. She didn't have time to heal every heart and mind in the world, she stated – she wanted a change that would change everything, for all time, and for it to happen now."

I nodded. It was a monstrous vision of course – and one that I had first-hand experience of, as there were villages and towns in the South that I had fought that were entirely choked by Deadweed. At least now I knew *why*. That this Saheera the Sea Witch was trying to punish humanity? What had humanity done to Saheera that was so terrible?

"But who made her the judge and jury?" I muttered under my breath.

"Precisely. She came to Selm to transmit the image of the world to her, believing that it would unlock her own powers, and help her become the witch that she wanted to be. But Selm would not, and instead offered to ease her hurting heart. This Saheera was riddled with guilt, regret, and grief, and although she would not open her mind to Selm if he would not do the same for her – Selm got the impression that since the disappearance of Chabon and her coven, Saheera must have suffered a terrible loss of faith. She felt abandoned, and alone, and she carried a deep hurt within her – she was in mourning and it was *that* pain that would fuel her subsequent magics, not a love for the balance of the world…" Tian said, and I saw immediately what he meant.

"And instead, if she can't balance the world with force, she will simply attack it, wiping humanity off the face of the map…" I said, feeling a certain unavoidable horror as I did so.

"Yes. Saheera is already proficient with encouraging plants to grow, and fruit, and respond to her," Tian explained. "And Selm can see all of that in the battles that yet live in your memory."

Just like my abilities, I thought, *which are a part of that same 'new' current of magic as well, had manifested through looking after the herd animals of my youth.* I had always had a way with animals, and it was only later had I realized that it was an *unusual* way with animals – as I had been able to tell which ewe was pregnant within days, or the baby goats, chickens, and anything else would be happy to be fed by me and return to their mothers later without their mothers rejecting them.

But – did that mean that my powers were being fueled by my pain as well as my love? I wondered, thinking of the younger Saheera – what she must have been like before she even came here to see Selm. Had the Sea Witch (before she was the Sea Witch) been a person of love, of wanting to heal the world as my powers had come from a place of connection and trust?

But something happened to her, which made her react through hatred and anger.

"But Selm could sense that great pain she carried, and cautioned her against her plans. It seems that, instead, Saheera has continued her studies into the living world and has instead created the Deadweed."

"And the Water Wraiths," I added. *No wonder she hadn't stopped from attacking the South, and Dagfan – and now the North as well!* I thought. Saheera had created an unnatural-natural army, and wasn't going to stop no matter how many times I managed to drive them back – because, to *her* – Dagfan and the South and the entire North all had to be remade anew…

"Where is she?" I asked suddenly. But we could stop her. If only we could find her, then I and Zarr would go there ourselves, if it meant being able to put a stop to her madness!

"Ah. That is something that Selm cannot help you with, as what a visitor does once they leave this place is up to them," Tian stated. "Saheera did not say where she was going, or what she was going to be studying, I am afraid…but there might be one place where you can find out…"

"Really?" I said. *Did he mean Sebol?* That was where the Western Witches had lived, and no matter its current state – wasn't it at least a little likely that Saheera had gone back to make it her lair?

But no… I thought. The Sorcerer of the Whispering Rocks had never said anything about meeting a dangerous, powerful witch on the mostly-abandoned island.

"The Cave of Truth," Tian said.

"The *what?"* I had never heard of it to be quite frank…

"It is a dragon place." Tian cocked his head to one side, giving the distinct impression he was paying attention to some other voice—Selm, of course. He nodded to himself, before going on. "A very special dragon place. There was once a time when the world was filled with many rare places where the natural currents of magic welled up of their own accord, and miraculous things could happen. There might be waterfalls that, like Selm here, could heal people. Or there could be eerie mists on certain abandoned moors in which, it is said, you could meet the shades of those departed…"

"You are talking about children's stories," I said.

"Dragon Tales, not stories," Tian corrected. "Many such lost mysteries become the myths or scare-stories for the next generation. They get turned into fantasy, or else get forgotten about altogether…but that does not mean that they never existed!" He gave a wry smile. "But perhaps the currents of magic in the world have changed, and there are not so many as there used to be, and maybe new ones are taking their place? Either way, Selm knows of one such special place that was still strong with natural dragon magic when he was a hatchling. It is called the Cave of Truth, and it was there that the dragons could go to seek answers to any question, and the cave would reveal it to them."

"How is a cave going to reveal the truth?" I asked. I had seen quite a few caves, and, so far none of them had ever talked.

"As I say, this is a place where one particular natural magic of the world wells up. Inside that cave is a lake whose waters are like blue crystal, and, or so Selm was told, if you peer into the lake and ask an honest question of its waters, then you will see your answer there," Tian said. "Selm believes that it is your only hope at finding the whereabouts of Saheera, and hopefully you will be able to find her and talk some sense into her.

Talk? I barely refrained from scoffing. Talking to the power-hungry, vengeful, and arrogant Sea Witch was the last thing that I wanted to do, but as I knew that these two creatures in front of us were probably some of the most peaceful that I had ever met, I wisely kept my mouth shut.

"Ah," Tian cleared his throat once more. "Selm tells me that the Cave of Truth lies far, far to the south of here. If it still exists. Across the Tall Mountains, south past Dagfan, and south still over the Burning Sands to the distant southern coast."

"The southern coast?" I asked. "Not the western coast?" The western coast I at least knew of— it was wracked with storms but was much nearer and led directly to the Western Archipelago and eventually the Haunted Isle of Sebol…

"The southern coast," Tian repeated.

"Okay," I said, even though I had never heard of it before and Tian might as well have been saying that it existed at the other edge of the world. As far as I knew, very few people had ever even attempted to cross the Burning Deserts. That was one of the main reasons why the Sorcerer of the Burning Rocks had chosen to live in their middle, as very few armies or assassins or busybodies would even survive the trek in the excruciating heat to get that far!

But Tian was talking about the *other end* of the Burning Deserts, where it was rumored that the people there were strange and different, and that they hated every one of their more northerly neighbors. I wasn't even sure that they had dragons there!

"How will we find it, apart from just 'head south'?" I asked.

Another pause from Tian as he listened to his instructions. "Selm tells me that the Cave of Truth lies against the Southern Ocean itself, directly under the red star, above the last cove before the mountain river."

Wow, great, I thought a little desultorily. *Cross the Burning Sands. Find some red star. And some mountains, and then a sea cove…*

I needn't have worried overly about my own abilities to navigate, however, as it happened…

"I have it," Zarr said, and I heard him thanking Selm in the back of my mind. *"Selm has given me the sense-picture of it. When we come close, I will be able to track it."*

Okay – I took back my earlier annoyed thought. *This* was why the dragon's pictures inside their heads were so powerful! Though Zarr had never been to the place, Selm had just directed memory of it—whether his own or some other long-ago dragon's— that was powerful enough to form a set of smells, sights, and sounds, that Zarr would now remember for the rest of his life– and always be able to find the way back to!

"Then, as much I hate to leave this fire," I groaned, "I guess we'd better get back to camp…"

Camp. I suddenly shivered in shock. I had left Akeem and the others fighting the Deadweed back there. What if they had lost? What if they had all been killed?

"Hush, Dayie-sister!" Zarr explained to me. *"Aida and Nandor are okay. I can hear them very distantly; they are travelling with the villagers to this place, bringing the wounded of the battle with them."*

The wounded? To this place? Could Selm truly heal us all? "Is Akeem alright?" I asked suddenly.

"I believe so…" Zarr said. *"I do not hear him gasping in pain, nor do I smell blood on him. But I smell a lot of soot and dragon fire! At their pace, they will arrive here by morning…"*

"They must have won the battle," I said and turned to Tian. "You're about to have a lot of people visiting, people from the same battle with Deadwood that I was fleeing…" I said a little gingerly, feeling as though I must be somewhat responsible for disturbing these two wise old beings' rest. "People who are coming for healing."

"Then they will be healed." Tian nodded slowly as he listened to Selm's words inside of his own head. "Although, if there are many of them, then they might have to stay at the lake for some days for Selm to rest and eat and build up his strength between each healing."

It was something that I was sure that anyone would be prepared to do, if the other option was dying of Deadweed wounds.

"Then, my friends, I beg you both to stay until morning at least, and then you can greet your friends and tell them of your plans to travel south to the Cave of Truth." Tian nodded and smiled, before creaking himself up to a standing position with the help of his staff, and proceeding to stumble and strut into the cave of Selm. The White looked as though he was dozing, still sitting on his haunches and breathing rhythmically.

"Is this the right thing to do, Zarr?" I whispered as I lay back with my shoulders against Zarr's warm belly. With the heat of the dragon around me, I had no need for a blanket – even up here in the Dragon's Spine Mountains!

"Is what the right thing? Sleeping in front of a warm fire? Enjoying your time with a friend who has healed you?" Zarr said.

"No, I mean flying all the way to the ends of the earth after this Cave of Truth?" I said, finally feeling sleepy and starting to blabber a little. "Especially when Dagfan is only just rebuilding, and Torvald itself was attacked. Now that we have the aid of Torvald's Dragon riders."

"But we would never have stopped the root cause – the Sea Witch's hatred for the world."

Or her love of it, I thought, feeling unsettled and anxious about what we had talked about tonight, and not entirely able to say why…

But Zarr was right, I could see that. From what we had learned – the only way to stop Saheera was to find this cave, and her, and perhaps make the Sea Witch see how her reckless and damaging dream was only harming everything, not healing it…

CHAPTER 18
AKEEM, THE POWER OF BELIEF

"The Cave of Truth?" I repeated. The place Dayie had described was nowhere I had ever heard of. "I have to say, Dayie, I'm more than a little worried about flying off to the far south when the whole world is in turmoil."

"But that is precisely *why* I have to go," Dayie said emphatically, though keeping her voice low amidst the hubbub and grumble of other people. Around us camped, stood, and waited the assembled shepherds and village folk of the mountains, some bearing wounds from the Deadweed attack but thankfully, most of them only suffering from the rigors and ailments of our hurried flight from the battle. We had marched through the night, following the path that the shepherds had pointed out to us, with me and Aida, as well as Captain Daris, his partner Jeonda, and their dragon circling back and forth to keep a careful watch out for the Deadweed.

It was invisible to dragon senses now, and my mind kept

circling back to how it had managed to almost take Zarr out. The Sea Witch had found a way to fool the dragon senses.

"It just smells like any other plant," Aida confirmed in my mind. I had wondered if that would make a difference – the dragon senses were so sharp after all, that they could differentiate the tang of a pine tree in a woodland next to the brackish, tannin-heavy scent of oak trees. Surely, they could identify the 'plant' of the Deadweed and track it like that – even if it had lost its darker, more curse-laden scent to them?

"It's not like that. It changes. At first it smells like watercress, then hogweed, billberry, water campion…" Aida told me. She didn't use these names for the various wildflowers and plants that we knew, but rather gave me the pictures and the scent of them in my mind, and I named them from my learnings with the Binshee.

"The Deadweed can camouflage itself, pretending to be other plants," I said to Dayie with a sigh. I knew in my heart that she was right about her decision to find this 'Cave of Truth' place. It was always just my head that made things difficult. I wished that Heydar was here to advise me. I wished that I didn't have to be weighing the actions and potential alliance with Torvald, against the mostly idiotic decisions of the Southern Lords; nor balancing the complicated tribal alliances I still had to secure within the Binshee with the far greater concern– the threat of the Sea Witch and the spread of the Deadweed and her Water Wraith army.

If she is attacking Deadweed in force and so blatantly, I

reasoned, *and she is able to camouflage her Deadweed now – then she is gaining in strength, not diminishing.*

Next to this realization was one even worse – maybe Dagfan had already fallen while we'd been in the North.

"No. My dragon-siblings are still at Dagfan, still fighting, every day and night," Aida informed me.

Of course. Aida had her immediate, mental connection to her brood-brothers and sisters that was as strong as any bond that I had with her. Could she pass messages to them for me?

"I could. But they are a very long way away," Aida informed me. *"At such a great distance, they will only reliably be able to feel a rough sensation that I send to them."*

Damn, I thought. I was hoping to be able to get the Wild Company dragons to talk to their bonded Riders and pass on information to me about what was happening in the South. But aside from the distance the dragon thoughts had to travel, there was also the fact that a dragon has different priorities than I did as Captain of the Wild Company. I wanted to know about numbers of troop reinforcements and the state of repair of walls – whereas the Vicious Oranges of the Wild Company would probably only be thinking in terms of flying, hunting, the smell of blood on their claws, or the release of fire onto the shores below…

"Fighting. Fire and fury." Aida relayed her impressions of her far-off siblings. *"Weariness. Some pain, hunger… The night is never truly black, as the dragon flames smolder still on the banks of the river."*

Right. It sounded like Dagfan had indeed been attacked again – and that the city of the South was in a hunkered down, siege sort of mode. Days and nights of fighting and clearing the Deadweed, hoping for a change of fortunes…

But how long could that even last? I thought. How long could any city survive under that level of harm?

"Okay." I nodded, raising my head. Only then did I realize Dayie had been watching me as I had conferred with my dragon. She nodded, and smiled a little. She had changed in the scant few seasons that I had known her. When I had first met her, she was a proud, defiant young woman – one I am sure wouldn't have waited patiently for me to have my internal conversation with Aida when she was urgently trying to convince me of why she was right.

Maybe it came from being a slave to that woman, and tasting freedom for the first time, I reflected. If all your power is taken from you, day in and day out, and you finally get a chance to make a difference – to do something that means something to you – then I guessed I would have been pretty insistent about my views and opinions as well!

But Dayie *had* changed – and it wasn't just the way that her limbs were slightly kissed by sun, or toned in different ways now after the months and seasons of training and fighting. There was an optimistic sort of light in her eyes that made it almost hard to look at her straight.

"It was Selm, the Oldest," Aida whispers into my mind, and I could sense the awe that she had in her voice for the dragon

that these people around me had come to see, and yet I had not.

"Selm healed you, I take it," I said awkwardly at Dayie, who nodded happily.

"You should see him, too, Akeem. He might be able to help you decide what you want to do – to rule the South or..." Dayie said in an earnest sort of way.

"To overthrow the Southern Lords?" I said, my earlier worries returning. *Why was everyone telling me that, recently?* I thought, not with a small amount of disgust. "I'm afraid that isn't going to happen, Dayie," I said heavily, much to her confused look.

"Oh, but I thought you wanted to..." she started to say, but I cut her off.

"No. I really *don't* want to try and rule a continent of people who regard me as little better than a usurper, and my father as a traitor!" I snapped. "It would mean a civil war with the three Southern Lords – and despite what the Queen-Empress of Torvald says— the poorer, everyday people of the Southlands will not thank me for throwing their lives into turmoil." I stopped then, though I could have said more, could have said how I wasn't certain how much the southerners even cared whether it was a prince or a council that ruled over them, just so long as their rulers got on with their business of keeping them safe, because when I looked up at those bright eyes, I found that she was looking troubled, as if I had stung her.

"I'm sorry," I mumbled quickly. "I didn't mean to snap at you…"

"It's alright, Akeem," Dayie sounded weary. Tired, even. "I understand. If you're not ready for it, then you don't *have* to do it."

Not ready? That needled at my pride. *Why wouldn't I be ready to rule the South? Had my father not taught me well?*

"Um… well…" I stammered, suddenly confused as to what I could say.

"But I think you're right, anyway," Dayie continued. "We need to concentrate on defeating Saheera the Sea Witch first, and then I am sure we can all worry about what happens next."

If we survive. I nodded.

But my gloomy thoughts were broken by a commotion happening on the other side of the crowd, where the shepherds and villagers were congregated around the lake. Muttered whispers passed backwards through the huddle, and I could feel a sense of hushed awe flowing back over me.

"He's here. The Oldest," Aida said in my mind, as her welcoming trill sounded far ahead of us in the skies where she patrolled.

We need to keep searching for the Deadweed, I thought, a little annoyed at this distraction from our duty. Even Daris, his partner, and their dragon were swooping in high over the lake to see the arrival of the largest sand's-damned dragon I had ever seen.

The head of the Giant White broke from the darkness of the cave, and his scales didn't gleam the pure and pristine white of a snow field either, but were discolored, faded, as if even the dragon was nearing the end of its long life.

At the side of this ancient dragon hobbled a man in a black robe on two stout sticks, *the Dragon Monk Tian.* I remembered what Dayie had told me of their meeting and last night spent up here in their company.

The effect on the crowd at the arrival of this legendary beast couldn't have been more pronounced. Not that they were noisy; the opposite was true, in fact. The crowd became reverent, and even the smaller children that were amongst their number looked up in stunned silence.

Selm was silent for a moment, and then, very slowly, lifted his enormous head up higher and higher, extending his neck until we could all see the glitter of silver from his scales where they caught the sharp mountain sunlight.

The dragon took great gulps of breath from the sky, and I saw his gullet swallowing them all down as if he could drink all of the scatterings of white clouds far above. For a small, very human moment, I was reminded of just how puny we all were compared to this great beast – and if he decided to sweep his head down and release a firestorm out onto us, then there would be little that we could do to run or hide before the entire crowd of fifty or so would be incinerated in a moment.

Selm *did* sweep his head down, when he had apparently had his fill of swallowing the sky – and I flinched when he opened his great maw and released—

Not fire and flame, but just breath. It must have been super-heated, however, as when it hit the surface of the lake below, there rose a great billow of mist, racing towards the crowd-

It was so eerie, and in the second before this wave of dragon-mist hit us, I confess that I closed my eyes and mouth. The waters of the lake rippled and waved with steam – and then we were engulfed.

It was like a refreshing summer rain. Warm at first, damp of course, but cooling instantly on the skin, and leaving a clear, light feeling behind it.

But as pleasant as this sensation was, it wasn't just a cleansing mist that hit us, it was a *feeling*. Something washed through my mind as easily as the mist rolled over the crowd of waiting villagers. It made me think of a time before all of my present worries and woes. Before the Deadweed and the Water Wraiths and foreign Queen-Empresses offering to start a civil war on my behalf.

It was a memory of my father.

'I believe in you, my son…' the memory rose in me as unstoppable and as inescapable as the mist had been. It was one of the last words that he had spoken to me, before setting flight for Roskilde and the Council of the Western Isles, to ask for aid against the Deadweed attacks.

I had never seen him again, and the Southern Lords that ruled as regents had quickly acted to strengthen their position and to sow discontent between the people of the South and the Binshee people of the mountains.

Where did you go? Why didn't you ever try to contact me? I thought at the memory of the strong man, the man whom I had admired so much. My father had been the one to first tell me about dragons, and he had been the one to encourage me to go 'find my dragon' in the wilds – which had been Aida, of course. He had believed in the power of what would become the Wild Company. Of the South acting together, strong, undefeated, as one.

'I believe in you, my son...' the memory repeated. I wanted to argue with it, I wanted to ignore it, I wanted to scream and cry and tell him that his faith had been misplaced – the South was in ruins, the Southern Lords cared even less for the outcast and minorities in their realms like the Binshee – and even the Binshee had split over my leadership!

'I believe in you...' but the memory was implacable. No amount of whining or arguing was going to change the inevitable: that my father had believed in me and had only allowed himself to go to the Western Council when he knew that he had no choice, and he knew that I was strong enough to do the right thing. To look after myself, and to look after the South.

With that memory came a sort of peace, a sort of confidence that I hadn't felt in a long while. *Why now?* I thought. I had remembered those words many times since my father had disappeared, but now it seemed that I could see them clearer, to understand what my father was really saying – that he loved me, and respected me.

"You get it, don't you?" Dayie surprised me by saying in a small voice next to me.

I opened my eyes and shook my head, feeling as though I had been in a daydream – but a pleasant, nourishing one, and now that I was awake, I felt healthy and whole, and what was more – I felt like I knew what I could do. *That* I could do it. That I could be the man that my father had wanted me to be – that my father had seen in me.

"Actually," I frowned, "I feel amazing."

I rolled my shoulders and stamped my feet a little, surprised at the warm feeling of strength that flowed through my limbs. Gone was the exhaustion and weariness of flying through the night and yesterday's battle with the Deadweed. I felt as if I could run a marathon!

"Yeah, it's not only you either, look…" Dayie seemed to read my thoughts as she nodded around us to where the other shepherds and villagers were starting to gasp and laugh in wonder at the magical effect that Selm had on them. Kids screamed in joy and started running in circles, and at least one old shepherd was standing up and laughing, loudly daring everyone to look at the wound he had suffered on his arms – now healed.

"Selm did this?" I said in awe, looking across the lake to the cliff above, and following the line of rocks to the ledge and the cave—

But Selm and the mysterious Dragon Monk Tian were gone, vanished as fully and completely as if they had never been there at all. I rationalized that they must have, of course, used the magical steams and fog that Selm had created to retreat back into the darkness of the cave – but with the sun now rising clear and warm in the sky, and the lake as placid as it had been just moments before – it almost seemed as though we had been party to a dream. Only one that left people healed, and happy.

"The Cave of Truth," I said, turning to grin at Dayie at my side. I was filled with a new sense of optimism. Maybe we *could* find the southern coast, and maybe we *could* defeat the Sea Witch, and maybe… but no. It was enough just to think about those two things.

CHAPTER 19
DAYIE, THE JOURNEY SOUTH

Although I was impatient to start on my journey, I saw the sense of Captain Daris's insistence that we return to Torvald with him, at least to re-provision. Akeem apparently *wasn't* so impressed with going back to Torvald, and I was thinking that maybe it was more of the same 'son of the South' stuff that he believed in, until I saw the final audience with the Queen-Empress Nuria.

She received us not at the palace, but once again in the Academy of the Dragon Riders, where she had been helping the clerks and scholars research more about Deadweed and oversee the production of more of the 'liquid dragon fire' they had invented.

"Of course, Lord Akeem – you will be pleased to know that Torvald will be dispatching a full shipment of the bottled Liquid Fire to the South forthwith…" she promised, her tone grave. "We received word from my brother the duke yesterday, and it seems that he is stuck in Dagfan. The sea roads have become unpredictable and impassable thanks to the Deadweed – and even I cannot guarantee him safe passage back to the citadel were he to land safely on Torvald shores." She looked annoyed.

It seemed that the Duke Robert was trapped, and that Dagfan was indeed still under attack. It became ever more important for me to fly south, as fast as possible!

"But the Liquid Fire will not be arriving by boat or by caravan," the woman with the dark hair and the small frame said. "Instead, two of the Wings of Dragon Academy Riders will be bearing it to the South, which means that they will arrive much sooner than any other form of travel. They will help the South defeat this Deadweed in any manner they can, and they will work to secure my brother," she stated. "After which time, their orders are to stand at ready should Dagfan – or *you,* Lord Akeem," she said very pointedly, "have need for them."

"I won't," Akeem said stiffly, earning a glare from Captain Daris. I was surprised at his strong defiance, but with the way his eyes sparked and his cheeks blushed with twin spots of deeper color, anyone could see he was truly upset.

"No?" The Queen-Empress Nuria appeared not to notice or care about Akeem's passions. "We shall see, I am sure."

After that, we were eager to take our leave, with Akeem seeming more insistent that we go now than even I was – but unfortunately, Queen-Empress Nuria had already outplayed us.

"It will be an honor to have you ride at the head of our Southern Expedition, along with the good Captain Daris here." Nuria nodded, and although I was prepared to argue that it would slow our flight time down – I realized that I hadn't told her or any of the other Torvaldites about what Akeem and I were *really* going to be doing – travelling to the distant south, in search of the Cave of Truth.

Why hadn't I told them? I asked myself as I felt stuck between courtesy and need. *Because the Cave of Truth was a sacred place to dragons, not people...* I decided. Selm hadn't explicitly or specifically told me not to tell anyone about the cave, but Tian's talk of how rare this place was – how ancient— it made me feel protective of it. I *didn't* want humans of any nation or city tramping there too easily – if even *we* could find it!

I also didn't want to have to explain to Queen-Empress Nuria that I would not be fighting to defend Dagfan, but instead seeking the Sea Witch. Maybe I was nervous of her opinion – of whether she would scoff at such a foolish quest, or take over my mission and send her best trained Riders to do what I knew *I* had to do. I had to go to the cave to find out the exact location of where the Sea Witch was, and I had to put a stop to her. Mengala and the Sorcerer of the Whispering Rocks had been right in a way – me and Saheera the Sea Witch were two sides of the same coin. Hearing Tian's story about the wandering Saheera had made me see that. She had started out just like me, a friend to plants and animals. For some reason, this made me feel even the more insistent that *I had to be the one to make her stop – and I would do that in any way that I could.*

We flew out of the citadel that afternoon, after an interminably long wait as the Wings of Torvald Dragons readied. Not that they didn't run a tight ship, I had to admire their efficiency. There were staffers and servants of the academy who brought out water and dried meats for the dragons to feast on, while the Dragon Riders saw to their own tack and saddles. That, I approved of!

But what took the longest twas the pomp and ceremony of everything. The Riders had to be assembled by their Captain Daris, all of whom roared some oath that they knew by heart – and then their individual orders and groupings were shouted out. After this, the Dragon Riders went to their dragons to spend a few moments alone with them, before mounting.

And then, I sighed, it was the Queen-Empress Nuria herself who came out to 'rally' the already-rallied Dragon Riders. She gave a short speech extolling their bravery and praising their compassion for flying to Dagfan's – and her own brother's— aid. It seemed that having the Queen-Empress herself here was a big deal not only to the human Dragon Riders, but also to their dragons as well, as if Nuria held a special position in their regard as the ruler of the *human* half of Mount Hammal.

Akeem grew more and more impatient by the moment, jostling in his saddle and scowling appallingly at the proceedings – but eventually, with the booming roar of the Dragon Horn, we were allowed to fly.

BWAAAARRM!

Akeem and Aida were the first to launch into the sky, with me and Zarr following close behind. This apparently caused a stir amongst the two flights of Torvald Riders, as there was a sudden clashing of wings and angered squawks from the Enclosure Dragons as we disturbed their carefully timed and perfectly choreographed take off.

Ha! I thought, and found my amusement mirrored in Zarr.

"We'll show them how we fly in the South!" He snarled joyously, as in answer, Aida gave her high-pitched, piercing screech.

Not that I wasn't impressed with how the Torvald Riders flew – they certainly had all the precision that we lacked in Dagfan, and I wondered if it owed to the fact that most of their enclosure dragons had grown up together, and so must have known each other—

"And their den mothers…" Zarr added, with a hint of regret.

"Do you miss her?" I asked him as the citadel grew smaller and further underneath us. It was customary, it seemed, for an 'outbound' flight of Torvald dragons to circle the Dragon Academy and the Sacred Mountain itself in wide, swooping spirals that wound higher and further – while Akeem and I opted for flying directly in a southward direction, using the benefit of the academy's height just under the top ridge of Mount Hammal to give us impetus and speed.

"How can I miss someone I never knew?" Zarr informed me, with what I thought was a characteristically draconian practicality.

I wondered at the truth of this. Did I miss the woman that I didn't even remember? My hand instinctively moved to the shell necklace that I now wore permanently around my neck. My mother's last present to me, and I felt...*something.* A snatch of song? *Mamma-la, Mamma-la...*

"I think I miss whatever should fill that space..." I mused, feeling a little awkward and complicated as we put the Dragon Mountain behind us. I thought of how Queen Jexia had told me that I would never master my magic until I reconnected with my mother, and how Selm the Oldest and his guardian Tian had told me that memories themselves were powerful – that they could be passed down from dragon to dragon, and able to heal even the worst of wounds...

"Ha. That is where I am luckier than you," Zarr said, enfolding my mind with his fierce, warm-charcoal affection. *"My first egg-memories were of you. I have no gap in my heart."*

Oh, Zarr... I thought, feeling more grateful than I had in a long time. And with a renewed sense of peace that was almost as strong as when Selm the Oldest had breathed his gift on me, we tore through the skies, heading towards the war-torn South.

The Torvald Dragons *were* good, apparently – they caught up with us easily, flying on the high thermals in the 'geese formation' that Akeem had used (I wondered how he felt about the fact that the Binshee weren't the only ones to discover that flying technique!)

"Ho! Lord Akeem!" Captain Daris shouted down to us as they matched our flight above. We had spent the entire day flying due south over Torvald lands, and for the first time I had some time to concentrate on what I was seeing underneath me. The Northern Kingdom was a green, lush, and fertile land, strewn with meadowlands, woods, and plains and lined with rivers that were studded with picturesque bridges. We had barely passed out of sight of one cozy little town before we saw another on the horizon – always with a tall tower on its walls with dragon platforms stacked along its sides.

That is what the South needs as well! I thought. If we managed to help the everyday people of the South accept dragons, then their oases and villages could also have platforms like this, welcoming the dragons, and helping them defend their villages.

But the Northern Kingdom of Torvald wasn't all roses and countryside, I saw in the next breath. It clearly was suffering from some of the same problems that the South was– with great scorched areas by the banks of rivers and lakes where the dragons had to set fire to the ravages of the Deadweed.

The farther south we travelled, the more prolific these dead patches became, always clustered at the rivers, and spreading back towards the Deadweed's arrival from the distant coast.

Captain Daris and his partner drew up alongside us, as the

afternoon was giving itself over to purpling twilight. “We have a way station by the Great Southern Road!” he called. “Dragon platforms, and with provisions kept stocked!”

It sounded like a good idea, so I was surprised when Akeem shook his head and instead pointed a little farther southwest of us.

The pass, I thought, remembering the route that we had flown north through the mountains on the way here. The Binshee in general, and Akeem’s Wild Company in particular, knew the High Mountains like the backs of their hands, and I gathered from the gesticulating Akeem that he didn’t want to waste any more time with Torvald customs when he could take a short-cut, straight to the South.

To be honest, I was surprised that Akeem was even agreeing to lead these two Wings of Torvald Dragons through one of the Binshee’s passes. Wasn’t Akeem always worried about whether Torvald would one day turn on the South?

“Aida says he isn’t happy about it, but it was her idea anyway...” Zarr informed me, with a slight note of humor to his voice. *Ha!* I thought, covering a wry grin with my hand. It was clear to me now who had the upper hand in the Aida and Akeem relationship!

The conversation continued for a while between the two Dragon Captains, but finally ended when Akeem shrugged, looked back at me with a nod, and allowed Aida to swoop lower underneath the Torvald Dragons and head for the Binshee pass. I could have stayed with the Torvald dragons and tried to figure out some more of their tactics I guessed –

but no – I wanted to get South as fast as I could as well. With a mighty beat of his wings, Zarr followed Aida, and we swept into the foothills of the High Mountains, their heads crowned with dark clouds and storm.

"No, I don't like bringing the Torvald dragons this way at all!" Akeem confided that night, after we'd settled on one of the narrow plateaus that cropped up here and there in the High Mountains. It was raining, and all of the dragons were subdued, huddling into their wings against the cliffs. Like nesting birds, the Torvald dragons roosted side by side, sharing body warmth as they huffed smoke into the airs. Aida and Zarr, however, seemed to be excluded from their company and had instead decided to huddle on the rocks above me and Akeem and our small campfire, battling the rain by the lee of a rocky outcrop.

"But what can I do?" Akeem looked annoyed—though that wasn't entirely unusual. His dark and curly hair was plastered to his forehead from the rain, but somehow, he still managed to look strong in his robes and leathers – not as bedraggled as I was sure that *I* looked, huddled in my flying blanket by the fire!

"We need to get you South, as quickly as possible – and these dragons need to get to Dagfan. Aida tells me that they've been fighting nearly every day. She can sense the anger and disquiet of her siblings, still there with Heydar," he said.

"Sand and Stars!" I swore, feeling suddenly ashamed of even

sitting here, as Latifa and Abir and Mengala, and the sorcerer – even Chief Talal—were right now fighting for their lives.

"I know…" Akeem was surprisingly perceptive, his dark eyes softening from the angered glare as they met mine over the firelight. "But there was something my father once said to me – that there are going to be plenty of times when you have to fight without food or water or sleep and with your very last ounce of strength…so when you can, you have to be sure to give yourself – and your dragon – those comforts."

It made sense, and so I nodded, knowing that we would need to be in good position for whatever waited for us at Dagfan or the flight south. But still, as I rolled up in my blanket by the fire's edge, I still couldn't help feeling guilty.

CHAPTER 20
DAYIE, WHO RULES DAGFAN?

"Aida wasn't joking, was she?" was all I could say when we saw the dark clouds on the horizon of the South. If Torvald had looked *scarred* by the ravages of the Deadweed, then the great Taval River – the mighty artery that cut across the top of the Southern Kingdom – looked *dead.* Its banks were black with soot and char, and its sluggish waters were dirty with flotsam of burnt Deadweed and the ruins of the small river towns.

"Skrargh!" The Torvald dragons appeared to be agitated by this sight, and for a moment I wondered at how numb I and Zarr, Akeem and Aida, Nas and Nandor had gotten to this sort of sight. It was terrible, of course, and my heart leapt into my throat with worry – but we did not shout our alarm and our dragons didn't keen reassuringly at each other as the Torvald dragons did.

Until, of course, the first wave of anger and despair rolled from Dagfan and through Zarr, Aida, and Nandor and washed right into me.

"Hyurk!" I gagged. Behind and above us the Torvald dragons started to lose their careful 'v' formations as the wave of dark emotions roiled through them, too.

"What is that?"

"Our dragon-brothers and sisters are under attack," Zarr growled at me, and in that moment, Akeem gave out a loud, victorious cry and surged ahead on the back of Aida. Even if the Vicious Orange was one of the smaller breeds of the dragons, (though their longer necks made them larger than the turquoise and green Sea Dragons) it didn't show as her wings blurred and she threw herself forward faster than a speeding desert falcon. With a roar of flame and smoke, Zarr tried to match her – and failed. But it wasn't a race. Not against each other, anyway.

It was a race against the Deadweed itself.

Dagfan grew on the horizon, its outer, ancient brick walls now dirty with soot marks. The small promontory that it straddled on the banks of the Taval River was a mess of embers and ash, with great piles of old bonfires still smoldering where the soldiers of the Southern Lords must have been attempting to burn the chopped-up plant parts.

Efforts had been made to clear stretches between the river and the nearest of the outlying settlements – it looked awful! A wasteland, as if nothing could live there ever again. Instantly, my eyes swam to the clutch of buildings on the other side of the rocky headland to the city of Dagfan – where the ring of the Training Hall still stood.

Thank the sands, I thought, seeing that it was still intact, and that it appeared to already be in full action.

CLANG-CLANG-CLANG! Our Dragon Gong was ringing, calling all our dragons to battle. Irafea and her two reunited Sinuous Blue daughters rose from the platforms, and the smaller Vicious Oranges of Akeem's Wild Company joined her in the air.

"Skreeeeee!" Aida let out a shriek of greeting, to be loudly met with raucous cries from her fellow Binshee dragons.

And out there, rising like a dark wave, was what everyone was so concerned about: a bank of Deadweed, lashing at the water and quickly eating up the already-scorched leagues between the shore and the city.

"Company! On me!" Akeem shouted, and Aida echoed with a ululating call – even if the distant Binshee Riders couldn't hear him, I knew that their dragons would follow Aida all the same. He plunged down towards the Taval River as if Aida were about to catch fish, before flattening into a whisper-fast charge, straight at the wave of the Deadweed.

I didn't need to ask if Zarr was ready, of course –he flared his wings to throw himself after Aida, as the other Binshee Riders joined us in their boiling, crow-attack flight.

Aida was the first to hiss her jet of dragon flame at the

approaching wave of Deadweed, before opening her wings out to swoop up and above the matt. I saw the rising, ponderous heads of the yellow flower-gourds attempting to follow her, knowing that they would open out into sickly-yellow petals to 'fire' their pollen-toxins into the air.

"Not if I can help it!" Zarr snarled, adding his own jet of flame to the fireball that Aida had created, and we were suddenly spiraling, rising on the thermals of our own dragon's flames, as our attack burst against the front vines.

The first wave of Deadweed flower heads withered in an instant, and the forward reaching, swinging, beating vines blackened and exuded their foul toxins into the air.

"Scarves!" Akeem called out, and I knew that he would be tugging down his gauzy, black scarf that he wore over his face as he flew above me, to cover his nose and mouth. I had a similar scarf ever since I had ridden with the Binshee Wild Company and was quick to do the same as Zarr banked high over the river, about to return for another attack.

I knew the scarfs wouldn't completely stop the toxins. Definitely not if the clouds of resin and oil and flower-dust hit any part of our exposed skin or eyes, but it would mean that we could breathe for a little longer.

Below us, the Binshee Wild Company were spilling their flames on the Sea Witch's attack; the fires that the Vicious Oranges could produce were sharper and more focused, not the rolling clouds of inferno that a Crimson Red like Zarr created – but they were like burning spears that chopped into the heart of the monstrous, water-borne thicket, hitting with such ferocity that they splintered vines and exploded knots of the weed at the same time as burning them.

But it wouldn't be enough, I thought, as I spared a glance back down the Taval to the west. *Where were the Torvald dragons?* I thought desperately, my eyes finding them flying high in two v-shaped wings. *Why weren't they attacking!* The Deadweed had formed a long mat that extended not quite as far as my eyes could see – as there was still the sparkle of dirty, greying water behind it – but it was a lot. Almost a half league's worth of the plant choking the river, from the looks of it,

Another new tactic from the Sea Witch, I thought, noticing that as they were burned, the 'front' of the Deadweed was constantly being replaced by the twirling, writhing vines from behind. Even with all of our dragon flames – could we manage to totally incinerate such a long stretch of the stuff?

"Skreyargh!" The Deadweed had almost reached the small, shattered, burned, and broken harbor next to Dagfan's promontory. I noticed that there were now *no* piers in the water (Dagfan had been busy to hastily build a new one after the last attack), just as there were now *no* intact boats anywhere to be seen – just the bobbing wreckage of timbers. *I guess that's why Duke Robert couldn't leave,* I realized. The boat that he and the Torvald trade delegation had arrived on must have been destroyed during one of the attacks, and that was why Queen-Empress Nuria had sent her Torvald dragons to 'rescue' her brother…

And just what *were* the Torvald dragons doing up there, anyway? I thought in annoyance as I looked up to see that the

Torvald Dragon Riders who had been following us had broken off from our mad charge and were instead high above the Taval River, circling and forming into two large, outward-pointed 'v' flights.

"Come on!" I hissed in frustration. "Do what you came here to do!"

The Wild Company were now rising from their own attacks, and I saw in alarm as several only barely managed to get away from the Deadweed vines that shot out to attempt to grab a reptilian ankle or two…

"wwwwiiii—"

That was when I heard it. The crashing sound of water and spray, like a dull roar in my ears, and beginning to form words once again…

"wiiiTTTCHHH!"

It was Saheera, I knew it. Exactly the same as before, she had found a way to lace the Deadweed with a curse directed solely for me, it would seem – or that was what Mengala the Old had thought…

"*WITCH!*" The riling water had an echoing snarl all of its own; an inhuman voice that rose above the battle and hit me like a wave of fog, bringing with it the waves of nausea, vertigo and dizziness, just as it had done before.

"*Dayie!*" Zarr said, and I felt his worry as he reached towards my pain with his mind.

"No!" Not this time, I begged him, closing my eyes as I let the waves of sickness hit me. I wondered if I was going to throw up. *No.* I am stronger than this. I can do this…

"Mamma—" One of my hands had risen in the air, and I was already mumbling my mother's song, the key to my magic, before I clamped my teeth down on my tongue and refused to let the words out.

Not yet, I promised myself. After my experience of wholeness – or wellness – with Selm the Oldest, I must have also been given some sort of perspective. Yes, the Sea Witch was hurting me. Yes, the Sea Witch was much more powerful than me, and she appeared intent on destroying me…

But I am stronger than this, I knew. I didn't have to use my magic yet, and risk transmitting my pain to Zarr. I would try to win this battle first without magic, and then, if all else failed…

"WITCH!" The roar grew into a crescendo, as I saw the Dead-weed starting to do *something* far below me…

It appeared to have stopped its forward charge to overwhelm Dagfan and instead was writhing and twisting around itself in a vortex, as more and more of the half-league long mat of the weed added and rolled over the frontrunning vines…

It formed a mound of weed at the mouth of the harbor, taller than even the Torvald galleon had been. And then the mound grew higher, vines interlacing each other and crawling over each other, their own thorns puncturing their own leaves as it rose into a tower, a mountain—

Climbing towards me.

WHOOOSH!

Flame exploded from around the base of the rising tower of Deadweed, and for a moment it was hard for me to see what it was that was causing it, as dragon flame always has a long tail of smoke and fire from where it ignites just outside the dragon's maw, arcing to its target. These were *explosions* of fire, great gobbets orange and red that burst open like the flower heads of the Deadweed itself, and then – *didn't go out.*

Even when they hit the surface of the rolling water, the brackish and soot-laded froth between the constantly twitching vines – the flames appeared resistant to the water, forming a dull glow *underneath* the ripples longer than any normal flame should.

"Watch out!" a voice cried, and I turned my head to see that the Torvald dragons, and, more specifically it was Captain Daris, angling his Stocky Green into an attack run – and not allowing his dragon to release her own fire against the Deadweed, but instead his second Rider – the blonde woman, half-stood in her saddle and threw something down, past Zarr's angling wing and belly.

It looked like the javelin the Dragon Riders of Torvald favored, along with the Great Bow. But this wasn't any javelin I had seen before – either in the North or the South. Instead of a wickedly sharp point on the end, it had instead a very large, bulbous 'teardrop' object.

Why are they throwing over-sized mallet things at it? I thought, an instant before the projectile weapon struck one side of the Deadweed tower and exploded into liquid flames.

Instantly, I saw what it was. A clay 'head' which had been attached to a javelin – slightly longer than any other I had seen, which I guessed must be so that the weight flew true when thrown. Inside that clay compartment must be the 'liquid dragon fire' that Duke Robert had been loudly bragging about, and, as Zarr continued to circle up, away from the reaching Deadweed and the hissing curse of the Sea Witch, I had a chance to see just how effective it really was.

The Torvald Fire was like lamp oil in many respects – but a hundred times more flammable. Lamp oil could be used to burn on the surface of water or buildings, but it evaporated quickly. The flames below us were thicker somehow, and able to last underwater.

The Deadweed recoiled from where it had been hit, and the mutated weed reacted defensively—an observation which alone was enough to shock me, for it was one of the first times that I had ever seen it do so— as it rolled those burning tentacle vines underneath itself into the water, to be replaced by newer vines –

But the water was still steaming! I saw and laughed despite my spinning head. The Torvald fire was still burning, and still strong even in the areas where it sat stubbornly on the water, looking impossible in small, eddying and floating mats of its own to rival the Deadweed. The Sea Witch's creation would recoil from one strike, only to roll its leafy body into a still floating, still burning patch of Torvald fire, and thus would continue to burn!

"Yes!" I said, as the second wing of the Torvald Dragons

rushed in, this time in perfect 'v' formation, breaking apart at the last moment to fly both to the right and left of the tower of Deadweed, each of the 'second' Riders on the Torvald dragons to throw their own Torvald fire javelins.

Flames stuck to the base, and then the walls of the Deadweed tower, and the edifice started to buckle, its body weakened by its own shriveling, charcoaling limbs. My nausea started to subside, my shaking and aching limbs started to return to normal as I realized what was about to happen.

With a mighty crash, the Deadweed fell, leaving its wrecked body – still green and yellow in some parts— to be easy pickings for the Wild Company, the Training Hall, and the two wings of Torvald dragons themselves.

The Deadweed attack was only one of our problems, I realized almost as soon as we landed at the Training Hall.

"How many?" Chief Talal's worried, pinched-red face met me as I dismounted from Zarr on one of the Training Hall's wooden landing platforms (which I myself had asked to be installed – they were flimsy things compared to the stone balconies, turrets and perches that Torvald provided, but we were getting there, I thought).

Just not getting there fast enough, not for my or anyone else's liking, for we didn't have anywhere near the space needed to accommodate the Torvald dragons. I knew that we had the caverns below to house dragons – but as soon as I thought of it, Zarr let out a grumble of anger behind me.

You won't have to ever sleep down there if you don't want to, I confided in him. as I turned to answer Chief Talal. Zarr could nest with Aida and the Wild Company dragons if he preferred.

"Two wings of twelve, so… twenty-four new dragons!" I said with glee.

"Twenty sand's-blowing four?" Talal, already beleaguered just with the responsibility of running the Training Hall, looked ready to pull what little was left of his pepper-grey hair out. "We haven't the supplies to feed twenty-four! Dagfan has been without any trade goods for almost a week – and that means no salted fish from the river communities, no cured goat from the northern highlands, no…"

It was a problem, I knew, but it was hard for me to put too much weight into it, as my head was filled with the recent victory – and on the back of that victory, I knew that I had to be gone from here soon – to travel south. Akeem, too, appeared impatient to be going, as he landed on the platform adjacent to mine, hopped lightly down to speak to the seconds of his Wild Company – but waved off the Dragon Handler's offers to tend to Aida's saddle.

Chief Talal was a soldier first and foremost – well, a dragon rider of Dagfan first, I should say – but he had been elevated to his position by the Southern Lords, and it was clear to everyone that the worst part of this new job for him was the administration of tasks such as arranging the dragon supplies, and writing requests to the Southern Lords.

"We have brought provisions for our men, so you don't need to worry about that, sir," Captain Daris of the Torvald Dragon Academy said, dismounting from where he and his partner had landed their Stocky Green on the same platform as Zarr. A ripple of unease spread up through me from Zarr, echoed in the rattle of wings from the Training Hall dragons below. To its credit, the Stocky Green Torvald dragon appeared completely calm as it nonchalantly sat in the middle of another dragon territory.

"And I must thank you for your offer of hospitality," Captain Daris said as he took off his horned helmet and gave a bow to Chief Talal. I wondered briefly if Daris was being sarcastic, but the formality seemed to make Talal uncertain of how to act.

"That's all very fine. Thank you, sir…" Talal gave a short, head bob of a bow, before throwing a glaring look at me. "But I must admit that I don't know how we can house and feed your dragons…"

"I've already told them to camp out in the plains and rocks beyond," Daris said. "As I say, my Riders have camp rations on them for a few days easily, and the dragons are no stranger to hunting their own food when they need. You have a great river there, I see…"

"Useless," Talal said quickly. "We daren't fish in it anymore – which is a sore blow to our dragons, because of, well, it's fairly obvious…" He threw a look over the walls at the clogged, brackish banks of the Taval River.

The Deadweed, I nodded in alarmed agreement. There was

still so much of the burnt body of the weed in the waters that it would take days of uninterrupted effort if not weeks to dredge it all out. Who knew what terrible poisons even the burnt and rotten bits of the weed still held?

"We will find a way, sir," Daris said with a stern grin. "We are Dragon Riders of Torvald, and we are used to long and difficult campaigns..."

I winced, expecting the effect of that braggadocio to be met with as much suspicion and hatred from Chief Talal as they would be from Akeem, but I was pleasantly surprised when it wasn't.

"Well, the Training Hall dragons here have also seen several campaigns..." Chief Talal said, and I was sure that he was sounding a little embarrassed, as when you might meet a favorite hero of yours, and struggle to match up. "But – were you at the Siege of Rilke's Island? I heard that the dragon battles there lasted for three days!"

It was not a campaign that I had ever heard of, but Captain Daris apparently had.

"I led a squadron of dragons and Riders myself, rooting out the bandits who had occupied Rilke!" The Torvald captain soon warmed to the subject. "They had set up some devilishly clever trebuchet traps that fired rocks and metal spikes – and, being on an island, they had a ready access to water to douse our dragon flames..."

"Oh, I had heard..." Chief Talal seemed impressed.

Oh great, I rolled my eyes. *At least these two will be getting on!*

"Excuse me, chief..." I butted in, my mind turning to the next worrying point. I nodded down to where the Training Hall Arena wasn't filled with resting or training dragons, as should be the case, but was instead half-filled with canvas-stretched camp tents. "Are we training up more recruits?" *Maybe they've turned this place into an emergency barracks...* I reasoned.

"No, ah..." Talal's earlier enthusiasm was wiped off of his face in an instant, and instead was replaced by a dark look. "That's Lord Qadir's troops."

"Lord Qadir?" I thought. He was the youngest of the Southern Lords, the younger brother who never appeared to be much interested in what I had to say when I had given my audiences with the three de-facto rulers of the South. I was about to venture what Qadir was doing stationing his troops here, when there was a strident shout from Akeem as he marched atop the battlement wall towards our platform. His scarf was pulled down, and I could see the anger in his tight features.

"And *why* is Lord Qadir declaring himself the Lord of the South now, Chief Talal?" the Southern Prince barked as he jogged up the wooden steps to the platform. He didn't stop moving until he was standing almost toe to toe with Talal.

To his credit, the chief did not budge or quaver in his stance, and I saw some of the old soldier's steel in his eyes and in his voice, as he said. "*Lord* Akeem," (he used the title with obvious distrust) "while you, Rider Dayie, and Lieutenant

Rider Nas have been gone, Dagfan has been at a state of almost constant war. Waves of the Deadweed, alternating with rivers of the Water Wraiths. Many things have changed, and we have lost many lives…" he snipped back.

Ouch. The disapproval that Talal held our northern mission was clear. That was going to make it ten times harder to convince him that I had to fly south again if I was to find and put a stop to the Sea Witch for good.

"Then don't tell them…Just go…" Zarr beside me huffed some smoke. He was always so straight-to-the-point. I sometimes wished that I could be as honest as a dragon.

"That doesn't explain…" Akeem started, but Chief Talal cut him off.

"Lord Ehsan is dead," Talal said.

"What!?" I couldn't stop myself from bursting out. Admittedly, I hadn't known Lord Ehsan all that well – or at all, really – but he had seemed eager to seek solutions to this crisis, rather than his brothers who had both seemed intent on arguing.

"I'm afraid so," Talal said. "He foolishly decided to sally forth from his tower inside the city with a ragtag fleet to try and clear a path for trade ships to get through. But they failed, and Ehsan and all of the available fighting or trading ships that Dagfan had went down with him."

"Why didn't he wait for us to return!" Akeem looked shocked. "Or why didn't he approach Heydar, my second? And ask my Wild Company to help?"

"The Wild Company have been invaluable in defending Dagfan," I heard Talal say in clipped tones, "but that does not mean that the Southern Lords cannot choose regular Dagfan soldiers to fight at their sides..."

"Regular Dagfan soldiers who got killed?" Akeem seemed livid. It was probably about time that I stepped in, as there seemed to be a lot more going on in this argument than just the fact that the eldest – and nicest, I thought sadly – Southern Lord had died. And Akeem needed his friends to help him sometimes, just like he listened to Aida.

Chief Talal still mistrusts the Wild Company, and Akeem thinks that the Dagfanites are fools... I wondered how Aida would make Akeem see that he couldn't just be angry – he needed to be clever...

"Gentlemen, enough!" I said firmly.

Akeem looked at me sharply, but to my surprise, he held his tongue and waited for me to speak.

"We can discuss why things happened after the fact, but please, for the sake of the South – we must find out *what* has happened first! If you will, Chief Talal – continue with your story." I cast a look at Akeem to see if he was going to over-ride me, but he nodded.

Talal licked his lips, appearing stubborn for a moment, but he inclined his head and began. "With Lord Ehsan dead, the next thing we knew, Lord Kasim was imprisoned, and Lord Qadir had ordered a martial law – *his* martial law on all barracks and storehouses, and, of course – here. He claimed that Lord Kasim was trying to take over Dagfan and the South."

"And Lord Qadir quickly rushed in to save the day?" I murmured, not believing it for a second. Not that I didn't doubt that Lord Kasim *might* have tried to take over Dagfan and the Southern Lords all by himself – he had appeared the most militaristic of any of the three brothers – but it was all too neat. Why would Qadir of all people, Kasim's own younger brother, care about whether Kasim was in charge or not?

Unless he had the same ambitions, of course…

"Well, all I know is that Lord Qadir is in charge of Dagfan now, and he has troops everywhere he can, rationing the supplies to feed the people and the troops," Talal glowered. He had always enjoyed a bit of a free rein out here to do as he wished – even if he had to always write up the scrollwork to justify it. The thought of having Qadir's troops here, inspecting his scant resources or telling him what to do would clearly be an anathema for the proud man.

"And what of Duke Robert, sir?" Captain Daris said, eloquent and courteous, but filled with restrained emotion. One look at the older man's face (he must have been about an age with Chief Talal, I realized briefly) was enough to tell me that he was *highly* concerned what these new developments must mean for him and his Torvald dragons.

The Torvald riders had, after all, come to rescue Duke Robert from the Deadweed. I wondered if they would have to rescue him from human dangers instead–and even sooner than they might have anticipated after our successful battle.

"The Torvald Duke is still a guest of Lord Qadir," Chief Talal stated quickly. "I believe that he has elected to stay out of southern politics, but…"

But anyone with half a brain could see where this could lead. Lord Qadir had seized the South when it was at its weakest, and he now had the Training Hall and its dragons under his eye, as well as the second most powerful person in the Torvald kingdom under his roof. Qadir could use Robert as a bargaining chip, or even a ransom against Captain Daris and his dragons, or Queen-Empress Nuria and her future trade deals.

"I want to see him." Captain Daris apparently came to the same conclusion. "And, sir, if you will not escort me to my duke's side, then I will fly all of my Torvald dragons to that city of yours, and *demand* that I see him."

Woah! I thought, feeling like I was stuck in the middle of a nightmare, and that it was only about to get worse. I don't know why I intervened at that moment. Maybe it was the still-lingering memory that Selm the Oldest had given me just a brief taste of.

The land, and all of its denizens, from humans to dragons, where once whole and at home. There was no strife between people, and we all lived a magical life…

Far, far different from the posturing and machinations of the world today. And besides which, every one of us here had almost died fighting a far greater enemy.

"Captain Daris, Chief Talal, Lord Akeem…" I looked at each one in turn. "These are difficult and stressful times… But there is an enemy somewhere out there who will stop at nothing until all traces of what we are, what we were, and what we have come to love has been wiped off the face of the land," I said with certainty, remembering what Tian had told me of Saheera's 'cleansing' ambition. "However insulting, or grievous our politics appear to be, we must remember that fact."

The three men didn't particularly look that convinced. Which was fair enough, as I wouldn't have been either – if I were advocating peace with Lord Qadir. Which I wasn't at all.

"None of us, from Torvald to the Southern Lords, the Binshee or the Training Hall can afford to lose *one* more life, let alone soldiers and dragons in a possible battle," I stated. "So, what you three men and I are going to have to do is to find a way to…*deal* with Lord Qadir which only involves *him,* and *us.*"

"Oh." Chief Talal looked surprised at my suggestion, whereas Chief Daris appeared to grudgingly approve.

Akeem on the other hand, was grinning.

CHAPTER 21
AKEEM, PARLAY

Dayie's plan was a simple one, if dangerous. I wasn't entirely sure if dangling me in front of Qadir as bait was something that Heydar would approve of – so I didn't ask him. Instead, I stood on the wide battlement of the Lord's Tower with Aida at my side. As soon as we'd landed, a host of Qadir's archers had rushed up to the top of the tower, arrows nocked and ready.

"Sssss!" Aida hissed at them, making the soldiers nervous and jittery. But there was only me. And a dragon.

"I've come to seek an audience with Lord Qadir," I called out to them, waiting for the one who must be their sergeant or captain to identify themselves.

"He's not taking visitors, Binshee--" a stony-faced woman started. She wasn't armed with bows, but with a short spear – and I took it that she had to be the superior officer here.

"He'll want to see me," I interrupted before she could finish whatever insult was on her tongue. "I'm Lord Akeem J'ahal-lid, rightful heir to the southern throne."

There was a murmur of whispers from the soldiers – none of whom had seen me before, but probably would have known of my existence. What rumors and nightmare stories were moving through their minds? *The exiled, renegade son of the old prince…the old prince who abandoned the South…the outcast captain of the Wild Company…* I waited until I saw the stories mix and settle in their minds. How true were those stories, they must be thinking. Had I come back to demand my throne?

There was a commotion at the back of the guard complement as messengers were dispatched, and I waited patiently.

Okay, time for phase two, I thought, lifting my hands in a welcoming gesture to the soldiers. As soon as I moved, I saw the archer's attention flicker as they tracked me, in case I were to call for my dragon to set fire to all of them, right here and now…

"I don't like this plan," Aida confided in me.

"I know," I murmured, raising my voice to speak to the guards. "Look, as a gesture of good faith I will even send my dragon away!" I clapped my hand and earned a scowl from Aida – I would pay for appearing to boss her about later, I was sure, but with her characteristic shriek, she jumped into the air, circled around the tower once, and flew back towards the Training Hall…

"I see you have come to your senses, Akeem!" snapped a sharp, critical voice as Lord Qadir appeared. He must have been hiding below, waiting for the threat of the dragon to disappear. "You have come to parlay?"

Coming to my senses? I thought. Was the Lord Qadir really so delusional that he thought that I had come here to parlay with him? Did he not know who I was? By all rights of birth and blood – *I* was the one who had the right to be here, while *he* was the usurper!

He walked up the stone steps to the top of the tower, surrounded by his guards. There was no way that I could get to him even if I wanted to…

The Lord Qadir was a small man, and a young one at that. He had changed from his tight-fitted jerkin and trews to the more opulent greens and indigo robes that his late older brother Ehsan had favored. At the small man's hands and neck sparkled gold and silver trinkets. It looked as though Qadir was taking his new position very seriously.

"Parlay?" I frowned, hopping lightly from the battlements until I was level with the soldiers. An easy target for them. If someone was going to die here, then the very least I could do was to ensure that it was me rather than any other…

"Akeem!" Aida shrieked in the air and in my head.

Have no fear, my heart – nothing will happen, I promised, but she knew that I could not make such a bald statement. "I suppose that I would be willing to hear your terms of withdrawal from the Training Hall," I said good-naturedly. "And your release of Lord Kasim and Duke Robert."

"But…what…bah…!" Lord Qadir looked stunned at my apparent arrogance. "You have *no* idea who you are talking to, do you?" he called out. "I am the *only* Southern Lord left. All of the other soldiers have sworn themselves to me. *Seize him!"* he barked at the soldiers, who hesitated for just a briefest moment, probably thinking it's never wise to anger a man who is friends with a dragon. I capitalized on that moment as I called out to them.

"You *can* seize me and lock me up just like you did with your brother, Qadir – but then things would go *very* bad for you indeed," I said, repeating what Dayie had told me to say.

"Lies and foolishness! Seize him!" Qadir demanded, and the archers stepped forward with their arrows nocked, as the soldiers at their rear reached for their swords.

Two can play at that game, I grinned, flicking my father's sword from its scabbard and settling into a defensive crouch.

"Hah!" Qadir seemed, if anything, entirely amused by my display of defiance. "One swordsman against ten or so archers? Are you so good that you can knock ten arrows from the air, Akeem?"

Try me, I glared at him. "You need to reassess your situation, Lord Qadir. I will not allow you to imprison me, so you will have to kill me – and as soon as you do, you will start a war that you cannot win."

"Pfagh!" Qadir seemed amused by my posturing, as well he might be – as powerful as the Wild Company were, they were only a small force, and Lord Qadir now commanded every able-bodied soldier in all of the South.

"I speak of the war against the *Deadweed,*" I said in a low tone, my eyes flicking between the first archer and the next, trying to gauge which was the most nervous and the most likely to fire accidentally.

"The Deadweed? I have the Duke Robert Flamma-Torvald, right here in my very own halls!" Qadir stated. "With his new Liquid Fire, we will be sure to defeat it!"

"If you harm me, my Wild Company will seek revenge, Qadir," I stated tersely. "Can you afford to fight a war against my dragons and the Deadweed?"

"The Torvald dragons will never allow your Vicious Oranges to attack me while I have Duke Robert!" Qadir crowed with apparent victory. Clearly this had been the gambit that he had expecting. He wouldn't be expecting what came next, however…

"You mean *those* Torvald dragons?" I nodded over the assembled heads.

"Skreach!" There was a roar of defiance from farther out, over the Training Hall as first one wing of twelve glittering dragons swept into the air, immediately followed by another. They banked in the warm breeze, and started to power their way northward. Away from Dagfan.

"What are they doing? Where are they going?" Qadir burst out, and I could hear the worry in his voice. He only had the Training Hall dragons – ten with Riders at best. He would have been counting on the Torvald beasts for his protection against the Deadweed.

"Torvald does not parlay with kidnappers or tyrants," I said. "Those two flights under Captain Daris will return to their own lands, where they will seek to destroy their own invasion of the Deadweed, and, if you harm the duke, I am sure that when their job is done, they will return to wreak their revenge on whatever is left of you."

"But their duke will die!" Qadir said in horror.

"They still have their queen. And I guess they think that it is up to you to keep him alive now, on your own. Against the Deadweed, and without my Wild Company," I said.

The young man looked apoplexed between rage and confusion. He wasn't a very clever man, I saw – just a greedy one. He had thought that he could bargain the life of Duke Robert for the service of Torvald. To be honest, I had no idea just *what* Queen-Empress Nuria would do at the news that her brother was being held prisoner – but Dayie thought that this gambit would work, and, I trusted her.

"I have a counteroffer for you, Lord Qadir," I called out. "Release Lord Kasim, and release Torvald's Duke – and you can remain a Lord of the South." *For a while,* I thought to myself. "But you won't be the only lord. You will be joined by Lord Kasim, and Chief Talal, and the Chieftains of the

Binshee tribes, and together you will help each other rule wisely."

"What?" Qadir didn't appear to understand.

"The South must stand united against the Deadweed," I said, echoing Dayie's words almost exactly, and knowing that they were true. "Dagfan *can* be protected – but only if you agree to work with Lord Kasim, the Training Hall, and the Binshee."

Qadir's eyes squinted as if he were trying to work out the catch.

Which was the beauty of Dayie's plan. There was no catch. It was just showing the man the simple truth.

"These are your choices, Qadir… Stand down your troops and agree to share power, or be left on your own against the Deadweed," I stated.

Really, I was offering him no choice at all.

"Release Lord Kasim from the dungeons," Qadir garbled angrily, looking dejected. He must have known that there was no way that he could fight the Deadweed and the Water Wraiths on his own. And when faced with a certain death, it is surprising how fast even the most stupid and arrogant of men can swallow their pride. "And tell the Duke Robert that it is safe for him to leave the tower."

Aida? It's done, I thought at my dragon-sister, to hear her flush of anger flooding through my mind.

"You humans and your politics! Always so complicated!" But despite her scorn of our ways, Aida transmitted her message to

the apparently retreating Torvald dragons just as we had discussed earlier, and they wheeled around in the sky, ready to return. They had never any intention of leaving the South without Duke Robert of course, but Qadir wouldn't know that.

Yes, us humans and our politics, I had to agree with Aida. These games made me feel tired, and even more certain of what I had decided.

I have given up the throne of my father, the thought circled around my head just as the Torvald dragons were circling around Dagfan. It made me feel light-headed, dizzy even. Not even Lord Qadir or Talal or Dayie and any of the others had realized what I had just done and what its implications were – but *I* knew.

I had agreed to give Lord Qadir a place on a Council of Lords along with every other major power-broker in the South, including the Binshee Chieftains. *Even after Queen-Empress Nuria had promised a helping hand in getting me to the throne; a throne that was rightfully mine...*

But I didn't want it. I had tried to rule the Binshee but it had led to that brute T'Lad splitting from the rest of us. Some people weren't ready to let go of their pride and their resentment, and, as crazy as it sounded – I knew that *I* was a figurehead for that hatred and jealousy at the moment.

If I wanted to be true to Selm's vision of me – of a man who fulfilled his father's wishes for peace, then I had to swallow *my* pride as well. What was best for the South was not necessarily having a divisive renegade prince try to force everyone together. I had to put the South first as my father had wanted and known that I could do.

And this was how I would do it. I would ensure that there would be a balance of power between the Southern Lords and the Binshee, and that no one group would ever have power over another again.

CHAPTER 22
DAYIE, AND THE TRUTH

"Do you think the truce will hold between Qadir and Kasim?" I asked Akeem that very evening. He looked doubtful, but I had to put my faith in something. "It has to," I muttered. "For Dagfan's sake," and I earned a morose grumble of agreement from Akeem.

The Lord Qadir had indeed removed his troops from the Training Hall, which allowed more of the Torvald dragons to at least take turns perching with and greeting the Dagfan dragons. The Duke Robert had been 'released' – he was never implicitly held hostage but had appeared only too glad to camp with Captain Daris and the rest of his men, as Akeem and I took our leave.

It felt like we were sneaking away from the battle – as the expectation of bloodshed hung heavy over the entire city – but I knew what we were doing was right. We had to find the Cave of Truth if we were to stop Saheera.

"Ready?" Akeem interrupted my thoughts as he looked over at me from where he sat upon Aida's back. We were perched on the side of the Training Hall as the sounds of feasting swam up to meet us from below.

The rightful Prince of the South looked different, I saw. His eyes were brighter, and he was looking around him, looking at *me* as if he were really seeing us for the first time. Usually he was so clouded in his own thoughts. What had changed?

The new Council of the South, I realized. That had been his idea – to offer Lord Qadir back his lordship along with inviting others. Which, quite frankly, had shocked me. *I* had only pressed on Akeem the idea of the Torvald dragon ruse, and making Qadir see how isolated he would be if he continued. It had been Akeem who had reinstated him as a lord.

"Are you okay?" I asked him. *How could he be? He's just given up any chance of his father's throne, hasn't he?*

"Actually – yes, yes, I am." Akeem said, and his tone was lighter and easier than it had been for a long time.

Why? I thought, but I didn't have to mouth my confusion, as Akeem was already chuckling at what he saw in my face.

"For once, it feels like a weight has been lifted off of my shoulders," he said. "I think it was Selm who showed me the way forward. I had been beating myself up about whether or not I could rule the South, whether I could fill my father's shoes when the entire South was so divided…" Akeem shrugged as if it made no difference now.

"And?" I prompted him. "What changed?"

"I realized that *I* don't have to save the South. Not on my own," he said, looking over at me quickly and away again.

Was he talking about me?

"It will take many years for the South to heal," Akeem continued, not looking at me. "And the best I can do is to help that happen. To bring the Wild Company and the Binshee out of their mountains and let the rest of the people know that we're here to protect them – all the while helping the new Council of Southern Lords make the right decisions. One day, in time – maybe the South will be ready for its own ruler – a prince or a king or…" Akeem coughed as if embarrassed.

Wow. I thought, surprised at the change in him. "Well," I said, equally as flustered for some reason although I didn't know why. "I think that you are the most noble man I have ever met," I said, and meant it. Who else would give up their chance at a throne for the good of the land?

"*Pfagh!* Not if there isn't any land left to save!" Akeem said abruptly, meaning that we had a long way to go yet, and he was right. We still had to find and stop Saheera.

Several key people had been told what we were about to do: Nas, Talal, the duke, and Daris of course. But I didn't want to make a big thing of our mission. There was no guarantee that we would even be able to find this cave, or that we would make it there and back in time to help!

"Pfagh! Have you so little faith in my abilities?" Zarr underneath me asked.

"Oh, it's not your abilities I worry about, wyrm – it's mine," I leaned over to give his neck as much of a hug as I could. I took a deep breath and straightened up, before nodding at Akeem.

"Ready." I said, and at that, we leapt into the night.

Our journey south was mostly uneventful – if you didn't count the rising sense of panic that I felt every time that Zarr's senses jangled with the smell of scorched earth. Even in the dark of night, it was possible to see that great swathes of land had been fired and burned either by the Training Hall Dragons or the villagers themselves. Akeem pointed out what used to be important oases for his people, now nothing but blackened ruins.

The Deadweed had stretched further into the deserts than I had thought possible, and it seemed the Water Wraiths must have helped it to 'hop' from distant creek to oases, following the watery army's moisture.

Neither of us slept much on that first night, as I was constantly wondering if at any moment a shadow in the night would suddenly twitch and rear up to reveal that it was a hiding mat of the weed, just waiting for us.

By the time that dawn had broken, Akeem told me. "I know where there's some cover!" And we flew toward a promontory of rocks on the edge of the deep deserts, where we would wait out the hottest part of the day. As the horizon was disturbed by the darker rise of rocks, Akeem signaled that we had made it, and led us in.

The day spent under the cool shade of the rocks was, for me, disturbed by dreams of wild water and falling – which was odd, because I was on the edge of the desert, and the only time that I had ever seen the ocean had been on the back of Zarr – and he would never let me fall!

"Never." He breathed his reassurance into me, as the ground started to lose its heat, and a fresher breeze from the north eddied around us.

"We should go now, while the winds are up," Akeem told me. He must have only had a little sleep during our siesta, as he had also been busy rationing the water into separate pouches, and setting up a gauzy sort of awning on one side of our camp. Seeing him like this, working patiently and quietly in the desert showed me a side to the young man that I hadn't seen before. He was a different man when he was just being a Rider, not the rightful Prince of the South. And, I had to admit, I liked *this* Akeem, the one comfortable in his own skin, the one who was quietly skilled rather than arrogantly prideful, much better. His decision to remake a fairer, truer Council of Lords appeared to only be agreeing with him.

No wonder he didn't want to challenge Qadir to the rulership of the South, I admitted as we packed our things and got ready to fly again. I knew that he could have – that had been my second plan to free the duke – for Akeem to announce that he had the support of Torvald and the Training Hall of Dagfan – but it was something that he had been adamantly against.

I allowed these worries to occupy my mind as we leapt into the air to resume our desperate flight south. It was easier to think of Akeem's problems than it was the Cave of Truth, for no sooner did it cross my mind, then all my worries came crowding in. What if it didn't work? What if the cave had been destroyed in the many long centuries that Selm himself might have been there? What if the cave was already covered with Deadweed? What if I wasn't strong enough to defeat Saheera?

But we flew on, into the cooler evening, and then through the night, because there was only one way to learn if any of my doubts had merit.

The deep deserts were freezing at night, a fact I had known but was never quite prepared for after the day's claustrophobic heat. Luckily, I had a full-bodied Crimson Red to keep me warm, as he flew southwards at a steady but taxing pace, heading for that dragon sense image inside his head that Selm had given us.

The blackened scorches on the pale sands grew fewer and farther between as the sands gave way to rolling dunes. We passed an oasis every few watches, but it wasn't until the sun had already crossed the horizon and was climbing towards midmorning that Akeem allowed us to stop once more, at an apparently untouched oasis with a scattering of trees and rocks, and an ancient brick well. There was enough shade for both us and the dragons, and we flung ourselves down into it greedily.

The water of this place was fresh and inviting, and the dragons took great lapping draughts of the stuff, so much that I was scared that they would drink it dry! But of course, they could not, as Akeem told me that these oases were fed by deep underground rivers and lakes, so deep that they were always fresh, and never contaminated by whatever was happening above.

After another day of sleeping fitfully and uncomfortably – with dreams of crashing waves all around me— Zarr woke me up with the prod of his snout as soon as the sun started to lower itself towards the horizon.

"It's time. We're not far," he told me, and I could sense a change in him.

"What is it?" I asked, to which he raised his snout and sniffed at the air.

"There is something…different in the air."

It was some watches later, past the middle of the night and towards what I thought had to be the early morning, when I knew what he meant. The ground below us remained the deep, rolling waves of pale sand dunes, unchanging and yet constantly complex and dizzying to the eye. And yet, there *was* something different in the air– a freshness, a tang of salt

As we flew on towards the horizon, it was at the first break of sunlight that I realized what it was.

There were clouds on the horizon – and it had been a long time since we had seen any.

And, it seemed, there were birds as well. I could hear their distant cries further ahead of us, and it wasn't long before I could *see* distant flecks of white and grey swooping and spiraling the clouds.

"Gulls," Akeem shouted over. "That means water."

That meant the coast, I thought. The southern coast. The *extreme* southern coast of the entire Midmost Lands; a place of legends and scare-stories. We had made the journey with great ease, I thought. Far easier than I had anticipated the journey to be.

"Selm's sense-map," Zarr informed me, and I knew he was right. The picture of this place that Selm had given to Zarr had included with it all of the easiest rivers of air to take, as well as each and every oasis to stop at. Selm's map had avoided any peril that could have befallen us in this journey, and once again, I thanked the stars for the opportunity we'd had to meet that noble and wise creature.

It was easier to fly through the rising morning this time, for despite the sun's fierce heat, it was tempered with a freshness from whatever waters we were approaching. The horizon, too, took on a different color. Green, which meant life, vegetation.

Both mine and Zarr's spirits rose as we saw that the southern coast was indeed rich with life. There was some sort of wood-land – but filled with no tree I had ever known. These had large, wavy fronds and scaled bark – and beside their grove rose a headland of rocks that eventually swept upwards into a mountain range…

The last hill of the mountain range, I remembered Selm's directions.

Which was over a bay, just as Selm had said.

"We found it," I said to Akeem, and wondered why I didn't feel happier. Instead, I felt a sick sort of apprehension in my stomach that I couldn't explain.

The little bay by the last hill of the mountain range wasn't tranquil and quiet, however – not that I knew what to expect of ancient mystical locations. Instead, it was filled with more seabirds than I had ever seen in one place– more so than the other western coasts I had visited. The water was thick with grey and white-winged gulls, and every available rock, cliff-face, and tree limb was noisy with them.

"Skrargh!" Zarr roared his challenge or greeting – I couldn't be sure—and, as one, the entire flock of seabirds took to the skies, filling the air with a raucous cacophony as they swirled into a vortex of wings and beaks, before finally rising into the skies and giving us the cove in peace.

"Did you have to disturb them like that?" I asked Zarr irritably.

"Of course!" Zarr said enthusiastically, but I wasn't listening – I was already looking at what had been revealed by the rising birds.

A cave, there in the cliffs above the cove. It had to be the one, and I nodded at Akeem, who was already gliding Aida down to one side of me while I led Zarr straight for the Cave of Truth.

There weren't any ledges here, none wide enough for both dragons to perch on, anyway. Instead, Zarr and Aida landed on the top of the cliff, facing the hills and the odd, spiked trees.

"I'll come with you…" Akeem said immediately, one hand on his sword.

"No," I said just as quickly. For some reason, I wanted to do this alone. And besides which, "We need a lookout." I nodded to the distant mountains and the trees. "We have no idea what sort of people live here."

Akeem didn't look as though he liked this idea – but really, I didn't know what harm he thought I could come to at a place that was sacred to dragons! I lowered myself to the side of the cliff where there was the faintest of tracks leading down through the tangle of rocks. It was an easy scramble, and I noticed that the rocks were worn smooth. I wondered how many people had made this journey before me, and how recently… I cast a last look back up at Akeem before I disappeared completely from view, to see him nod in my direction. *He trusted me.* He trusted that I could do this – whatever it was I had to do.

Realizing that made me feel more confident in myself. It was a far cry from when I had first met Akeem in the High Mountains, when he had been convinced that I was inept!

The cave mouth was large, large enough for a dragon to walk into, of course, but it wasn't dark. Instead, the air was filled with a shimmery pearlescent which I couldn't identify, and when I stepped into the cavern, there was a soft crunching beneath my feet.

The floor of the cavern was dusted with a fine, silver-black sand, and the ceiling was high, and yet the large hallway-like front of the cave turned, so that the light from the cove outside was hidden from view, to be replaced by-

"Earthstars?" I thought, thinking of the glowing mineral rocks that can be found deep underground. No, these were a different sort of crystal – but it was clear that they had some of the same properties. Not blue, but white. The walls were veined with sparkling lines of this quartz-like, pearly stone that seemed to emit a dull, milky glow – strong enough to see by. And what I could see was that there was only one other feature of this cave: an underground pool.

This had to be it, I thought, before immediately feeling the cold seep of anxiety in my legs and stomach. *Was I good enough to beat Saheera even if I found her? How was I going to stop her in the end?*

At first, I thought that the waters had to be made of liquid silver, as they shimmered and shone with light – until I realized that they merely caught and reflected the glowing light of the rocks all around. It gave the cave an eerie, otherworldly feel – and I didn't know if it was just all the strange rocks.

I'm starting to feel giddy, I thought, recognizing the forerunner sensations to the aches, shivers and pains that always came after I had used my magic. But I wasn't using any magic – so what was causing this feeling? *Would I be able to fight off the magic-sickness enough to get the job done?* I suddenly felt very small, and very young, facing powers that were far more ancient that I could even dream of.

My eyes were drawn to the silvered pool itself. Its constantly eddying glows and hues caught the eye, making me feel sleepy. It was *almost* peaceful down here, in a slightly eerie kind of way.

Now, what did Selm say? I thought, my heart in my throat as I settled down beside the side of the pool, the black-silver sand slightly damp under my palms. "That dragons came here for answers, to look into the waters…" I did so, seeing nothing but a ghost-like impression of myself, etched in silver and light. My reflection constantly morphed and changed, reconfiguring and breaking apart as the water ebbed and moved.

But there were no revelations forthcoming.

Did you have to be a dragon to get it to work? I thought in dismay, thumping the sands at my side in frustration. No, surely Selm the Oldest and supposedly wisest dragon would have known that? And those steps outside had looked as though they had been worn by smaller people – humans, not dragons.

I stared once more, trying to let my mind drift and be ready for 'wisdom' to fall on it.

Which also didn't work.

"Oh, come on!" I rocked where I sat, almost shouting into the water, as-

Splash. My mother's shell necklace slipped from its place tucked into my vest and hit the surface of the water, still attached to its cord around my neck. The white and silver light below me swirled and eddied, and suddenly –images arrived in my mind, as strong and as clear as dragon-senses.

The shell necklace. The one that I wore about my neck. I could see it in my mind, in intricate detail, and I remember thinking how pretty it was, as warm and rough hands tucked it into my hands. Those were a man's hands, and ones that I knew only too well. I knew that they would be scarred by the snags and burrs of fishing hooks – because I was looking up at the face of Obasi the fisherman, the man who had adopted me.

Suddenly, I was lifted up, clear from the water, and I realized that this was the day that I had been found. The Cave of Truth wasn't showing me the location of the Sea Witch, but instead my own past!

My foster-father was carrying me in his arms, the shell necklace clutched in my small hands as he lifted me high against his shoulder, so that I could see behind us – the long curve of a beach that had been recently storm-wracked. Great timbers and drifts of seaweed scattered the high shoreline, and I knew that I had to be looking at the day that I was found.

But then the vision changed, and I was looking at a different place, a different time. I was peeking around the edge of someone's deep green skirts, and the smell of my mother – my real mother – filled me. I knew this in a way that I knew that I was hungry, or happy. It was written inside my very bones.

"Witch! Witch!" But my mother (and I) were surrounded by an angry horde of people, some bearing torches, others spears, all wearing the robes and leathers of the people of the South.

This was how my mother died? I thought. But I had been told that my mother must have been in a boat, which had capsized in a storm-

That was clearly not what was happening in the memory, as my mother – with her long and pale hair and her green skirts – turned to me quickly, murmuring something over and over again as she pushed the shell necklace over my head.

"Mamma la, mamma la..." she whisper-sung the melody at me, and I felt myself rising from the ground, my vision of her diminishing and growing fainter before me.

"Mother!" I cried out, but suddenly I was shooting backwards, and falling into the sea, enclosed in an orb of my mother's magic…

"No!" I wanted to scream and shout, to drag that memory back – but it was gone, dissolving, to be replaced by a pregnant woman, walking along a sea path, overlooking the quay of a small village, where boats were disembarking. The woman was pretty and young, and did not seem to mind the burden of her belly as she walked hurriedly to get a last glimpse of the disappearing boat.

Or galleon, I thought. That was the name for those types of vessels, wasn't it? Three-masted and tall, with at least three different 'floors' or decks. The woman herself, with her pale hair that was just a tad blonder than my own, was unmistakably my mother, but it was before I was born. She was waving down at the boat, but there was no one waving back. I wondered who had been aboard – her husband? My father? My real father?

There was a wave of sadness wash over me, not just the loss of whomever my real father was – but I thought that it was the same sadness, loss, and dumb anger that my mother had felt that day…

And then, the last image. An island with two narrow and spear-like peaks, with a dense mat of trees clustered at their base. This was somewhere in the Western Archipelago, I reasoned, seeing the distant dot of other small islands on the horizon.

And the image drew in, to where there was a cave in one of the twin peaks, from which smoke was curling. I flew towards and into that cave against my will, seeing that it was inhabited. There were heavy rugs on the floor, as well as old wooden benches made out of ships timbers, and a fire in one corner of the cave 'room.'

There was a form hunched over on the rugs near the fire, at her side were two stone bowls, one filled with water, and the other filled with strange moss and leaves and green plant matter. The form was shaking and twitching, muttering words I didn't understand, but that hurt my mind just hearing them. It was a woman with greasy blonde hair streaked with silver, and a tattered, threadbare green dress.

It was my mother, I recognized in a flash. My real mother, the witch, I gasped in shock. She hadn't died at all! Then, where was she? What was she doing? Why did she look so ill?

I watched in horror as she turned, and I caught sight of a deeply lined, troubled face – her magic had aged her, clearly – and she grabbed a few pieces of the various plant matter, muttering and whispering over it as she dipped it once into the water, twice, three times…

And the little knot of leaves and roots and tendrils suddenly started to sprout, growing at a fast pace, putting forth fleshy green leaves and thorns…

"No!" The Deadweed. My mother was the witch who had created the Deadweed.

My mother was the Sea Witch.

CHAPTER 23
AKEEM, NOT YOUR FAULT

"Dayie? Dayie!" I scrabbled down the rocks, recklessly vaulting those that turned a corner to make my mad dash into the Cave of Truth that much quicker.

Just a few moments earlier, a strange feeling had blossomed through Aida and, therefore, into me. It was the sort of feeling that I got around magic – around Dayie's magic, anyway – a sort of grinding teeth, anxious feeling in my limbs. But it wasn't that which made me so frantic to get to her, it was the images that swept into my mind at the same time. Of a woman, Dayie's mother— it had to be, for she had the same light hair, the same sharp features— on the shoreline, of Dayie as a child being thrown into the sea to save her from a crowd of angered fisherfolk – and finally, of Dayie's mother herself, creating the Deadweed.

What? I thought for a moment, before realizing that I wasn't shocked. I was surprised, yes, but I wasn't shocked. Had a hidden part of my heart guessed this fact and refused to tell the rest of me?

If the normal people of Dagfan finds out – they'll lynch her, I immediately thought as I raced through the tunnel in the cliff. I couldn't let that happen. I wouldn't let that happen, and I knew that if Dayie wanted me to, I would keep her secret and take it with me to the grave if I had to.

Maybe I should have been surprised at my fervent commitment. But I could already hear all of the sorts of cruel assertions that others would throw Dayie's way: *'If the mother is evil, then so must the daughter be!'* and the like. Well, I had spent my entire life living under the shadow of my father, and I had only recently found a way to be myself.

I wasn't going to let Dayie's parentage smother the person that she could be.

It was Zarr who gave Aida these images, who shared them with me. Zarr was able to see just what Dayie was seeing, after all, even now the Crimson Red had taken to the skies to swoop around to fly to the entrance of the cave – but he had known that I would be able to get in there faster than the time it would take him to launch, turn, and scrabble at the rock walls.

Please let her be alright! I thought as I raced ahead of the screeching dragon coming to land behind me…I found her lying by the side of the pool, unconscious, one hand still clutching onto the shell necklace.

"Dayie… Can you hear me?" I reached for my water pouch,

dampening a cloth and carefully wiping it over her brow - I didn't trust the oddly glowing water of this pool.

"Dayie?" I asked gently. She opened her eyes and coughed a little, as if she really *had* just been thrown into the sea by her mother.

"How… Why…" She shook her head as she rolled over, looking as though she had just crawled out of a three-day battle.

"It's okay, it's going to be okay," I said to her gently, knowing how much this truth must have hurt her. If only she could see what I saw in her, what I knew about her? That she was no monster. She was brave and capable and beautiful. How could I make her see that?

"You don't know." Her eyes filled with tears. "This is never going to be okay…" I saw her hesitate, wanting to tell me what she had seen and afraid at the same time, not knowing that I already knew.

"Dayie, listen to me," I said firmly, reaching out to hold her hand and draw it to both of my own. "I saw. Zarr shared the images with Aida because he was worried about you, and she shared them with me." I let that knowledge sink in for a moment, saw the fear cross Dayie's features, and then the angered determination to get through whatever it was I was about to throw at her. It broke my heart to see her in such emotional turmoil. If I could take away all of this pain for her, I would— in a heartbeat.

"Dayie. It's not your fault. Whatever your mother had done, or became – that has nothing to do with you."

"But maybe if I had searched harder for her— If I had found a way to get a message to her—" Dayie said. "Maybe she wouldn't have made the Deadweed." Suddenly her face paled. "All of those lives lost. All of that pain and upset she's brought…"

"It's not your fault." I repeated. And kept on repeating.

"No…" Dayie shook her head, but I wouldn't relent.

"You were thrown into the water. You could never have known where your mother was," I said, as Dayie collapsed against me, sobbing in my arms. It was only then that I said nothing and just held her until her crying stopped. *I would do anything to keep the woman safe,* I thought. *Even from herself.* I don't know how long we stayed like that, but it felt like no time had passed at all when she finally took a staggered breath and broke away from me.

"Thank you," she said in a small voice, wiping her eyes. "I guess now I'm going to tell my mother that she doesn't have to hurt anyone anymore…"

CHAPTER 24
DAYIE, REUNION

"You are sure you can find it?" I asked Zarr, again, as we flew westwards over the blue waters. I was anxious, the revelation about my mother was preying on my nerves.

"I have the image. It is like the Cave of Truth. Once a dragon has a scent, they will never lose it," he said, his voice in my mind sounding a little exasperated with me for questioning him.

"I'm sorry," I said after a moment, Of course Zarr could find it. He could do anything.

"Ha! Not anything. But almost," he said, now pleased with my confidence in him.

Strangely, it had been Akeem who had been insistent that we go to my mother's island as soon as we could. I would have thought that he might want to return to Dagfan, to rally more of the dragons there.

"But no. There is no time to lose," he had told me seriously, and I knew that he was right. Besides which, he had Aida tell her siblings using the connections in her mind what we were doing, and he knew that Heydar's dragon and several others of the Wild Company were already making their way, following the image and the scent of the island with the twin peaks just as we were.

But we would get there first, as it turned out.

We spent the rest of the day and the night following the southern coastline of the desert lands until Zarr seemed to catch a fresh wind and set off in slightly northwesterly direction. The coast of the Southlands became a blur, and then a haze, and then vanished from view altogether as we flew nonstop into the next day. It was impossible to know how fast we were travelling, but Zarr could sense my urgency, and he kept himself to the high and chill airs, gliding when he caught a favorable wind, and beating his wings when not. By the middle of the day, we started to see clouds on the horizon, followed by the indistinct shapes of other islands.

"Is that it?" I asked the Crimson Red.

"No, but we are getting close," Zarr informed me, and within a few minutes of him saying that I saw that he was right. It wasn't the sight of my mother's island that alerted me – but rather the darker shadows on the water. Banks and drifts of the Deadweed, floating like rafts in the deep ocean, their yellow flower heads waving and bobbing.

They're heading to the Southlands, I thought, seeing their gradual drift to the east far below us. I wondered how long it would take each separate flotilla of the monstrous weed to reach shore, and at the destruction each would bring.

And some of those mats were as large as the one that had clogged the River Taval, I realized in horror. Dagfan had only barely survived that last attack, and now there was easily three or four more of a similar size coming their way…

And with the Deadweed's ability to re-sprout and spread itself wherever it landed, I thought, how long before the entire lands were covered?

A jolt to my awareness from the dragon underneath me, and I looked up to where the sky was starting to darken, leaving just enough light to see the rising shape of an island, rising fast on the northwestern horizon and from which the drifts of the Deadweed seemed to be coming– and it had two thin peaks of mountains.

We were here. We had found my mother's island.

"Dragons!" Zarr informed me, and I looked around to see their shapes on the horizon – but there were none.

"Where?"

"On the island. Underground. In a cave." Zarr sniffed the darkening air as we swept lower and lower towards the island. *"And they are Vicious Orange dragons. From the South, not Sea Dragons... And humans too... Sleeping, But not natural sleep. They're enchanted!"* There was greenery everywhere,

and I recognized the yellowish, bulbous dots of Deadweed. My mother's creation was even strangling the life from her own home, I thought, as I watched the trees and rocks of the island slowly, lazily, being covered by the weed. It grew a lot slower out here, and moved sluggishly – and I wondered if that was because the weed knew that it didn't have any rivals.

Or maybe it was designed to just attack the South, I thought, still appalled at my mother's actions.

Appalled? I caught myself on that word. Was that really what I was feeling? I had to wonder as the island drew larger in our view. She was a woman who had apparently lost her lover and had to throw her child away in an effort to save her… Maybe she deserved my sympathy, not my anger, I argued with myself. She must have believed for so long that there was nothing left in this world for her. That everything had been taken from her. Was it really so strange that she would seek to take revenge against the whole world?

That I was taken from her, I realized. Was *that* the great wound that Selm had seen in her? Was it really the loss of her baby – *me* – that had caused all of this?

Which meant, is some small way – that I had a part to play in all of this. Perhaps I was even responsible in some small way…

"Not responsible," Zarr roared into my mind.

"Involved," I settled for. I was *involved* in this torment that my mother had caused – and if it was her mourning me that had caused it, maybe by showing her that I was here, and that I could return, would mean that she would drop her attacks of the mainland…

No, it wasn't strange why she did what she did, I considered. *But it was still wrong.*

I remembered Akeem's words. That it wasn't my fault, and that whatever my mother had become – that wasn't my doing. I thought then that she could have tried to find me, all alone out there in the world. She could have tried to see what had happened to me, with all of her impressive power… But she hadn't.

"Vicious Oranges?" Akeem called out to me as soon as Aida relayed news of the other dragons to him, and I could hear the hope in his voice, along with the worry. "My father – or my father's dragon—might be amongst them," he said. "That might be why we never heard from them!"

"Go," I said to him immediately. The last few years of his life had been about this. The loss of his father. I couldn't stand in the way of him finding that out.

"No. Your mother…" Akeem looked at the other mountain and then back at me. "The Sea Witch – I can't leave you to face her alone!"

"I said *go,* Akeem!" I shouted at him. "Those dragons and people – whoever they are – will be just as trapped if we're both dead. At least this way you can be sure to save them! Now go, while I distract my mother!" I said, already turning Zarr towards the first, nearer mountain, where my visions had told me my mother's lair was.

"Skrargh!" Zarr coughed a warning as trembling yellow flower heads rose from below to greet us. As we neared the base of the mountain, the cave was clearly visible above us, but the mat of Deadweed between us and the entrance was thick and convoluted. We would have to burn our way through, I thought as Zarr took great gulps of breath—

Unless.

"Zarr, wait. I have an idea…" I said, raising my hand and half-closing my eyes, finding in me that quiet and still space that was always humming a simple little tune…

"Mamma la, Mamma la…" I called out, feeling the waves of peace and security start to rise in me, as old as the oceans in my blood…

"Mamma la, Mamma la…" My voice gained in strength, losing its quavering timbre and instead became a lilting, haunting melody as I sang the refrain over and over, feeling the song's power course up and through me, spreading like cooling summer rain on the angry heads of the Deadweed below.

In response, the already lazy Deadweed seemed to flag and bob, their flower heads curling back in on themselves as if they were sleeping – and even the vines lost their shivering intensity and started to crawl backwards, leaving a path for Zarr to land on-

No sooner had Zarr's paws touched land, then a stern voice split the night airs.

"Who sang that? Who are you, witch?"

Standing above us, in the mouth of her own cave, stood my mother.

No – *hovered* my mother, I corrected, as I realized that the woman up there wasn't even touching the ground. She still wore the green dress, but it no longer looked so tattered and threadbare and was instead a deep, luxurious verdant green. Her hair was a radiant silver, and constantly billowed around her as if she were underwater – and she was young.

Almost as young as me, I thought with a faint hint of disgust. This had to be a charm, I thought. A guise to lure or intimidate visitors.

"It's *you*, isn't it?" My own mother snapped at me from where she floated.

"Yes, it's me…" I started to say, my eagerness to be recognized as her daughter blinding me temporarily.

"The witch who seeks to thwart me? The one who would protect the South from its rightful destruction!?" she said, her voice rising into a shriek.

Well, yes, that was me, I thought. But it wasn't *just* who I was. "Mother," I said.

"Gah!" my mother screeched in fury, and I didn't know if she had heard me – she couldn't have, could she? Because she was sweeping her hand down and, in response, the Deadweed at our side burst into life once more, curling and unfolding, the flower heads opening once again—

"Mother!" I shouted up at her again. "Who else knows that song? Who else could it be?"

"Ssssss!" Zarr hissed, flicking his tail and unfolding his wings, meaning to jump out of harm's way (with me on his back) should he have to…As well he might at any moment, as my mother's Deadweed was towering and growing above us, forming an archway, a thicket of thorns and poison-

But she hadn't ordered it to kill me, yet… I clutched onto that thought.

"You wore a green dress when you threw me into the ocean. You gave me this!" I held up the shell necklace high into the air.

"Impossible…" Saheera, my mother, faltered where she hovered, her form flickering. Her hair stopped billowing around her and became lank, her feet touched the floor, and her skin started to look older. "No, no – you died…" she repeated again, and the indecision my words had inspired wavered, strengthening into resolve…

"Dayie…" Zarr hissed urgently into my mind, for the Deadweed had now formed a tunnel completely around us, leaving just a window of hope at the end, occupied by my mother.

"It's me. I promise. I've come back," I said, even though my words broke my own heart. "You need to stop this, Mother. You need to stop hating the world."

"No. *Lies!*" My mother threw out both hands suddenly as she shook her head, causing the Deadweed to suddenly creak and groan and creep closer…

I sang my mother's song even as tears rolled from my eyes. I was going to die, here, by my mother's own hand and her creation. And what was worse was that I had brought Zarr here to die also.

Fly away, my dragon brother... I thought as I choked back tears between song verses – struggling to hold the Deadweed back.

"Never," Zarr said in my mind, roaring and slashing at the monstrous weed around us with his tail and claws.

I was exhausted, and my throat was sore from singing. The song wasn't working. It wasn't strong enough. "Mother! I don't want to lose you again!" I shouted.

"But – but…" The older woman stumbled back against the outer wall of the cave, shock and surprise a better weapon than any other that we could have used to stop her.

"*Mamma la, Mamma la...*" I repeated, my head throbbing with pain as the Deadweed struggled against my calming commands, but the aperture widened without my mother's baleful intelligence. I kept on singing despite the headache, and soon the opening was large enough for Zarr to hop through, up the banks of the mountain, to where my mother was panting and holding her chest.

“Child?” she whispered. “Can it really? Can it…?”

“It is,” I said, hopping from Zarr’s back to kneel at her side. She looked ancient. Far too old to be my mother, but I knew that it was the curse of the powerful magics she had been weaving. They were sucking her life dry… “We need to reverse this,” I said softly, “we need to stop the Deadweed and the Water Wraiths… You don’t have to do this anymore.”

My ancient mother looked at me with tears in her eyes, squinting and blinking. “But you see it has to be this way… We have to remake the world…” she whispered up at me.

“We already can. We don’t need the Deadweed to do that,” I said to her, reaching out to touch a hand to her hair. It felt dry and knotted. She had given up on herself long before she had given up on the world.

“What are you talking about?” I saw my mother try to regain some of her temper, try to scowl at me, but her lower lip was wavering with barely-suppressed emotion.

“We change it by what we do. Now. Here. We change it by being ourselves. Who we were meant to be,” I said to her, relaying in my heart what I knew the secret message of Selm’s vision had been. “We change it together, by being here for each other.”

My mother took a hitching breath, as if she had been hit in the stomach although no one had touched her. Her eyes widened before sadly shaking her head. “I cannot stop it, my daughter. I have given too much of myself to this work. It lives on without me now…” She sighed, screwing up her eyes for a moment, before bursting out, “I have been so stupid!”

“No…” I said, knowing that what she said was true, but not wanting her to suffer any more pain than the decades of hurt and heartache that she had already gone through.

“Yes. But I know a way. *You* can stop the Deadweed and the Water Wraiths with our song. And the dragons. Get them to sing it, too…”

My mother cleared her throat and started to sing in a high-pitched and thin voice.

“Mamma la, Mamma la…”

And I joined in, adding Mengala’s counter melody to my mother’s own voice as the waves of magic started to flow and interact between us. I felt peace. I felt calm.

I felt whole.

The song rose in strength, although I couldn’t say if that was because of our voices or because of the magic that we were spinning together, my mother and I. Beside us, Zarr started a low, throaty growl, in perfect pitch with a lost bass melody I hadn’t known existed. Waves of power flowed down the mountainside from us, washing over the rocks and the trees and the Deadweed—

“Skreee! Skreeee!” Suddenly, from the darks opposite us, shapes flashed into the skies. Sea Dragons and Vicious Oranges who had clearly been the Sea Witch’s prisoners. I heard confused, groggy shouts as their Riders on their backs awoke, shouting in alarm and joy as they realized that they were moving and flying once again… These must have been the patrols of Roskilde and the Western Isles, I thought. Whenever they had found the source of the Deadweed, my mother had merely imprisoned them.

And what of Akeem? Had he found his father? I scanned the skies, but I could not make out which of the Vicious Oranges was Aida beside the others.

"Sing with us!" I called out desperately, breaking the melody for but a moment. The victorious Sea Dragons were only too glad for a chance to celebrate. They lifted their high-pitched, whistling cries to join the melody that we were making, and the song rolled further and further out…

Everywhere the song touched, it seemed to make the Deadweed at first fold into itself, and then shiver and wilt. It was a monstrous plant, born of a curse, and its healing would be this: to return to the earth from which it was made.

The song seemed to last forever, as other dragons arrived and added their voices to ours – Heydar and the Wild Company dragons who had flown through the days and nights to get here to save their prince. They saw what was happening in an instinctive way that dragons did, and repeated and amplified the song out over the waters. Everywhere the song struck, the Deadweed and the Water Wraiths fell back into their elemental parts, never to return.

"We've done it, Mother, we've done it!" I said, turning to see that my true mother had stopped singing a long time ago. The magic that she had wrought with me had claimed her life, but she looked as though she was sleeping, peacefully.

I cried then, and for a long time, I think, until Akeem's arms once again found and wrapped themselves around me, just as he had before, in the cave – and before that, when Zarr had been sick.

I leaned into him and let myself cry, hearing him make small noises, soothing noises, and even say things – but I didn't know what they were. After what seemed like a long time, something nudged my hands, and I saw that it was Zarr's great snout in front of me, as Akeem held me.

"Dayie... Look. The sun is coming," he said, and I wiped my eyes to see that the dragon was right. The sun was rising over the eastern horizon, and it was revealing a shining, sparkling sea, clear of Deadweed.

"You did it, Dayie," I heard Akeem murmur behind me, his voice gruff as he carefully disengaged.

"We did it," I corrected him, meaning him, me, Zarr and Aida, and even my mother. "But Akeem – your father!" I pointed out. "Did you find him?"

Akeem's face was similarly tired and his eyes puffy as if he too must have been crying. "My father wasn't there, but the other Sea Dragons – the patrols of Roskilde, say that they have news of where he went. He came to their island years ago to seek help and said that he was going to try to take the Western Track to find the last of the Western Witches." Akeem said, looking to the dark of the western horizon where still the last few stubborn stars hung over a dark sea.

"You think he found it?" I said in awe. Despite all of this chaos and torment that surrounded us, I was surprised that I *could* still feel surprise, even awe at what he said. The Western Track was a magical road through which the Western Witches had fled these lands for another stranger land far away. It was the same magic that the sorcerer and Mengala had used to hurl me and Zarr across the deserts in a fraction of the time it would normally take.

"I think he did." Akeem said hopefully. "I think my father and his people are still out there somewhere, on new adventures…"

"And we can find him…" I said. Now that I knew there was a way – by using the sorcerer and Mengala's magic – then I knew I wanted to give to Akeem what I had been given: the gift of family, even if I had my mother back again for just a short while.

I knew that we would have a lot of work ahead of us to do, to carry my mother's song out to the rest of the South – and the North, and in so doing, undo the evil that she had wrought – but it was a task that I would be proud to do – and that *she* would be proud of me in doing as well.

I would make the world whole again, I thought, before realizing that this great magic hadn't brought with it this time any pain, or nausea. It seemed that the healing of the world would also help to heal me as well.

END OF DRAGON SONG

DEADWEED DRAGONS BOOK THREE

Dragon Called, 24 April 2019

Dragon Magic, 29 May 2019

Dragon Song, 26 June 2019

PS: Go back to the very beginning. Keep reading for exclusive extract from ***Dragon Trials (Return of the Darkening Series Book One).***

THANK YOU!

I hope you enjoyed **Dragon Song**.

Please don't forget to leave a review.

Receive free books, exclusive excerpts and be kept up to date on all of my new releases, when you sign up to my mailing list at AvaRichardsonBooks.com/mailing-list.

ABOUT AVA

Ava Richardson writes epic page-turning Young Adult Fantasy books with lovable characters and intricate worlds that are barely contained within your eReader.

She grew up on a steady diet of fantasy and science fiction books handed down from her two big brothers – and despite being dog-eared and missing pages, she loved escaping into the magical worlds that authors created. Her favorites were the ones about dragons, where they'd swoop, dive and soar through the skies of these enchanted lands.

Stay in touch! You can contact Ava at:

facebook.com/AvaRichardsonBooks

amazon.com/author/avarichardson

goodreads.com/AvaRichardson

bookbub.com/authors/ava-richardson

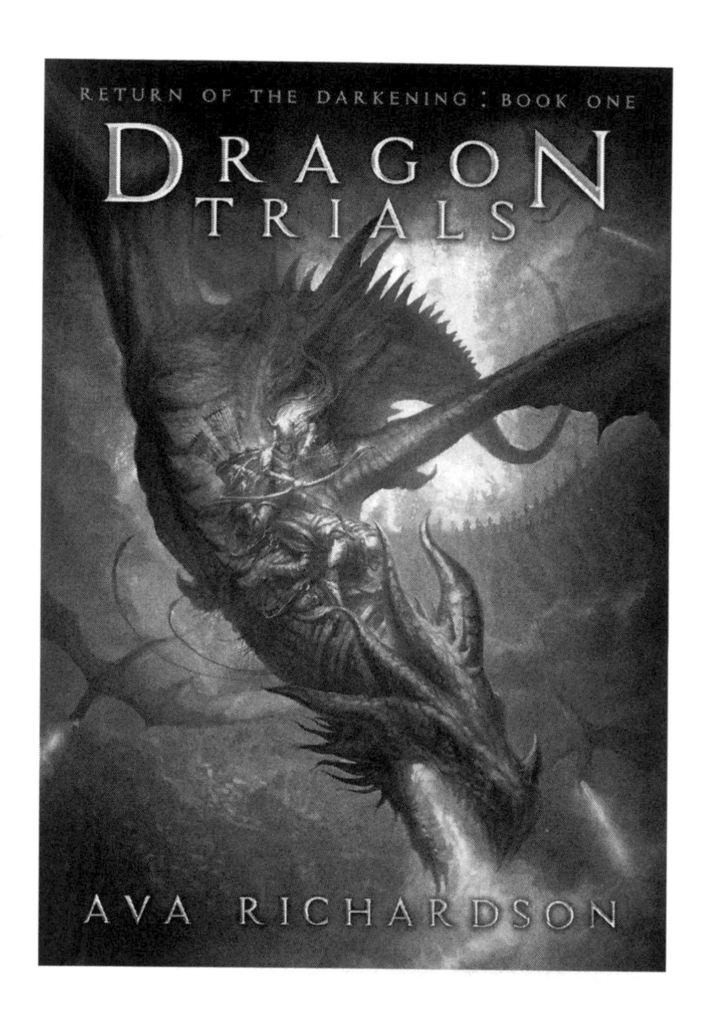

BLURB

High-born Agathea Flamma intends to bring honor to her family by following in her brothers' footsteps and taking her rightful place as a Dragon Rider. With her only other option being marriage, Thea will not accept failure. She's not thrilled at her awkward, scruffy partner, Seb, but their dragon has chosen, and now the unlikely duo must learn to work as a team.

Seventeen-year-old Sebastian has long been ashamed of his drunken father and poor upbringing, but then he's chosen to train as a Dragon Rider at the prestigious Dragon Academy. Thrust into a world where he doesn't fit in, Seb finds a connection with his dragon that is even more powerful than he imagined. Soon, he's doing all he can to succeed and not embarrass his new partner, Thea.

When Seb hears rumors that an old danger is re-emerging, he and Thea begin to investigate. Armed only with their determination and the dragon they both ride, Thea and Seb may be the only defence against the Darkening that threatens to sweep over the land. Together, they will have to learn to work together to save their kingdom…or die trying.

EXCERPT

High-born Agathea Flamma intends to bring honor to her family by *Every fifth year, the skies over the city of Torvald darken as large shadows swoop over the city, dark wingbeats blowing open window shutters and their bird-like cries disturbing babes and sleeping animals alike.*

The city folk of Torvald are prepared for this ritual however, as the great Dragon Horns—the long brass instruments stationed along the top towers of the dragon enclosure—are blown on those mornings. Farmers and market folk rush to guide their skittish cattle out of sight, whilst children flock to the narrow cobbled streets or crowd atop the flat rooftops.

Choosing Day is a time of great celebration, excitement and anticipation for Torvald. It is the time that the great enclosure is unbarred and the young dragonets are released into the sky to choose their riders from amongst the humans below. It is a day that could forever change your fortunes; if you are brave and lucky enough. It is a day that heroes are made, and the future of the realm is secured.

"Dobbett, no! Get down from there right now." Dobbett was a land-pig, although she looked somewhere between a short-snouted dog and a white fluffy cushion. She grunted nervously as she turned around and around atop the table, whimpering and grunting.

She always got like this. I wasn't very old the last time that Choosing Day came around; I must have been about thirteen or fourteen or so, but I remember how my little pet ran around my rooms, knocking everything off stands or dismantling shelves. I couldn't blame her: land-pigs are the natural food of dragons, and if she even caught a whiff of one, she went into a panic.

"No one's going to eat you, silly," I said to her in a stern voice, making sure I picked her up gently and set her down on the floor where her tiny claws immediately clacked on the tiles as she scampered under my bed.

Good Grief! I found myself smiling at her antics, despite myself. Dobbett was a welcome relief to the butterflies I was feeling in my stomach.

Today was Choosing Day, and that meant that today would be my last chance. If I wasn't picked now, then by the time another five years rolled by, Father would probably have married me off to some annoying, terribly fat merchant or nobleman.

Memories of the prince's last Winter Ball flashed through my mind, filling me at once with the most curious mixture of disgust and hopelessness. The prince, and all the royal family, had been there of course, and my older brothers too—Reynalt and Ryan—looking splendid in their dragon scale jerkins.

They managed to do it, I thought. *They got their own dragon.* My two older brothers were chosen almost as soon as they were old enough to sit on the saddle—even though it is always the dragon itself that does the choosing.

"*As close as egg and mother, is a Flamma to a dragon,*" I mouthed the well-known Torvald saying desperately hoping it would prove true. I wanted to declare: I am Agathea Flamma, or more properly, *Lady* Agathea Flamma. Our household had sired Dragon Riders for the last hundred years, and the rooms of Flamma Hall were filled with the statues, busts and paintings of my great-uncles and grandfathers and great-great grandfathers who rode the mighty drakes into battle in defense of the city and the realm.

My brothers were chosen, why not me? Everyone had expected them to be chosen. No one expected me to be.

I am a girl. They say I am better suited to marrying well, running an estate, raising little Dragon Riders all of my own... "Ugh!" I snorted in disgust, throwing open the patio doors to the balcony of the tower and walking out into the fresh morning air.

The last of the Dragon Horns just finished their mournful cry. I could already hear cries and screams of excitement as the shapes flew out of Mount Hammal, the dragon enclosure far over the mountain from here. They looked so beautiful. Long, sinuous necks, powerful; each one a different colour. Today there are green, blue, black—even a red.

They swooped and soared over the city, skimming over its rooftops and around the many terraces to the cheers and cries of the people below. I saw some people trying to entice the dragons to choose them by waving colourful flags or roasting land-pigs right on their rooftops.

Not for these beasts, however. These great ones were reveling in their freedom: performing barrel rolls and turns in the air, one after another. Then some smell would catch their nose and they followed the scent like a lightning flash to their chosen rider.

No one really knows why or how the great wyrms chose their two riders. Some say it's magic, others say that dragons can read your soul, so they choose the ones that they know they can live and work with the best. You have to have two riders for every dragon though: a navigator and a protector. The navigator is like the pilot and the guide; some say they can almost sense their dragon's emotions. The protector is the one who gets to fire arrows, throw lances and use swords to defend both dragon and the navigator when they are on patrols.

Not that Torvald had gotten into any wars over the last hundred years. The fact that we had the dragons—or should that be the other way around?—meant our enemies rapidly sued for peace. We still have trouble with bandits and cattle rustlers of course—last summer all it took for my brothers to scare them off was one low fly-by. There has always been one threat, however—that of the Darkening returning.

My father swore the old stories were true, but my mother did not like to hear him speak of those tales. I have only heard the old legends once. My father's stories left me with such nightmares—where I dreamed of being claimed by darkness, where I was lost in a deep blackness—that it left me unable to do more than curl into a shivering ball and cry.

I have forgotten most of the old tales, but I still remember the fear they left in my bones. My brothers told me they are just stories to make children behave, but I wonder at times if they are right, for we still have Dragon Riders patrolling against the return of the Darkening.

What would Father think if I was actually chosen to be a rider? I scanned the horizon, searching for the dragons. *Where are they? Have all the riders already been chosen? Is my chance over?* It couldn't be. It just couldn't. I imagined the look on my father's face if he heard the news. He would be delighted, surely, that all his children had been chosen. It would make the Flamma House a force really to be reckoned with.

And I just want to make my father proud of me. I realize this, running to the balcony and turning around, hearing the telltale caw of the giant lizards; not being able to see them yet.

He wants me to get married, another part of my mind kept thinking. *He wants me to 'do the right thing' and bring some respectability to our family.*

"I can't do it," I whisper, shutting my eyes tight against tears threatening to spill over my lashes.

There was a breath of fresh air against my face and my hair lifted. A round of cheers and shouts rose up from the city below. I felt heartbroken. The last dragon must have made its choice—and it wasn't me.

Suddenly, it went dark. I opened my eyes—and almost fainted.

A red wyrm slowly descended to our tower. It was young, its forehead horns barely as big as my hand at the moment, but in fine shape. And a red, too. I knew they were fierce and rare. The wyrm made a twittering noise in the back of its throat. I could see its throat expanding and contracting like a bellows as it raised its wings to catch the thermals and hang in the air. Its eyes were a brilliant green-gold, a colour I had never seen before. It was holding me in its steady gaze. Now I could really understand why everyone thought they had the power to hypnotize.

Its great head with an elongated snout was still, almost calm, as it lowered its claws to grab onto the side of the tower, splintering rock and the wooden windowsill as it did so. Half of its bulk was atop the tower and the other half gently lowered onto the wide, semi-circular balcony beside me.

"Uh…h-hi?" I said, feeling a rush of panic as the beast slipped a forked tongue into the air, tasting its choice. All thought of the correct etiquette went out of my head as I stared into its great, golden-green eyes.

I got the incredible sensation this young beast was smirking at me as it tasted the air again and *huffed* gently into the space above my head. Breath smelling like wood-smoke mixed with something aromatic, like basil or pepper.

"Dear…dear dragon, my name is Agathea Flamma, of the H-House Flamma, and I th-thank you…" I tried to stammer through the traditional greeting that every child in Torvald learned by the time they were ten.

The beast nudged its head forward, slowly inclining it until it was just a foot away from me. I stretched out my hand, feeling a curious heat radiating from its scales. It was so shiny and new. The only other dragons I had seen were the ones that my brothers or the prince rode; they were much older, with scales that had lost some of their luster or become cracked, scratched and broken with time.

Incredibly, and I could hardly breathe, the creature bumped its head against my hand. Despite the heat radiating from its breath, the scales felt cool and smooth to my touch. Not cold, but not blistering hot either. Like a cool lake on a hot summer day.

"I-I," I tried to speak, finding myself unable to gather my thoughts or articulate just what I was feeling. *Me. A Dragon Rider. I'll be one of the very few women riders in the whole service.*

Before I could concentrate my thoughts, there was a buffet of strong air almost knocking me off of my feet and the dragon was in the air. *Am I wrong?* I thought for a moment the dragon must have made a mistake—maybe it had been sensing my older brothers and became confused.

But then the tower dropped away. I was yanked upward with a wail. The dragon had lightly clasped me in its two, warm-and-cool talons and I was being carried through the air like a precious prize, back to Mount Hammal and the dragon enclosure.

WANT MORE?

WWW.AVARICHARDSONBOOKS.COM

Printed in Great Britain
by Amazon